FOXDEN ACRES

Madalyn Morgan

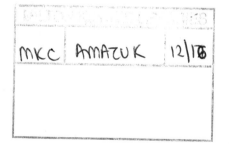

A CIP catalogue record for this book is
available
from the British Library.

ISBN: 978-1489505019

Proofread by Alison Neale, The Proof Fairy
http://www.theprooffairy.com/

Author photograph – ©Michael-Wharley
2013
http://www.michaelwharley.com/

Formatting by Rebecca Emin
www.rebeccaemin.com

Cover design by Charles Carter

Foxden Acres is dedicated to the memory of
my wonderful parents,
Ena and Jack Smith.

I also dedicate Foxden Acres to all the brave
servicemen and women (British and
Commonwealth) of the Armed Forces: Royal
Air Force, the British Army and The Royal
Navy. The home guard, air-raid wardens,
nurses, doctors, hospital auxiliaries and
volunteers, ambulance drivers, men and
women of the fire brigade, factory workers,
farmers, and wartime correspondents. And
the women: The mothers, daughters, sisters
and wives who kept the home fires burning,
so our heroes had a home to return to. Last
but by no means least "Britain's secret
weapon," the hardworking women of the
Land Army.

ACKNOWLEDGEMENTS

I would like to thank my mentor, Dr Roger Wood, for his continued help and encouragement. David Chapman, editor of St. Peter's Review, who published my articles when no one else would – and still does. Author and friend, Debbie Viggiano my beta reader. I would also like to thank my soul sister Dianna Cavender, my aunt Dianne Ashton, and friends, Jane Goddard and Valerie Rowe, whose faith in me has never wavered. As well as authors, Theresa Le Flem, Jayne Curtis and Gill Vickery.

Thanks also to Jacky Willks, aged 7.

PROLOGUE

Bess and Annabel, each holding one of Charlotte's small hands, crossed the road from the car park to the railway station at Rugby. They were early. The northbound platform was deserted but for an elderly ticket collector and the station's resident pigeons. As they approached him the sprightly old man doffed his cap. Then, looking down at Charlotte with a twinkle in his eye, he said, 'Good morning, sunshine.'

Charlotte smiled shyly, 'Good morning.'

Returning the smile, the old man carried on along the platform, while the pigeons, perched high in the ornate rafters, cooed sleepily. The once transparent roof had been painted black at the beginning of the war to fool the Luftwaffe. Today the only creatures fooled were the pigeons that, until woken by the thundering approach of a train, dozed peacefully, believing sunrise was at noon.

'I'll ask what time the train's due,' Annabel said, and disappeared through a door marked Enquiries.

Bess looked at her wristwatch for what must have been the twentieth time that day. Then she checked it against the clock hanging above the ticket office. Its round moon-like face and brass numerals were half hidden by a hooded shade and its chimes – like the station's signposts and platform numbers –

had been removed in 1939 and not yet replaced.

The clock's rusting hands met at twelve. The antiquated timepiece emitted a loud thud, and a pair of pigeons flew their illusory night.

'When will my daddy's train be here?' Charlotte asked.

'Soon, darling. In about an hour. We have to be patient for a little while longer.' An hour was nothing, Bess thought, not when they'd waited for years, but it could seem like an eternity to a child. Looking into Charlotte's enquiring eyes, Bess reflected on how bright the little girl was for her age. She stooped until they were on a level. 'I know you've been waiting a long time, sweetheart.'

Charlotte nodded.

'But you won't have to wait much longer, I promise.'

At that moment Annabel came out of the Enquiries office. 'The station master says the train left London on time and he doesn't expect any delays.' She threw her arms around Bess and laughed with relief.

'I don't know about you, but I could do with a cup of tea,' Bess said. 'What would you say to a glass of milk and some chocolate, Charlotte?'

The little girl's face lit up. 'Yes please.'

The cafeteria was bright and cheerful. The blackout blinds that had stifled the light for so many years had been replaced with colourful curtains. Paper chains in red, white and blue

7

were looped across the ceiling and long white banners with bold red lettering that read, "BLESS 'EM ALL" and "WELCOME HOME BOYS" had replaced solemn posters that had warned, "CARELESS TALK COSTS LIVES" and asked "IS YOUR JOURNEY REALLY NECESSARY?"

Seated with their refreshments, Bess and Annabel chatted excitedly. Charlotte, Bess noticed, sat quietly admiring her black patent shoes which she had chosen herself, and took great care to eat her chocolate without dropping any of the delicious treat on her new coat.

The room quickly filled, but Bess and Annabel were oblivious to everyone as they reminisced about land girls, backbreaking work, young servicemen, Jewish evacuees – and how, amid the fear and turmoil of war, they had each fallen in love.

CHAPTER ONE

Bess was falling through the air in the pitch of night. The earth was getting nearer, beckoning with gnarled fingers. Before she hit the ground she heard a short grinding noise followed by a sharp clang! Then the familiar chimes of the library's long-case clock struck the quarter hour. Bess opened her eyes, relieved to be out of the terrifying world of dreams.

Bess put down the book she'd been reading before falling asleep, climbed onto the window-seat and looked out of the window. She traced the familiar snow-covered hills, the backdrop to Foxden Hall, across the windowpane with her finger as a flurry of snowflakes, the last of the afternoon's fall, floated out of the blue-black sky to the courtyard below.

That morning the courtyard, a cobbled quadrangle with stables on one side and the entrance to the servants' quarters on the other, had been ankle-deep in snow, which Bess had crunched through purposefully, taking care to leave her footprints clearly defined. During the day caterers, wine merchants and musicians, arriving in a variety of vehicles to prepare for Foxden's New Year's Eve party, had trampled the crisp white snow into dirty brown slush. Now even that was gone and the wet cobblestones glistened beneath the headlights of chauffeur-driven motorcars.

'Oh, no!' Bess gasped. She stumbled from the seat and ran to the window overlooking the drive. A convoy of a dozen motorcars was heading towards the Hall. She had meant to leave before any of Lord and Lady Foxden's guests arrived. Apart from anything else, she had promised her mother she'd be home by half-past six – to sit down to a family supper at seven. At that moment the clock began to chime again. The hour was seven. She was late. Her mother would be furious.

Quickly Bess put back the books she had been reading, each in its original place, on the tall mahogany bookcases that lined the library walls. Then, after replacing the guard in front of what was left of the fire, she put on her coat, hat and gloves, and threw her satchel over her shoulder. Satisfied that she had left the library as she found it, she switched off the reading lamp and made her way to a small panelled door at the back of the room, which would take her down a narrow flight of stairs and into the servants' hall. She lifted the latch, but the door didn't budge. She tried again and this time leant her shoulder to it, but the door held fast.

Bess had no choice now but to leave the Hall by the front door - and, she hoped, without anyone seeing her. Taking off her hat and gloves and stuffing them into the pocket of her coat in an attempt to look less conspicuous, she made her way to the library's main entrance. Reaching for the handle she pulled open the heavy oak-panelled door and silently stepped out onto the first floor gallery.

She was alone. She wondered for how long. Below she could hear the orchestra and the chatter of people meeting and greeting each other, but there was no one in sight. Quietly she closed the library door, tiptoed to the edge of the balcony and looked over the banister. Beneath her shards of shimmering light, reflections from the huge mirror-ball that hung from the ceiling of Foxden's elegant ballroom, darted through the open door, lighting up a giant Christmas tree. With its brightly coloured Victorian characters and shiny baubles, the magnificent fir was the centrepiece of Foxden's marble hall.

To her right a party of latecomers arrived. A footman was relieving them of their coats when one, and then another, looked up. Bess ducked. She felt sure they'd seen her. To her relief they were admiring Foxden's seasonal décor – and carried on doing so all the way to the ballroom.

Bess was angry with herself for not having the courage to simply walk down the main staircase. For ten years, since she had passed the eleven-plus and won the Foxden Scholarship to attend Lowarth Grammar School, Lord Foxden had allowed her to use the library. When he learned she was about to take her teaching certificate he had sent a message with her father – who was his head groom – inviting Bess to use the library during the Christmas holiday. In his words, she was to come and go as she pleased. Even so, Bess felt sure that tonight Lord Foxden would have preferred her to go, as she had come, via the servants' stairs.

Crouching, Bess inched her way along the balcony to the top of the stairs and peered through the spindles of the banister. This time there was no one in the hall, not even a footman. Before she had time to change her mind she leapt to her feet. Taking hold of the stair-rail, she fled down the stairs and, without making a sound, ran across the marble hall to the front door. She turned the handle, flung open the door and was through it in a flash. She spun on her heels and pulled the large brass knob on the outside of the door until she heard the door click shut. Holding onto the doorknob to steady herself, she caught her breath. 'Done it!'

'Done what?' someone standing behind her demanded.

Bess froze. A wave of panic went through her. She needed to compose herself – and quickly – so she lifted her head, stood as tall as she could, and turned to face her inquisitor.

'Who are you and what are you doing?' he barked.

Bess opened her mouth, but was too shocked to speak. The man standing in front of her was James Foxden, her brother Tom's childhood friend and heir to the Foxden Estate. She made a dash for the semi-circle of stone steps that would take her down to the drive, but James Foxden sidestepped and blocked her passage. He threw down the cigarette he'd been smoking and, without taking his eyes off her, ground it vigorously beneath the sole of his shoe. 'I asked you a question. Who are you and what are you doing here?'

'That's two questions... Which would you like me to answer first?'

James Foxden didn't reply but kept looking at her, the frown lines on his forehead deepening.

Bess felt the colour rise in her cheeks. I've gone too far, she thought. 'I'm sorry, I--'

'Just a minute...?'

Bess watched the expression on James Foxden's face turn from a scowl to a look of surprise. Then he roared with laughter. 'It's young Elizabeth, isn't it? Tom's sister?' he asked, extending his hand in formal greeting.

Bess's eyes flashed. 'I'm not so young now,' she snapped, 'but yes, I am Tom's sister.' Taking his outstretched hand, she thought how full of himself Tom's old friend had become. 'Bess Dudley, how do you do? Your father invited me to study in the library,' she exaggerated slightly, 'and I lost track of the time. Goodbye.'

'Don't go. I haven't seen you for years, not since I moved to live in London. I hear you're down there too, at a Teachers' Training College. How are the long and lonely corridors of academia? How are your parents, your sisters? How's Tom? Father tells me he's doing a terrific job in Suffolk.'

Bess wasn't sure whether James Foxden was being patronising or whether he was genuinely interested in her family. She gave him the benefit of the doubt. 'My parents are well, thank you, and so is Tom. He'll be at home now; he's here for the New Year.'

'Good, perhaps we can--?' At that moment an elegant young woman with black hair styled in a fashionable bob, wearing an evening gown of cherry-red velvet, appeared at the door – and James let go of Bess's hand.

Acknowledging Bess with a smile that was more polite than friendly, the young woman looked coquettishly at James. 'James, you promised me this dance.' Then, without waiting for a reply, she half-walked, half-waltzed back to the ballroom, but didn't enter. She stood in the doorway, swaying to the music.

Bess turned to leave. 'Do you have to go?' James asked. 'Come and join the party.'

'Thank you, but I'm not dressed for a party.' Bess held her only winter coat firmly in place so the simple grey shift beneath it couldn't be seen. 'Besides, my parents are expecting me.'

'Of course, I wasn't thinking. Wish your family a happy New Year and give Tom my best, will you? Tell him to come up when he has time and we'll go to the Crown for a drink - it would be good to catch up.' James stood aside to let Bess pass. 'Will you be safe walking home on your own?' he asked as she drew level.

Her heart was thumping so loudly in her chest, she felt sure he'd hear it. 'Yes, I'll be fine. I love walking home on nights like this,' she said, gazing up at the full moon in the clear winter sky. Sensing James was watching her, she brought her focus back to earth and for the longest moment found herself looking into his eyes.

Embarrassed by the intimacy of the situation, she said, 'Happy New Year,' which broke the spell, and she ran down the steps.

'Happy New Year. By the way,' he called after her, 'what was it you'd done?'

'Done?'

'Yes, when you left the Hall you said, "Done it!"'

'Oh, that!' Bess didn't stop. 'I'd left without being seen.'

'But you haven't…' His words were lost in the cold night air.

As she walked away from the Hall hundreds of butterflies were flying round in the pit of her stomach. Excitement surged through her. She had an uncontrollable urge to run, to scream, to shout with joy. Instead, she walked calmly and with purpose along the drive until she was beyond the arc of light that surrounded the building. When she was sure no one could see her, she stopped and looked back.

The French windows of the ballroom, which opened onto the peacock lawn at the side of the house, stood ajar. A narrow beam of light shone along the footpath leading down to the lake, and the sound of the orchestra rose into the night. Hugging her satchel to her chest Bess swayed to the gentle rhythm of a waltz, which she recognised as "The Blue Danube." Then the tempo changed and the beat quickened. The orchestra began to play "Swing as You Sing" and Bess began to dance. She could feel the wind biting cold against her cheeks, feel it tugging at her hair, pulling it from its neat bun and forcing it to fly wildly like a banner of silk. Faster and faster she twirled until she was out of breath. She wondered what it would be like to dance with James Foxden. And she stopped.

James Foxden had a dance partner. Besides, why would the heir to the Foxden Estate be interested in the daughter of one of his father's estate workers, a schoolteacher – and not even that, yet – when he could have any one of a dozen beautiful society women?

Pushing her hair from her face as if she was pushing James Foxden from her mind, Bess turned her back on the Hall and started for home. It was at that moment she thought she saw a light in the library window. It was no more than a flicker followed by a tiny red glow, as if someone was lighting a cigarette. Was someone watching her from the library window, she wondered, or was it a spark from the fire? She caught her breath. The thought of going back to the Hall sent shivers down her spine. She must think. She remembered quite clearly placing the fireguard in front of what remained of the fire – in case any dying embers spat – before she switched off the reading lamp. Or was it the other way round? No, it was definitely guard before lamp. She strained her eyes and looked again. This time there was no light in the window, but the full moon was in the sky. That was what it must have been, she thought, turning for home – the moon reflecting on the library's stained glass window.

Bess had barely stepped through the door of her parents' cottage when her brother Tom ran down the passage, picked her up and swung her round.

'You're getting heavy,' he said, pretending to stagger beneath her weight. 'Must be the lazy life you're leading in London.'

'I don't think so!' Bess greeted her handsome older brother with a kiss. 'We students work ten hours a day and live on bread and cheese.' It wasn't far from the truth. 'Anyway, cheeky, you don't call driving cars and riding horses for a living hard work, do you?'

'No, but it's good work if you can get it,' Tom said, laughing.

Because Tom had come home for the New Year, Bess's three younger sisters, eager to be near their brother, helped their mother prepare the tea. Bess's mam forgave her for being late. Truth was, if she hadn't apologised her mam probably wouldn't have noticed.

During supper, Tom complimented his mother on her cooking and ate every morsel she put in front of him with enthusiasm. Bess, not as hungry as she had been before meeting James Foxden, ate like a bird and refused pudding.

'Have mine as well, why don't you?' Bess said when her mother scraped the enamel dish to give Tom the last helping of apple pie.

'Must be all that fresh air,' he teased. 'Gives a bloke an appetite. Not like you student types, sitting at a desk all day.'

'Right! That's it!' Bess countered. 'I challenge you to a race across the Foxden Estate. Be at the stables tomorrow morning at seven and we'll see who's the fittest and who can ride a horse the fastest.'

It was good to have Tom home. Bess watched as her sisters – all completely captivated by their older brother, with his dark hair and good looks, smart suit and wicked sense of humour – oohed and aahed and agreed with everything he said.

Margaret, Claire and Ena – second, third and youngest of the Dudley girls – were enjoying the fact that, because it was New Year's Eve and Tom was home, their father hadn't enforced the rule of no talking at the table. They nudged and shushed each other while Tom recounted stories of his travels to Ireland and France, where he had bought horses for Lord Foxden's stables in Suffolk, and they giggled at the tall tales their brother told about the grooms and stable lads who had accompanied him.

Laughing, Bess said, 'You can certainly tell a good story, Tom. Kiss the Blarney stone while you were in Ireland, did you?'

'Ah, that was her name, was it, Miss Blarney Stone?'

Claire and Ena looked at each other and giggled again.

'So what's been going on in Woodcote, girls?'

'Next door's had another baby--' Claire began.

'And he's still not working!' Margaret said, her tone judgemental.

'That's because the poor man's been ill,' Ena explained.

'Not too ill to get his wife in the family way.'

Ena's cheeks flushed and she began to giggle.

'Shush, Ena!' Claire elbowed her younger sister in the ribs.

'Ouch! That hurt!' Ena turned, glared at Claire and hit her on the arm.

'As I was saying…!' Margaret shouted above the noise of Ena and Claire squabbling. 'I don't know how old she is, but --'

'Mam, Claire dug me in the ribs,' Ena said, interrupting Margaret to make sure she got her complaint in before Claire, who had already opened her mouth to tell her mother that Ena had hit her.

'You big baby, I hardly touched you!'

'I'm not a baby. Fatty!' Ena hissed.

Margaret rolled her eyes and waited for her sisters to stop bickering. 'As I was saying... She looks older than her years, but that's what having kids so young does for you.' Margaret pursed her lips, indicating she was an authority on the subject.

Bess and Tom, doing their best not to laugh, were saved by their mother. 'I think you're right, Margaret. I was young and slim, and I didn't have a grey hair in my head until I had that pair,' she said, frowning at Ena and Claire.

'That's enough!' their father said, standing up and pushing his chair away from the table. 'Of one thing I am sure,' he added, taking in his three younger daughters, 'Mrs Barnett won't be sitting next door gossiping about her neighbours!'

Claire and Ena, allies now, stood up without saying another word and began clearing the table. While their mother covered the leftover food and put it in the larder, Bess and Margaret washed the dishes and put them away.

After banking up the fire, Tom poured his mother and each of his sisters a glass of sherry, his father and himself a glass of stout. Then, as they had done on so many New Years' Eves in the past, the family sat round the fire and listened to the wireless.

Sitting on the corner of the fire surround, Bess watched her father take his old pipe from the mantelshelf. It had belonged to his father. He only smoked it at Christmas and New Year. The rest of the year he smoked Capstan Full Strength cigarettes, or rolled his own. He placed the empty pipe in his mouth and held it between his teeth while he took a piece of the grainy block from its wrapper and rubbed it between the palms of his hands until it was shredded. He then filled the bowl of the pipe, pressing and patting the coarse flakes of tobacco with his thumb, while he listened to the BBC's National Programme. At last he struck a match, put it to the pipe's bowl, and sucked slowly and deeply. Once the ritual was over Bess's thoughts turned to events earlier in the evening and to James Foxden. Smiling, she hummed The Blue Danube and recalled how James had asked her to join the party. If only, she thought, and wondered if she would see him again during the holidays.

Before the New Year message, the BBC crackled its nightly news bulletin highlighting the collapse of Germany's economy, the threat it posed to Europe and the possibility of war. Thomas Dudley tapped his pipe on the hot-brick at the side of the fire. 'They told us there'd never be another war,' he said, running his thumb round the bowl of the pipe to make sure it was empty. 'They said the Great War was the war to end all wars.'

No one spoke. Their father had fought in France with the Royal Mounted Engineers from 1914 to 1918 and was lucky to get out alive. A bullet went through his right knee and into the heart of the horse he was riding. The horse died instantly.

It was Tom who broke the silence. 'It's the only way to stop Hitler and his Nazis from taking over Europe, Dad. From what I've been reading in the papers, another war is inevitable.'

The wireless crackled and went dead. Tom tapped the Bakelite case and it burst into life in time for the BBC's New Year message: 'Peace in our time and goodwill to all men.'

'Except to Herr Hitler,' Claire shouted and everyone cheered.

On the stroke of midnight the mood lightened, a toast was made to absent friends, Tom and Margaret led the family in a verse of Auld Lang Syne and Big Ben chimed in the New Year of 1939.

Early on New Year's morning, Bess walked up to the stables at Foxden Hall with her father. She saddled her favourite horse, a black mare called Sable, and when Tom hadn't arrived by the time she was ready to leave she set off alone.

'I'm going up to Rye Hills, Dad,' she called to her father, who was saddling Sultan, a handsome five-year-old Irish hunter. 'Tell Tom where I'm heading when he gets here.'

'Will do! Oh, and Bess?' her father called after her. 'Don't forget the horses have to be groomed and on stable parade for Mr Porter to inspect at nine. The hunt's at ten. You bear that in mind now.'

Bess shuddered. How could she forget? For as long as she could remember she'd been taken up to the Hall on New Year's Day to watch the hunt – and if the kill was close she'd been taken to that too. She shook the memory from her mind. 'Don't worry,' she shouted back to her father. 'I know what a stickler for punctuality Mr Porter is.' She didn't like the old man very much, but as Mr Porter was the estate manager and her father's boss, it was up to him who rode the horses out, so it was wise to keep in his good books.

Bess walked Sable round the lake and trotted her back through the woods. Once they were in open countryside she allowed the horse to gallop at her own pace until they came to the river.

What a beautiful morning, she thought, looking back at the Hall. The early morning sun penetrating the frozen marshes produced a fine silver mist that shimmered and rose before evaporating into the cold air. The Hall looked as if it was floating on a glistening sea. It was while she was watching the illusion that Bess noticed a horse and rider on the horizon. Putting her hand up to shade her eyes, she recognised the horse as Sultan, but she wasn't able to see the rider because the sun was directly behind him. It must be our Tom, she thought. I'll teach him to be late. She took off her neckerchief and waved it in the air encouragingly. As the rider started towards her, she galloped away, laughing.

She dismounted to rest Sable at Bonn's Hole, a picturesque part of the River Swift where, as a child, she had spent many sunny afternoons - first with Tom and his friends and later with her sisters. The water was clear then but now, after the recent snowfalls, the current was fierce and the river muddy. Legend had it that on a winter morning many years ago a farmer and his wife, named Bonn, were taking produce to market in Lowarth by horse and cart when the horse slipped a shoe and stumbled into the river, taking the Bonns and the cart with him. Mr and Mrs Bonn and the horse were rescued, but the cart was stuck in mud on the riverbed and couldn't be pulled out. Eventually the cart disintegrated, leaving that part of the river wider and deeper, and it has been called Bonn's Hole ever since.

'Perhaps it was on a morning like this, with the river ready to burst its banks, that Farmer Bonn's horse lost his footing,' someone called to her.

'Yes-- perhaps it was,' Bess said, unable to hide the surprise in her voice. Bess felt her cheeks flush so to give herself time to recover she took two carrots from her pocket. She gave one to Sable and the other to Sultan, before looking up at James Foxden and smiling.

'You're an early bird,' he said, dismounting and following her along the bridle path that linked the Foxden Estate to the Rye Hills and Lowarth.

'This is the best time of the day,' she replied, stroking Sable's nose. 'It's peaceful and quiet out here early in the morning. Sometimes I feel as if Sable and I are the only people in the world – if you know what I mean. Then I see a rabbit or a fox and, well … I love to ride out at dawn and watch the sunrise.'

Laughing, James said, 'You must get up very early in the summer.'

Bess shot him a look, but soon saw the funny side of what she'd said and, laughing, kept walking. She didn't feel the need to make conversation. It was enough to breathe the morning air and be with someone with whom she had riding in common – if nothing else. Nor did she feel self-conscious because she was the daughter of a groom and James the son of a lord. Everything was equal out on the Estate; there was no class or gender difference.

She was miles away, savouring the freedom that the open fields allowed, when James said, 'Why did you ride off when you saw me?'

'I thought you were Tom. I challenged him to a race this morning, but he didn't show up.'

'I'll take up the challenge on Tom's behalf,' James said. 'But I think it only fair to warn you that I have never been beaten racing Sultan across the Estate.'

'Yet!' Dare she challenge James Foxden? Yes, she dare! 'I'll see you back at the stables.' And before he had time to reply, she was astride Sable and galloping towards the Hall. With the wind in her face, exhilarated and excited, she raced across Foxden's fields and meadows. Of course she could beat James Foxden on Sable; Sable was the fastest horse in the stables; she loved to race and she loved to win, as much as Bess did.

'You're late, Bess! Mr Porter's looking for you,' her father shouted as she trotted Sable into the yard.

'Only by a few minutes,' she said, dismounting. 'Anyway we don't care, do we, girl? We beat James Foxden in a race,' she shouted over her shoulder as she walked into the stables – and into Mr Porter.

'If you wish to continue exercising the horses in my stables, Elizabeth Dudley, I suggest you abide by my rules,' Mr Porter said curtly.

'Yes, Mr Porter. I'm sorry I was late bringing Sable back.'

'It's not good enough. Mr James is leading the hunt today and it's my job to make sure the horses are as well turned out for him as they would be if it was his father wearing the Pink.'

'And they will be, of that I am sure, Mr Porter,' James said, walking into the stables behind the old man. 'Your horses are famous for being the best turned out hunt horses in three counties.'

'Thank you, sir; it's very kind of you to say so.' Mr Porter puffed out his chest and pulled himself up to his full five feet five inches. 'If you'll excuse me, I must get on. Miss Dudley? Sir?' he said with a nod, and left the stables.

Bess held her breath until he was out of sight, then burst into laughter.

'He's not such a bad old stick,' James said.

'I suppose not,' Bess conceded, taking off Sable's saddle, 'but he's always so damn miserable. I don't think I've ever seen him smile.'

'Do you ever smile at him?' James asked, grinning.

'No!' Bess replied, mimicking him with an equally silly grin before leading the way into the tack room.

'Perhaps you should. That face would reduce Ebenezer Scrooge to laughter,' James said, following her with Sultan's saddle.

While they fed and watered the horses they reminisced about their childhood and the sunny afternoons they'd spent at the river in the school holidays.

Shaking his head and laughing, James said, 'What a tomboy you were, always trying to compete with the lads, challenging them to jump across the river, or climb trees. The trouble you got into!'

Pretending to be shocked, Bess retaliated. 'What about the trouble you and Tom got into? Have you forgotten how the pair of you went scrumping in the vicarage orchard? How the vicar, taking his dog for a walk, had stopped to play throw-and-fetch beneath the apple tree that you two had climbed? When you were away at boarding school, Tom missed you. It wasn't so bad for me,' she said, turning away so James couldn't see the blush in her cheeks. 'I was much younger. Besides, I'd learned to ride a horse by then and progressed from jumping the river to jumping fences.'

By the time the third stable lad had nudged her and said pointedly, 'Excuse me, Miss!' Bess realised that she and James were in their way. The lads could hardly tell James to leave his own stables, so she intervened. 'James, do you think we should let the lads get on with grooming the horses for the hunt?'

'Perhaps we should,' he said, looking around at the frantic activity. 'Will you be riding out tomorrow?'

'Yes, if Mr Porter will let me ride Sable.'

'Oh, I'm sure he will,' James said. 'Until tomorrow then! Same time?'

'Of course!'

As she approached the cottage, Bess could see Tom's legs sticking out from under his Austin 7 motorcar. Tinkering, he called it. She opened the gate. 'And where were you at seven o'clock this morning?'

'Here, giving the car the once-over.'

'You'll never have any money while you've got that thing!'

'Perhaps not,' her brother said, edging his way out from beneath the car. 'But I'll have

28

plenty of girls.' With black and oily outstretched hands, he chased her into the cottage. 'I'll teach you to drive,' he said, scrubbing his hands in the kitchen sink with a brush and a block of green soap that stank like fish and carbolic. 'You can have a go now if you like.'

'I'd rather ride a horse, thank you.'

'But cars are the future,' her older brother argued.

'Then I'll learn to drive one in the future,' Bess said, pulling on the peak of his old cap until it covered his eyes before running upstairs to her room to get changed.

From her bedroom window Bess had a good view of the huntsmen and women as they arrived at the Hall for the meet. She scanned the crowd looking for Sable, hoping to see an experienced huntsman astride her rather than a novice.

She was watching the hounds running round in circles, annoying the horses with their excited yapping, when she noticed the dark haired girl from New Year's Eve on Sable, followed closely by James on Sultan. She hated to admit it, but they made a handsome couple. Today, because James was leading the Hunt, he was wearing a red jacket instead of his usual black. Hunting Pink, they called it, but it was more the colour of scarlet. Bess watched as James and the beautiful girl from the party led the meet down the drive towards the cottage.

'I hope she can ride,' Bess said from between gritted teeth.

'Hope who can ride?' Tom had come into the room and was standing at her side.

'The girl riding Sable.'

'What a beauty. Lucky old James,' Tom said, laughing.

'Can't you think of anything else, Tom?' Bess snapped, immediately regretting the way she'd reacted. Her brother might suspect she had feelings for James – something she was almost afraid to admit to herself. 'I'm sorry--'

'I know how you hate fox hunting,' Tom said, putting his arm round her shoulder to comfort her, 'but it's a country tradition, you know it is. Gentlemen--'

'Gentlemen? There's nothing genteel about thirty human beings on horseback and a pack of half-crazed dogs chasing one little fox to ground, frightening the life out of it or ripping it to pieces,' she said, all thoughts of the girl with James forgotten.

'I was going to say, gentlemen have been hunting foxes since the sixteenth century and --'

'Maybe they have, but it doesn't make it right!' Bess shivered. Watching the hunt reminded her of the day she was blooded. 'Go on,' the villagers shouted. 'It's lucky to be first at the kill – to be given the pad and to be blooded.'

'It's not lucky for the fox!' Bess had screamed back at them. But her mother, egged on by the village women, held her tightly by the wrist and dragged her through the pack of babbling hounds and the panting horses to the dying fox. She was six years old – and terrified.

Every year the memories of that poor fox lying at her feet, his eyes open and glazed, came flooding back to her. It had been fifteen years, but she could still smell the blood and feel it, warm and sticky on her face.

During the weeks that followed, Bess and James met most mornings, but they were never alone. Bess rode with her father, or the lads. James rode with the girl from the party who he introduced to Bess as Annabel, but who Bess's father addressed as Miss Hadleigh. Tom rode with them several times. And each time he made a beeline for Annabel. He had no chance, Bess thought. Annabel Hadleigh may throw her head back and laugh loudly at Tom's jokes, but she only had eyes for James.

On the evening before Tom returned to Suffolk and Bess to London, Tom and James arranged to meet for a drink at The Crown in the village of Woodcote.

'Are you coming with us, Sis? I'll buy you a glass of Vimto if you promise to be a good girl,' Tom teased.

The prospect of seeing James, spending time with him socially, thrilled Bess. 'I might as well,' she said as casually as her excited heart would allow. 'I've nothing else planned.'

'No she is not!' her father interrupted. 'A public house is no place for a woman.'

'But you take Mam to the pub!' Bess said.

'That's different. Your mother's accompanied by her husband!'

'And I shall be accompanied by my brother,' Bess argued.

'I said no, Bess! What on earth would Mr James think?'

Bess was crestfallen. James was a modern man. He wouldn't think it improper if she went to the village pub. But she didn't argue; locking horns with her father was futile.

The next morning, after waving Tom off, Bess walked up to the stables and took Sable out for what would be the last time for several months. 'Another beautiful day,' she said, leaning forward and patting Sable's neck as she took in Foxden's magnificent landscape. The meadows and pastures, no longer blanketed in snow, were lush and green. The River Swift, sparkling in the wintry sun, snaked its way south and the Rye Hills seemed to roll on forever. Bess sighed. She would miss mornings like this when she returned to London – she always did – until she got back into the swing of studying, then there'd be no time.

At Bonn's Hole she dismounted and looked back. There was no one on the horizon. James wouldn't catch her up today. Today she would ride alone.

Hoping to see him before she left for London, Bess spent longer than usual feeding and grooming Sable, but it wasn't to be. So, after saying goodbye to the grooms and stable lads, she thanked Mr Porter and walked home.

While she was packing her college work, she realised that one of the books she had brought home to study, a novel by Mary Webb called Gone to Earth, was missing. She searched the cottage upstairs and down, unpacked and repacked her suitcase and satchel, but the book was nowhere to be found. She sat on her bed, exasperated. It had to be somewhere and if it wasn't at home the only place it could be was the library at Foxden Hall. It was half-past twelve; she was cutting it fine if she wanted to catch the two o'clock train from Rugby, but she needed to find the book because it had to be returned to the Co-operative Lending Library in Kensington before the beginning of term. She already owed sixpence, because the book was three days overdue. She didn't want to pay three shillings and sixpence to replace it. She had no choice but to go up to the library and look for it.

Bess set off along the drive. In the worst case, she wouldn't find the book and she would have to take a later train. In the best case, she'd find the book and bump into James Foxden. Then to hell with the train, she laughed. As she neared the Hall, her heart began to beat faster.

To her relief she found the book almost immediately. It had slipped between the seat-cushion and the backrest of the window-seat on New Year's Eve. She had finished reading it and put it down to look out of the window, as she was doing now, and – her stomach turned a somersault – there was James, in the courtyard, standing by his car.

She scrambled onto the seat and watched him walk from the car to the house. Within seconds he was back carrying an assortment of cases and bags, which he strapped on the back of his car. He returned to the house as a young maid came out with a tartan blanket over her arm. The maid went to the passenger door of the car, opened it and, leaning in, wrapped the blanket around someone's legs. Bess wondered who it could be. It hadn't occurred to her that James would take someone to London with him. She leaned closer to the window, hoping to catch a glimpse of his passenger.

She didn't have to wait long. After tucking in the blanket the maid stood up and, as she stepped away from the car, the passenger leant forward and spoke to her. Bess took a sharp involuntary breath. The fur collar on her coat was turned up and the brim of her red trilby hat was pulled down, but when she lifted her head to speak to the maid Bess could see clearly that James's travelling companion was Annabel Hadleigh.

'Caught you,' James said, looking over her shoulder to see what it was that had captured her attention so fully.

Bess shrieked. So preoccupied was she with watching Annabel Hadleigh that she had neither seen nor heard James enter the library. 'You're going to have to stop creeping up on me, you know,' she said, moving away from the window.

'I'm sorry if I made you jump but I wanted to catch you before I left. I'm driving Annabel home to Kent but I'll be in London tomorrow and I was thinking that, since we're both down there, perhaps we could meet up... I could telephone you and...?'

Bess opened her mouth, but couldn't speak. There was no public telephone at her lodgings and Mrs McAllister, her landlady, didn't allow her tenants to make or accept calls on her private telephone unless it was an emergency. Nor did she approve of them having gentlemen friends. Of all her rules – and there were many – no gentlemen callers was at the top of the list. Besides, although the house was clean and tidy, the furniture was old-fashioned and the décor was tired. While it was good enough for her, Bess didn't want James Foxden to see where she was lodging. Nor did she want to subject him to tea and a grilling from Mrs McAllister.

'But if you would rather I didn't call,' James said, sensing that Bess felt uncomfortable at the suggestion.

'Oh no, it isn't that-- It's my landlady,' she said feeling an utter innocent and a fool.

'Then I'll give you my card with my telephone number and if you have a free evening you can call me. We could meet in town, see a show and have a bite of supper.

Or we could go to a dance at the Lyceum or the Trocadero.'

Bess accepted the small card. 'I would like that.'

'See you in London, then!' Smiling, James offered Bess his hand.

'Yes... London,' she said, taking his hand in hers.

'Goodbye.'

By the time she'd formulated the word 'goodbye', James had left. She heard his car start up in the courtyard and turned to look out of the window, but she was too late. She ran to the window overlooking the front drive in time to see the small green sports car, enveloped in a cloud of exhaust smoke, disappear down the drive and out of sight.

Unable to move, Bess stood in the empty library for some minutes. Did James Foxden invite her, Bess Dudley, to supper in London? Perhaps he was just being kind to the sister of his childhood friend. Did he, or did she imagine that he held her hand for a little longer than was necessary when he said goodbye? Well, maybe she did imagine that, but one thing she did not imagine was the small white business card with James's name and telephone number embossed in black, which she was holding in her hand.

Before she burst with excitement, Bess put the card between the pages of her book and ran home.

The train to London was ready to depart as Bess and her father arrived at Rugby station. The station attendant, Bess could see, had closed the last door in the last carriage and was standing with his whistle poised.

'Stop!' Bess shouted, running across the platform – and as she reached the train the attendant opened the door. 'Thank you,' she gasped, throwing her luggage into the corridor and jumping in after it.

She could see several empty seats in the adjacent compartment, so she left her case and satchel where they'd fallen, pulled down the window in the top of the door and hung out. 'Bye Dad, I'll write.'

Her father's farewell reply disappeared, drowned by the piercing sound of the steam whistle as the train began to move off, as did his image beneath smoke and gases from the train's chimney. After closing the window, Bess picked up her bags and elbowed the half-open door of the compartment until it was wide enough for her to pass through.

'Let me help you,' said a young man, jumping up from his seat and rushing to her aid as she stumbled in. Then, as if it were a feather, he lifted her suitcase and placed it on the overhead luggage rack.

'Thank you.' Breathless, Bess flopped down into the empty seat opposite, next to the window. And, after making a porthole in the condensation, she leaned forward and peered out.

A flock of sheep, fat in their winter coats, stood firm with their backs to the wind and a herd of cows huddled together by a sparse hedge which, without foliage, gave little shelter. It was a bleak picture.

A playful cry from the young woman sitting next to Bess brought her attention back to the train's interior. Her male companion was teasing her with a small red box. Pretending it was an aeroplane, he flew the box towards her - taking care to keep it out of her reach - and then flew it away again. Eventually, after making a series of staccato droning sounds he brought it crashing down onto her lap. Squealing with excitement the young woman opened the box to discover a small solitaire diamond ring, which her companion placed on her engagement finger.

Bess smiled, remembering the token of affection that nestled between the pages of her book. She opened the book and tried to read, but she couldn't concentrate. All she could think about was James. She closed her eyes and pictured his face, his strong jaw and high cheekbones, the outline of his mouth and his teeth – white and straight. His eyes were clear and blue and the skin around them wrinkled when he laughed... And she wondered when she'd see him again. She wondered too about Annabel Hadleigh. What was Annabel Hadleigh to James? What kind of a relationship did they have? And what kind of a relationship might she hope to have with James?

She took the small white card with its clear sharp lettering from her book and read the inscription: "The Honourable James Foxden, Barrister at Law." The telephone number was in italics, a little smaller than his name, in the bottom right-hand corner beneath "Foxden, Foxden and Hadleigh." She felt a tinge of unease as she nursed the book on her lap. Thinking how easy it would be to lose the card if it slipped from between the book's pages, she took her wallet from her handbag and placed it securely between two ten-shilling notes.

'Would you like a cigarette?' the young man sitting opposite asked.

'No, thank you, I don't smoke.' Bess couldn't put her finger on it, but there was something about the way he looked at her that made her feel uneasy. She knew that if she didn't occupy herself in some way he would try to make conversation, so she looked out of the window again. She didn't mean to be rude; she just didn't want to talk to him, or to anyone else for that matter. She wanted to sit quietly and reflect on everything that had happened since New Year's Eve. Once she was back in London, she would have little or no time to herself. With her final exams looming she'd be studying day and night, except for the evening James was taking her out. She wondered when and where that would be. Would they go to a show, or would they go to a dance, before they went to supper - or would they do both? Of one thing she was certain: wherever they decided to go, she would have nothing on her mind on that night except James.

With the card safely in her handbag Bess opened her book again and started to read. Within a few minutes her eyes grew heavy and she began to feel tired. The cha-cha-cha chum, cha-cha-cha-chum as the train sped south became hypnotic and she closed her eyes.

Rays of pale winter sunshine filtered through the train's dusty windows and cast a warm dappled light across Bess's face. She sensed the train slowing down each time it approached a station and knew when someone had boarded or left the train by a cutting draught that swept into the compartment each time the door opened. And when the train entered a tunnel the clear, sharp sound of metal on metal became dull and muffled and her eyes, although closed, sensed the daylight had been snuffed out. Once through the tunnel Bess felt again the mellow sunshine on her face. She dreamt of James standing by her side in Foxden's library, tall and handsome and...

CHAPTER TWO

'Excuse me, Miss,' Bess heard someone say. She opened her eyes and saw the ticket inspector. His face was level with hers and he was tapping her on the shoulder.

'We've arrived at Euston. You'll have to leave the train now or you'll end up going back to where you came from and that wouldn't do, would it?'

'No, it wouldn't,' Bess said, looking round, trying to get her bearings. The compartment was empty. Her fellow passengers had left and she could see a long queue of disgruntled looking people waiting to board. Under pressure to vacate the train as quickly as possible, Bess stumbled to her feet while the ticket inspector lifted down her suitcase.

'Is this everything, miss?' Without waiting for a reply, he handed Bess her satchel and hauled her suitcase to the door.

Turning, she picked up her book and then looked for her handbag. 'Wait!' she shouted. A wave of nausea swept over her as the realisation struck. 'My handbag has gone!'

'Perhaps you put it in one of your other bags,' he said, frowning.

'No! I didn't. I remember clearly, I was reading my book and I put my handbag on my lap for safekeeping. I put the book down, but not my handbag. I was holding it when I went to sleep. Someone has stolen it!'

In the station's cramped and shabby lost property office a small birdlike man with a beaked nose and dark piercing eyes produced an official-looking document with the words "LOST PROPERTY" stencilled across the top in red lettering, and "Euston Square Police Station" at the bottom in small letters. The man placed the sheet of paper squarely in front of Bess and handed her a fountain pen that looked old enough to have been used to list the animals in Noah's Ark.

'This form says "Lost Property." My handbag was stolen,' Bess said, and pushed the form back to the man.

'Head Office does not issue "Stolen Property" forms,' the man said, pushing the form back to her.

Bess sighed loudly and pushed the form back to him. 'If I fill out a form that says "Lost Property" how will the police know my handbag was stolen?'

'Because I write "STOLEN" on the top before I take it to them,' he said, and pushed the form firmly back to her.

Bess cleared her throat. 'If you'd have told me that in the first place--'

'I'm telling you now.'

'That's all right then!' she said, smiling thinly. 'Thank you!'

The man nodded half-heartedly that he'd acknowledged her thanks, which didn't make

Bess feel any better. 'I'm sorry,' she said, 'but there's something in my handbag that's very important to me, and--' Seeing the man's blank expression she stopped speaking. 'I'll just fill out the form, then.'

Under his watchful gaze Bess wrote a description of the brown leather handbag with its gold-coloured metal clasp shaped like a bow. She listed the bag's contents: the brown leather wallet containing three pounds – two pound notes and two ten shilling notes; the matching leather purse, which contained five shillings in change; her powder compact, lipstick, and silver comb with mother-of-pearl fashioned along the spine. Last, but by no means least, she wrote a brief description of the small white business card that James had given her earlier in the day – and she wished with all her heart that she'd left it between the pages of her book. After reading the description she signed her name and added her London address and telephone number.

'We report all lost property to the local police, so there's every chance your bag will be found and returned to you in due course, Miss.'

Bess did not share the Birdman's faith in human nature and wanted to scream, 'My handbag is not lost; it was stolen!' Instead she thanked him, picked up her suitcase and satchel, and left his stuffy office.

The sky, dark with the onset of dusk, looked as if it was ready to burst under the weight of ballooning storm clouds. Bess was cold and she was tired. 'What next?' she said aloud. Then she remembered she didn't have an umbrella.

Dragging her suitcase onto the concourse, she edged her way into the slipstream of people heading for the buses. But she couldn't take a bus. She didn't have the fare. How was she going to get to her lodgings? Perhaps the bus conductor would let her send the money on. She'd heard of visitors to London leaving their names and addresses with bus conductors and posting the fare to the bus company when they returned home. If she explained what had happened perhaps she too could… She stopped. On the far side of the concourse, next to the sign for taxis, she saw a telephone box. She had money in her room. She would telephone her lodgings and ask her housemate Molly to bring it to her. She would have to reverse the charges, but because it was an emergency her landlady wouldn't mind.

With renewed optimism, Bess sidestepped out of the bus queue, but before she had taken a step in the direction of the telephone box she was knocked off her feet.

'Sorry,' a city type in a bowler hat shouted without stopping.

'No you're not,' Bess shouted back at him, 'or you'd have looked where you were going.' She struggled to her feet, but before she'd recovered her balance a giant of a man swept past. His suitcase caught her suitcase with such force that the handle of her suitcase snapped and the case crashed to the floor, discharging its contents onto the concourse.

'Stop!' Bess shouted, but the giant didn't stop; no one stopped. Everyone was determined to get to a bus or taxi before the storm broke, and pushed their way to the exits, swerving to the left and right to avoid falling over her as she crawled around on the floor. When she had found and returned her clothes to the gaping suitcase she picked it up and held it in her arms as if it were a baby. Blind with anger and frustration – and with as much dogged determination as everyone else – she pushed her way through the crowd to the telephone box.

Triumphant, she stepped inside, and then burst into tears. Taped across the front of the black metal telephone unit was a piece of cardboard with "OUT OF ORDER" written in chalk. Unable to take any more, Bess gave up the heavy burden in her aching arms to the floor of the redundant telephone booth and sobbed.

'I think these are yours.' An attractive, well dressed woman in her early thirties handed Bess a brown leather glove and a white cotton underskirt.

'Thank you,' Bess whispered, accepting the articles of clothing. And in the comparative quiet of the telephone box, she told the woman about the theft of her handbag, which meant she had no way of getting to her lodgings, the obnoxious man in the lost property office and the brute that knocked her off her feet. 'You'll have to excuse me; I don't usually give in to tears.'

'Nor I, but I think I would if everything that has happened to you today had happened to me. But please dry your eyes,' the woman said, handing Bess a small white handkerchief. 'I have an idea. My husband will be here soon. Why don't you come home with us, have something to eat, and when my husband goes to work this evening he will drive you to your lodgings.'

'I couldn't,' Bess said. 'I don't-- I mean, you don't know me. You're very kind, but you don't even know my name – I don't know yours.'

'That is true, but easily remedied. My name is Natalie Goldman. How do you do?'

'How do you do, Mrs Goldman?'

'Please, call me Natalie.'

'Thank you, Natalie. My name's Bess, Bess Dudley.'

'I am pleased to meet you, Bess.' Natalie Goldman took Bess's hand, shook it, and laughed kindly. 'It is a bizarre situation in which we find ourselves, Bess, do you not think?'

Bess looked around at the out-of-order telephone and her old, now broken, suitcase, and then at the sophisticated woman with her smart case covered in stickers from a dozen foreign countries and laughed with her.

'There is a saying in my country. When two people have laughed together in the face of adversity they will be good friends.'

Sensing that Bess was still unsure, Natalie Goldman opened her handbag and took out her purse. 'If you would rather not come to our home, let me give you the taxi fare to your lodgings.'

'I didn't tell you so you'd give me money-- I don't want your money.'

'Then how will you get there?' Natalie Goldman asked sympathetically.

'I don't know,' Bess sighed, unable to stop her tears.

Natalie Goldman put her arm around Bess's shoulder. 'You look all-in, Bess. Please let me help you?'

A sob caught in Bess's throat. 'Thank you, Natalie, you're very kind. I should like very much to come to your home.'

'And you will be very welcome,' a tall handsome man said as he arrived at Natalie's side.

'Anton!' Natalie turned at the sound of the man's voice and threw her arms around his neck. 'Bess, may I introduce you to my husband, Anton?'

'I am very pleased to meet you, Anton. Your wife has been very kind to me. I don't know what I'd have done without her.'

Anton Goldman rolled his eyes good-naturedly, as if to say he was used to hearing people say such things about his wife. 'And I am pleased to meet you, Bess. We should get going before it rains,' he said, taking the safety strap from his wife's suitcase and buckling it round Bess's before carrying both cases to his car.

Bess and Natalie ran across the road behind Anton and while he put the cases in the boot they jumped into the car – Natalie in the front, next to her husband, and Bess in the back. As Anton steered the car into the traffic heading north, towards Hampstead Heath, it began to rain.

The Goldman's house was at the end of a narrow but well-lit lane on the south side of the Heath, a stone's throw from Heath Street, Hampstead's main shopping area. The journey took an hour and by the time they arrived it was blowing a gale and raining heavily.

'It's too windy for the umbrella; we'll have to run for it.' Anton leapt out of the car to get the cases from the boot and the women made a dash for the house.

At a downstairs window Bess could see three small faces peering out into the night. By the time she and Natalie had reached the front door the welcoming party had opened it and were tumbling out to greet them.

'Hello my darlings,' their mother said. 'I've missed you so much.' Natalie Goldman wrapped her slender arms round her three children. 'Come, let us go inside out of the rain.'

The children asked their mother about the train, the boat that had taken her across the sea, and about their grandparents. Then the smaller of the two boys asked his mother if she had brought anything back for him. 'Yes,' she said, 'there is something for each of you, but you will have to wait until I unpack. I promise to tell you every detail of my trip tomorrow, but tonight we have a guest. So children, after our guest has freshened up, would you please show her to the back sitting room?'

Natalie took off her coat, helped Bess out of hers, and hung both in the cloakroom next to the front door before showing Bess to a small well-equipped washroom further along the hall. 'I'll use the bathroom upstairs, if you can make do with this one, and we'll meet in the sitting room. Use anything you need, Bess,' Natalie called.

Bess filled the hand basin with hot water, lathered the bristles of a small nailbrush with rose scented soap and scrubbed the dirt from beneath her fingernails. Once her hands were clean she emptied the basin and refilled it with clean water. Then she washed her face, patted it dry with a soft white towel and looked in the mirror. Rogue curls had escaped from the bun at the nape of her neck and hung at the side of her face like a spaniel's ears. She didn't have a comb and she wasn't about to look in Natalie's cupboards, so she poked the offending strands of hair back into the bun with her fingers and secured them with a couple of Kirby grips that she found in the pocket of her skirt. Now her reflection showed a clean face and almost tidy hair, so she left the washroom.

Natalie and Anton's children were sitting at the bottom of the stairs in the neatly furnished entrance hall. 'If you'd like to come with us,' their daughter said, jumping up, 'we'll show you to the back sitting room. Come on,' she said to her brothers.

The boys followed closely behind their sister and Bess followed them along a short corridor with a door on either side. The oldest of the boys opened the door on the right, and then stood back to let Bess enter. Once she was inside the children trooped in behind her, followed by their mother.

Except for a gate-legged dining table and six chairs, Bess thought the back sitting room looked more like a front parlour. Thick rugs covered the floor, heavy brocade curtains hung from the window and, on the opposite side of the room, a large settee and two armchairs stood either side of a roaring fire.

Natalie's daughter showed Bess to the armchair nearest the fire and joined her mother and brothers on the settee.

'Bess, I would like to introduce you to my children,' Natalie said when the boys had stopped fidgeting. 'This is my daughter Rebekah, who is ten years old, and these two young men are my sons – Benjamin, who will soon be nine years old and Samuel, who is seven.'

The younger of the two boys sat up with a start and looked at his mother. 'I'm seven and a half,' he said indignantly.

'Forgive me, Bess. Samuel is seven and a half,' she corrected, putting her arm around her youngest son's shoulder and drawing him to her.

Benjamin gave Bess a welcoming smile but Samuel, concentrating on the small semi-circles he was making in the rug with the toe of his right shoe, didn't look up.

Bess smiled at Benjamin and Samuel, and then at Rebekah. Rebekah had inherited her mother's bright intelligent eyes and dark hair. Benjamin was from the same mould, tall and good looking with an athletic build. Samuel, on the other hand, was as short as Benjamin was tall and as chubby as his older brother was slim. He wore owlish spectacles that looked as if they were too big for his small face and he scowled - especially when he was being talked about or looked at.

'Hello,' Bess said, 'I'm very pleased to meet you.'

'And children, this is Miss Dudley.'

Smiling, Rebekah said, 'Hello,' while Benjamin, with a smile and Samuel, with a puckered brow said, 'How do you do?' as one voice.

'Boys, would you please go upstairs and find Nanny Friel? Ask her if she would bring in a selection of cold plates with tea. And ask her if she and Nurse Ambler would like to join us here in the sitting room.'

Without hesitating, the boys ran off to relay the message to their nanny while Rebekah sat quietly reading a book.

'I'm afraid we don't keep to tradition. Nanny used to despair of us when she first came to live here. The children and I take tea in whichever room is the warmest – often it's the kitchen – and she just about puts up with that. Today, because we have a guest, she will expect us to observe the correct etiquette. Tea and cold plates in the back-sitting room? Tut, tut! We must prepare ourselves for the frown of disapproval from our darling Nanny,' Natalie said, laughing.

'Do you like reading, Rebekah?' Bess asked when the young girl closed her book.

'Yes, I like languages too. I'm learning French. My friend at school has a French tutor. Son nom est Monique. Her name is Monique,' she said with quiet confidence.

'Well done, darling,' Natalie said, applauding her daughter.

'And, because Nanny Friel doesn't speak English – and talks to us all the time in German – I understand and speak a little German. Daddy speaks German too.'

Natalie laughed. 'Better than I speak English, Bess.'

Bess smiled, but said nothing; she wasn't sure she'd be able to keep the surprise out of her voice. Natalie spoke as if she was German, but surely not? She had an accent, but it wasn't necessarily a German accent. Bess was pondering Natalie's ancestry when Nanny Friel entered the room carrying a tray of crockery which she plonked down on the sideboard with a clatter, making Bess jump.

'Dieses ist nicht bequeme, Natalie. No!' she said, her starched pinafore crackling like autumn leaves as she dragged the oak drop-leaf table from beneath the window and extended it to its full potential.

'It will be comfortable enough, Nanny, don't worry,' Natalie said, smiling at Bess as if to say, I told you so!

'Wenn Sie so sagen,' Nanny capitulated, eyeing Bess with suspicion.

'I don't think Nanny likes me,' Bess said when Nanny left the room.

'Oh, don't pay any attention. Nanny suspects everyone of being a spy, or worse. She has been with us a long time and we love her very much, don't we, children?'

'Nanny was Mamma's nanny when Mamma was little,' Rebekah said.

'But she's old now,' Samuel whispered. 'So we mustn't make her run around after us. We have to ask Nurse Ambler if we want anything, don't we, Mamma?'

Natalie shook her head and smiled at her youngest son, but before she could answer him Nanny, followed by Nurse Ambler and Anton, brought in trays of food, which they lined up along the sideboard.

After introducing Bess to Nanny and Nurse, Anton went to the kitchen to fetch more chairs while the two women laid the table.

'Tea is ready, children,' Nurse Ambler called.

The three children jumped up and ran to the table where Nanny supervised the seating arrangements. When the children had settled down Nanny beckoned Bess to the table, pointing to a seat at the far end next to Anton and opposite Natalie.

'Help yourself, Bess, you must be hungry,' Natalie said.

Bess was hungry; it had been a long time since she had eaten anything. Because she'd gone up to the library at Foxden she had missed lunch. When she'd got home there hadn't been time to do anything but grab her bags and jump into the waiting taxi. And at Rugby station the train had been about to leave so she didn't have time to buy a sandwich from the cafeteria.

Anton handed her a dish of cold chicken and another of beef. Bess took a slice of meat from each and returned them to Anton who, before passing them to Natalie, forked another helping of meat onto her plate.

Bess cut into the beef, but before she had time to put her fork to her mouth, Nanny was at her side. 'Versuchen Sie bitte meinen speziellen Kartoffelsalat.' No sooner had she finished speaking than she raised her hand to Anton as if to say don't tell me! 'Please to eat it, my potato salat. It is food of my home,' she said, nodding and smiling in spite of the sadness Bess could see in her eyes. 'There is no one so good,' she concluded, and spooned a large dollop of creamy potato cubes with chopped onion and gherkin onto Bess's plate. 'Eat, bitte!'

Bess forked a portion of potato salad into her mouth. 'It's delicious, Nanny. I've never tasted anything like it.'

'Good,' Nanny said proudly and returned to her seat to eat her own food and watch over her young charges.

When it was time to leave everyone came to the front door to wave Anton and Bess off, including Nanny Friel and Nurse Ambler.

'Goodbye, Nurse Ambler and thank you,' Bess said to the children's nurse. 'And thank you for the delicious food,' Bess said to Nanny Friel. 'Will you send me the recipe for your wonderful potato salad?'

Natalie began to interpret, but stopped when Nanny shook her head. 'Nein!' she said 'It is the secret of my family. You come again here and I make for you.'

'Thank you. And thank you, Natalie. I don't know how I shall ever be able to repay you for your kindness,' Bess said, hugging Natalie Goldman as she would have hugged one of her sisters.

'I'm sure you would have done the same for me, Bess.'

'Yes, I would. And if there is ever anything I can do for you or for your family in the future,' Bess said, 'you only have to ask.'

Anton Goldman, having said goodbye to his family, had put Bess's case and satchel on the back seat of his Austin motorcar and was sitting with the engine running.

'I must go or I'll make your husband late for work. Thank you again.'

Bess walked down the path to a chorus of goodbyes from the Goldman children, opened the passenger door of their father's car and lowered herself onto the soft cream leather seat. As Anton reversed the car out of the drive, Bess waved a final farewell.

Anton Goldman drove along the lane, turned into Heath Street, and within minutes the quaint shops and cafés of Hampstead were behind them and they were heading for London's West End.

'What a wonderful wife and family you have, Anton,' Bess said. 'How kind and generous they are.'

'I think Natalie saw a kindred spirit in you, Bess.'

'And I in her. I liked her very much.'

Anton Goldman laughed. 'Sorry, Bess, I don't mean to be rude: That my wife liked you does not surprise me. That my children liked you was to be expected – what's not to like? But that Nanny Friel liked you means you must be a very special person, Miss Dudley.'

'I don't know about that, but I liked her too.' Bess wanted to know more about the elderly German woman, but thought Anton might think she was prying, so she didn't press him.

She watched the window-wipers as they swept backwards and forwards across the windscreen - swoosh shlap, swoosh shlap. Through the driving rain the streetlights looked as if they were flickering, as if the shilling in the electric meter was about to run out and at any moment the lights would flicker their last and the world would be plunged into darkness. They had travelled through London's suburbs for half an hour without speaking when Bess broke the silence. 'Where did you meet Natalie?'

'In Geneva, at the university. We had three wonderful years together, but once we had our degrees we had to return to our own countries, Natalie to Germany and me to England.'

'A long distance love affair,' Bess said. 'That couldn't have been easy.'

'It wasn't. We visited each other every few months, but it wasn't enough, so one morning I packed a bag, went to Germany and asked Natalie to marry me.'

Bess laughed. 'How romantic.' She looked at Anton, expecting to hear more, but his expression had changed from a smile to a frown. She wondered why. 'Were you married in Germany?' she asked after a few minutes.

'Yes, eventually, but while we were making the arrangements we encountered Nazis.' Anton cleared his throat. 'But I'm sure you don't want to hear about Nazis.'

Bess did want to hear about them, but she didn't want to upset Anton Goldman. 'My brother Tom and I talked about the Nazi party and Germany's chancellor, Adolf Hitler, at New Year,' she said. 'Tom thinks if Hitler has his way, there'll be another war. He says Nazis are bullies, and--'

'Oh, they're that alright. The month we were due to be married, fascists, men in brown shirts – so proud of their beliefs that they covered their faces with black scarves – painted swastikas and anti-Semitic slogans on the walls of the synagogue where Natalie's family worshipped and where we had planned to be married. Then, the day before our wedding, they burned the synagogue to the ground. The Rabbi was inside and died in the fire.

'My family and many of our friends had travelled from England and Switzerland to be at our wedding, so we had a civil ceremony in a neighbouring town. But the writing was on the wall, literally. I feared for our lives if we stayed in Germany, so I brought Natalie to England – and here we are.'

'Did Nanny Friel come to England with you?'

'No, she had retired by then. When Natalie went to university her parents bought Nanny a cottage in the village where her sister lived. She was happy for a couple of years. Then one day Natalie received a letter from her saying that her sister and several friends had gone missing - disappeared.' Anton paused for a moment, as if to regain his composure. Finally he said, 'Their bodies were found in nearby woods. They had been shot.'

'I'm sorry.' Sorry sounded pathetic, but Bess was so shocked she didn't know what to say.

'Natalie went to Germany immediately and set the wheels in motion to bring Nanny to England. It was almost impossible to get a travel permit for an elderly Jewish woman, but after bribing several local authority officials where Nanny lived, Natalie obtained a temporary permit for Nanny to visit Switzerland. It's too complicated to go into now, but that's why Nanny's wary of strangers. She's terrified the Nazis will find her and send her back to Germany.'

What had happened to Nanny Friel's sister and her friends was unthinkable. If she hadn't have heard it from someone who'd had first-hand experience of such horrors she wouldn't have believed it. Bess felt the bitter taste of bile rise in the back of her throat and swallowed hard.

When they arrived at The Strand Anton said, 'If you look to the right, Bess, you'll see the Prince Albert Theatre. That's where I work.'

Bess looked as directed and on the front of the theatre, high above the main entrance doors in letters standing six feet tall and illuminated by dozens of lights, it said "Goldman Productions".

'Would you like to come in and have a look round? I have to go to a meeting, but I can get someone to give you a guided tour.'

'I'd love to,' Bess said, 'but I ought to get to my lodgings. My landlady was expecting me hours ago. I know it isn't late, but I don't have a key and she'll be fussing. I'll take you up on your offer another time, if I may?'

'Of course,' Anton said and drove on down The Strand to Trafalgar Square.

'Anton, would you think me ungrateful if I said I'd like to travel the rest of the way by bus?'

'But I promised Natalie I'd make sure you got home safely. Besides, it's pouring with rain, you'll get soaked waiting for a bus.'

'I don't mind the rain. We don't have a car at home, so whatever the weather, if I want to go anywhere I have to walk or cycle.' Bess paused, searching for the right words. 'I can't explain it, but today has been an extraordinary day. It's been both awful and wonderful - and I'd like to spend a little time on my own. Does that sound strange?'

'Not at all, if you're sure?'

'Yes, I am.'

Anton turned into The Haymarket, continued to Regent Street, and at the junction with Oxford Circus pulled up at a bus stop.

Before he had time to put on the handbrake, Bess had jumped out of the car, opened the back door and lifted out her luggage. 'Thank you, Anton,' she said, returning to the front of the car.

'It's been a pleasure, Bess. I'll send you an invite to the opening night of our new show. You can sit in the Goldman family box with my favourite critic.'

'I should love that. Goodbye.'

'Goodbye, Bess.'

'Oh, Anton,' she said, before closing the door. 'Would you lend me six pence please, for the bus fare?'

Anton handed Bess half a crown and said, 'Don't leave town.'

'Thank you,' she called after him, 'I won't. Well, not before I've had a guided tour of the Prince Albert Theatre.'

Bess waved until the rear lights of Anton Goldman's car had turned into tiny red specks, put out her hand and waved down a bus. 'Arcadia Avenue, please!'

CHAPTER THREE

Bess gave the bus conductor the half-crown that Anton had lent her and he gave her two shillings change.

'Brand new, they are,' he said. 'Don't know where they came from but you want to keep them, darlin'. Bring you good luck, they will.'

'Thank you, I could do with some,' Bess said, dropping the two shiny shillings into her pocket. After putting her suitcase in the luggage compartment, she took the stairs to the upper deck and found a seat at the front of the bus.

What an extraordinary day it had been. It had begun ordinarily enough with breakfast, waving Tom off, and exercising Sable. The extraordinary part began when she couldn't find her book and had to go back to the library at Foxden Hall to look for it. And thank goodness she did, or she wouldn't have seen James and he wouldn't have invited her out, or given her his card.

She could have done without having her handbag stolen, her suitcase bursting open in the middle of Euston Station and the public telephone being out of order. But if none of that had happened she wouldn't have met Natalie and Anton Goldman – and she wouldn't have known how Jewish people in Germany were being treated by the Nazis.

In need of a distraction, Bess looked out of the window at the New Year displays that had replaced the Christmas friezes in the windows of the department stores. At Hyde Park Corner she watched as young and old alike, drenched to the skin, scurried along slippery pavements struggling to hold umbrellas above their heads in the downpour.

As the bus approached Knightsbridge the sky above Harrods glowed from thousands of coloured lights. Banners sporting the Harrods emblem flew from every corner of the building. Above the main entrance the flags of a dozen different countries boasted an international clientele and every window displayed a red and gold sale sign in a different language. Bess had no money for purchasing anything other than life's necessities – she certainly couldn't afford to shop at Harrods – but that wasn't going to stop her from window-shopping in London's most famous store before term started.

Excited about her last term at teacher training college and her prospects after she had passed her final exams, as well as needing to think about happier things, Bess allowed her imagination to run wild. When I get my teaching certificate I could teach in London, she thought. Her mind, like a butterfly's, flitted between her childhood ambition of teaching in a country grammar school to be near her family, Foxden and Sable, to working in London to be near James. Why not do both - first London and then the country? She laughed until she remembered James's card had been stolen with her handbag.

Handing Bess her suitcase once she had stepped down from the bus, the conductor shouted, 'Be lucky!'

'I will,' she said, by which time the bus conductor had dinged the bell and the bus was on the move.

Walking along Arcadia Avenue in the rain, a refreshing contrast to sitting in the smoky bus, Bess made a decision. As much as she wished it wasn't so, she couldn't telephone James because she no longer had his number. And he couldn't telephone her because, apart from telling him not to, she hadn't given him her number. There was nothing she could do until the next time she saw him at Foxden, which she hoped would be on her twenty-first birthday. So she needed to put James to the back of her mind and concentrate on getting her teaching certificate. She had worked too hard and for too long to be distracted now, however pleasant the distraction was. Besides, what she had learned earlier from Anton Goldman put the theft of her handbag and James's card into perspective.

Bess was the first of the paying guests to return to the semi-detached Victorian villa in Arcadia Avenue. Like Bess the other guests, with the exception of Molly, went home to their families for the Christmas holiday. Molly had no home and no family. Her only living relative was a distant uncle who spent his Christmases at a retreat in Ireland and didn't return to England until the New Year. But Molly hadn't been alone this Christmas; she'd spent it with Mrs McAllister, the landlady at number seventy-nine.

'Molly is visiting that uncle of hers. It appears he has returned from foreign parts,' Mrs McAllister sniffed. Bess wasn't sure why Mrs McAllister disliked Molly's uncle. It couldn't have been personal because she'd never met him. It was more likely to be that she thought he had abandoned Molly, who she was very fond of, to go off to "foreign parts," although Ireland was hardly what Bess would have called foreign. 'I'm expecting her home any time,' Mrs McAllister continued, as she led Bess upstairs to show her what she called 'improvements' to her room.

Improvements! Bess's heart sank. Knowing Mrs McAllister, who charged tuppence if you had a bath in the middle of the week, any improvements were bound to cost money - and money was something she didn't have a lot of.

On the landing at the top of the stairs Mrs McAllister flung open Bess's bedroom door and, with a gesture more akin to a diva taking a curtain call at the Royal Opera House, ushered her in.

'Well, dear, what do you think?' she asked, following Bess into the small room. Before Bess had time to reply Mrs McAllister swept past her, extolling the virtues of hot water on tap, and proudly opened what she called the airing cupboard to show off a new electric boiler. Bess's only thought was how much this new convenience was going to cost her.

Interpreting the worried look on Bess's face as disapproval, Mrs McAllister continued. 'Of course, the room is a little smaller.' As if Bess hadn't noticed. 'So I shall reduce your rent proportionately. Will two shillings a week be satisfactory, dear? And no charge for your mid-week bath.'

'Yes. Thank you. That will be fine, Mrs McAllister,' Bess said, shocked by such a generous reduction in rent and tickled by the carrot her landlady was dangling of a free bath mid-week.

'Good!' Mrs McAllister concluded. And, after giving the built-in cupboard a reassuring pat, she swanned out of the room.

The room was definitely smaller because of the flimsy-looking cupboard surrounding the boiler, but what struck Bess most was the temperature. Before Christmas the room had been uncomfortably cold to sit and study in, and there was a distinct smell of damp. Now it was warm. And even if the faint gurgling sound in the pipes persisted, as hot water was drawn off and replaced by cold, it was a small price to pay for a warm room and a two-shilling reduction in rent.

'Two shillings,' she said, which reminded her of the two shiny new shillings the bus conductor had given her. She took them out of her coat pocket, wrapped them in a sheet of writing paper, and put them in the middle compartment of her satchel – for luck. After hanging her coat on the back of the door and putting her skirts and dresses on coat hangers in the wardrobe, she put the clothes she'd retrieved from the concourse at Euston Station in a cotton wash-bag and hung it next to her coat. Underwear, cardigans and blouses she folded and placed on shelves designed for men's shirts in the small wardrobe: a man's wardrobe that was once part of the bedroom suite in her neighbour Miss Armstrong's room.

Of her housemates Miss Armstrong was the one Bess knew least well. She was a bookkeeper and worked for a chain of fashion houses called La Mademoiselle Modes in London's West End. She was tall and slim, attractive rather than pretty, with brown hair that she kept stylishly short. The girls didn't know her age, though she had once said that she'd lodged with Mrs McAllister for ten years, so she was probably in her early to mid thirties.

Miss Armstrong was a private person. She talked about work occasionally but never about friends, male or female. Molly thought she was walking out with someone because one Sunday evening, returning from a visit with her uncle, she saw Miss Armstrong getting out of a gentleman's car. When Bess asked Molly what the man was like, Molly said she daren't look, but by the sparkle in Miss Armstrong's eyes that night at supper she was definitely in love. That was typical Molly, young and romantic, with a vivid imagination.

Bess picked up a book and fell backwards onto her bed. But before she had read the first page, there was a knock on the door.

'Bess, are you there?' called a voice Bess recognised as her friend Nora.

'Yes. Come in.'

Nora Myers was Bess's closest friend at number seventy-nine. Not only because they were the same age and both came from the Midlands – although Nora was from inner-city Birmingham, which was about as far away from Foxden in lifestyle as you could get – but because they both attended the De La Salle Teaching College in Kensington.

'Happy New Year, if it's not too late,' Nora said, hugging Bess as she stood up.

'Of course it's not. Happy New Year. Did you have a good Christmas?'

'It was all right, but I missed everybody,' she said, blushing.

'You mean you missed Arthur McNaughton,' Bess said. Both girls laughed.

'And you?'

'Yes, it was lovely, thanks. My brother was home. We had lots of fun, and I went riding every day.' Bess purposely didn't mention James. She was excited enough just thinking about him. If she said his name she thought she'd burst.

'I'm starving. Are you coming down for tea?'

'Yes. Hang on while I put my shoes on,' Bess said, finding one shoe under the bed, the other on the opposite side of the room.

'Molly's back and she's brought a hamper of goodies from that mysterious uncle of hers,' Nora whispered.

'What do you mean, mysterious uncle?'

'Well, you know. I mean, no one's ever seen him, have they? He could be her sugar daddy for all we know. He's always giving her money and--'

'Don't say things like that,' Bess said. 'Think yourself lucky you have a family. Poor little Molly's all alone in the world, except for her old uncle.'

'All I'm saying is, no one's ever seen him and when he gives Molly money it's always in cash. I think it's a bit odd, that's all.'

'Perhaps it is, but it's none of our business,' Bess said, although Nora was probably saying what the other women had thought at one time or another.

In the small communal sitting room, Molly was rifling through a large hamper with childlike enthusiasm. 'Look what I've got, Bess,' she said, dishing out bags of buttered almonds, chocolate-covered Brazil nuts, toffees and fudge. 'Happy New Year!' she shouted, handing Bess a bottle of cream sherry. 'I bought that with some of the money my uncle gave me. I know,' she said, 'we'll toast my uncle's generosity, the New Year, and our continued friendship. Come on, Mrs Mac – oops, sorry – Mrs McAllister. Give us ya best glasses, lassie. Nothing but the best al dee the noo,' Molly said, in the worst Scottish accent Bess had ever heard.

Everyone laughed, including Mrs McAllister who, after allowing Molly to pull her into the middle of the room, took a bow. Still smiling, she took a red, green and blue checked tablecloth from the dresser drawer, opened it and laid it across the table, smoothing the creases with the palms of her hands. 'The colours of the McAllister tartan,' she said proudly, as she did every time she used the tablecloth. 'Although somewhere along the line – probably when the name became anglicised – we lost an A and gained an L,' she concluded, before placing the contents of the hamper onto china plates.

Bess poured generous measures of sherry into Mrs McAllister's best glasses and Molly shouted, 'Get the good stuff down you, girls, 'cause next week we'll be back on the cooking sherry.'

Bess wasn't hungry but she couldn't resist a little duck pâté on a Jacob's cream cracker followed by a truffle, which she had never tasted before. She told her housemates about her Christmas, her sisters and her brother Tom, and the presents she had given and received. She still daren't mention James. She couldn't trust herself to say his name without blushing. Nor did she tell them about the theft of her handbag, or meeting Natalie and Anton Goldman. It wasn't the right time; it would have put a damper on Molly's tea party.

Miss Armstrong said her Christmas with her brother, a country vicar, had been pleasant but a little too quiet and she was pleased to be back in London. Nora agreed, saying how much she had missed her sweetheart Arthur, and after a couple of glasses of sherry she declared her undying love for him.

When the party ended the girls banned Mrs McAllister from the kitchen. Everyone agreed that she had done enough for one day so, after a few 'Och buts' and 'Ah wells,' she retired to her private sitting room.

By the time the table had been cleared, the dishes washed up and the uneaten food covered and put in the larder, it was midnight and the house, usually quiet by ten, was still a hive of activity. While Bess, Molly and Nora jostled to be first in line to use the bathroom, Miss Armstrong came out of her bedroom, turned into the bathroom and closed the door. The three girls stood open-mouthed before bursting into laughter and applauding Miss Armstrong for her tenacity. Eventually giggles and whispers replaced the laughter and chatter and the last two girls, Nora and Bess, said goodnight and went to their own rooms.

'Good old Molly,' Bess said, as she climbed into bed. The vision of Molly pursing her lips and mimicking Mrs Mac's voice, and standing with her arms folded beneath her firm little breasts like Mrs Mac, whose habit was to fold her heavily freckled arms beneath her ample bosom, made Bess laugh aloud.

Molly reminded Bess of her young sister Claire. Like Claire, Molly was pretty with big blue eyes. She looked older than her years, and attracted the attention of young men. Claire was lucky, she had older sisters to look out for her, but Molly was an orphan and didn't have anyone until she moved to live with Mrs McAllister and the girls at Arcadia Avenue.

Molly was the youngest of the women and called herself an actress, although she had never trodden the boards. She hadn't worked at all during the two years she had lived with Bess and the other women but she was confident that one day she would be discovered. Until then she was dependent on her uncle for her lodgings and clothes, and a small allowance for books and elocution lessons.

Molly, like most eighteen year olds, preferred to spend her money going to dances or watching the latest film at the Alhambra Picture House. She said it didn't matter how she spent the old boy's money because she was only borrowing it and one day, when she was rich and famous, she would pay every penny back.

Bess thought about introducing Molly to Anton Goldman but decided against it. She didn't know Anton well enough. Besides, after helping her young friend to learn audition speeches, Bess feared it would be some time before Miss Molly McKenna was ready for the London stage – and probably even longer before the London stage was ready for her.

'There's a telephone call for you, Bess,' Mrs McAllister called from the bottom of the stairs.

Bess woke with a jolt and stumbled out of bed. Telephone call? Only her father had Mrs Mac's number. Unless somehow, James… Her heart soared. 'I'm coming, Mrs McAllister!'

'It's the police, dear.'

'Police?' Fear overwhelmed her as she pulled on her dressing gown and ran downstairs.

'I do hope it isn't bad news, dear,' Mrs McAllister said, pointing to the large black telephone on top of the bureau in her private sitting room.

'Thank you, Mrs McAllister.' Bess lifted the receiver as Mrs Mac left the room. 'Hello. This is Elizabeth Dudley.'

'Euston Square police station here, Miss Dudley. We've found a handbag that fits the description of the one you reported stolen in January. If you'd like to come down to the station and identify it--.'

Bess shook with relief. It had been three months since the theft of the bag. And, thinking she would never get it back, Bess had put it out of her mind. 'Thank you. Is the wallet still in the bag?' she asked, fearing it wasn't.

'Hang on, Miss.' Bess heard the telephone receiver clunk against a hard surface. 'Yes, the wallet's here, and so is the purse,' the policeman said. 'The money's gone, I'm afraid, but it looks like everything else on the list's here.'

Bess was on tenterhooks all the way to Euston. She knew it was an incredible bit of luck to get the bag back and was pleased the wallet and purse were still in it, but she so wanted James's business card to be there too.

'Good afternoon, Miss. Can I help you?' a ruddy-cheeked desk sergeant asked, pushing up a glass hatch that looked more like a serving flap in the take-out of a pub than the enquiries window in a police station.

'My name's Elizabeth Dudley. I believe you've found my handbag?'

'Yes Miss, it's here.' Reaching under the desk, the sergeant produced the bag. 'This is yours, I believe,' he said, removing a small luggage tag which Bess could see had her name on it. 'If you'd just sign the release form,' he said, handing her the bag and the form.

'Thank you.' Bess scribbled her signature, picked up her handbag and left.

There was a small grassy area in front of the police station with a couple of wooden benches facing a flowerbed of daffodils. When she arrived the seats were occupied by office workers eating sandwiches, but now the area was deserted. She sat on the nearest bench, opened the handbag and looked for

James' card. She took out the wallet and checked each compartment, but the card wasn't there. She knew it wouldn't be in the purse but she looked anyway. In the bottom of the bag she could see her powder compact, lipstick and comb, but there was nothing else except the bag's frayed lining. 'Damn,' she said, under her breath.

Pleased to have the handbag back but disappointed that James's card wasn't in it, Bess snapped the gold clasp shut and set off along Euston Road to catch a bus home.

Molly tipped the contents of Bess's bag onto the kitchen table. The wallet flew out first, followed by the purse and comb. 'These are real leather, Bess, you can't throw them away. And this comb is ever so pretty. It'll be as good as new after a wash.' The comb was pretty and Bess wondered why the thief hadn't kept it and tried to sell it. It was the only surviving piece of a dressing table set that had belonged to Bess's Granny. Bess had loved it for as long as she could remember but Granny said a silver comb was far too precious for a child. Then, when Bess started at the grammar school, Granny gave it to her as a reward for passing the eleven plus. It was her only personal possession, the only thing she could truly call her own, that her sisters were not allowed to play with – and she treasured it.

'All right,' Bess said. 'I'll keep the bag, the comb, and the wallet and purse, but I don't want the make-up. I know it was a man that stole my bag – and the chances are he didn't use the make-up but I still don't want it. Just the thought of him touching it ...' Bess wrinkled her nose. 'Bin it, Moll.'

Molly disappeared outside and shook what remained of the bag's contents into the dustbin. 'Bess?' she said on her return. 'Did you want this?'

Bess stared at Molly in disbelief. 'Where did you find it?'

'It fell into the dustbin when I shook the bag. It must have been stuck in the lining,' Molly said, handing Bess James's business card. 'Why, is it important?'

'Yes, my young friend, it is important.' Bess hugged Molly before running to find Mrs McAllister who, after hearing the urgency in Bess's voice, vacated her sitting room for the kitchen and the kettle.

'Holborn 1959 please?'

'One moment please,' the operator said, 'trying to connect you.'

Why was she taking so long? The clock on Mrs Mac's mantle gave the time as twenty past three. Bess didn't know James's office hours but it was the middle of the afternoon. Surely someone was there.

'There's no reply, caller. Please call back later.'

'But I can't call back later. Please try the number again,' Bess pleaded.

The operator sighed loudly and the line went dead. Bess held her breath and listened to silence. She was about to put the receiver down when the operator came back on the line. 'You're connected, caller.'

'Thank you--'

'Foxden, Foxden and Hadleigh, Temple Garden Chambers. How may I help you?' a young sounding female voice asked.

'I'd like to speak to James Foxden, please.'

'Who may I say is calling?'

'Bess-- Bess Dudley.'

'Bess...? I'm sorry, but Mr Foxden's in a meeting and doesn't want to be disturbed. Unless it's urgent of course, and then I can--'

'No! No, it isn't urgent. I'll call back tomorrow,' Bess said.

'I'm sorry, but James won't be here tomorrow. Would you like to leave a message?'

'Yes. Thank you. Would you tell him I phoned, and I'll try to catch him later?'

'Thank you. Goodbye,' the girl said, and she'd gone.

Bess returned the telephone receiver to its cradle and picked up the telephone directory.

Leaving the Underground at Aldwych, Bess walked along Fleet Street for about half a mile, and found James' chambers on the junction with Fetter Lane. Taking his business card from her pocket, she checked it against a list of names on a brass plaque by the main entrance. Foxden, Foxden and Hadleigh were on the third floor.

Returning the card to her pocket – she wasn't going to risk losing it again – Bess looked up at the third storey windows and felt her stomach churn. She was suddenly overcome by doubt. What was she doing, coming to see James when she'd been told he was in a meeting? She looked at her watch – it was half past five. If he wasn't still in the meeting, he'd have left the office by now. She walked away.

There was a chill in the air and it had started to spot with rain. She stepped into the first doorway, buttoned her jacket, and wished she had worn a coat. She had come all this way, she reasoned, it would be a shame to leave without trying to see him. What was wrong with casually calling on a friend who had suggested they meet up? According to the girl who answered his telephone, James wouldn't be in the office tomorrow, so this might be the only chance she'd get to speak to him before …. Before what? The girl hadn't said why he wasn't going to be there. Thinking about it, she hadn't said much at all.

Bess stepped out of the doorway and looked towards James's office – and there he was, standing on the steps outside the main entrance where she had stood minutes before. He was hunched over with his hands cupped, lighting a cigarette. He straightened, drew on the cigarette, and as he exhaled he began to walk in Bess's direction. Bess lifted her hand to wave, then let it fall when she saw a girl in her early twenties come running out of the building calling James's name. The girl caught up with him and took the cigarette from between his lips. She took a long drag, closed her eyes and exhaled slowly. She lifted the cigarette to her mouth a second time but James took it from her.

Bess watched as the girl linked her arm through James's and pulled on it until he was facing the opposite direction. They walked a short distance and stopped outside a restaurant called Ye Olde Eatery where, after what looked to Bess like a discussion on the weather because the girl pointed to the sky before pulling her coat round her, they went inside.

Bess crossed the road and walked to a bus stop that was almost level with the restaurant. She couldn't see James but the girl was sitting at a table next to the window, looking into the street.

Surrounded by dozens of men and women as they left the offices and chambers on Fleet Street, Bess felt less conspicuous. She joined a queue of people waiting for taxis and had a clear view of the restaurant. She looked across the road and into the restaurant window, hoping to catch a glimpse of James. Instead she caught the eye of the girl – who smiled.

Embarrassed, Bess looked away, took a step backwards and trod on the foot of a woman who was locking the door of a solicitor's office. 'I'm sorry,' she said. The woman glared at her and walked away. Bess ducked into the doorway. It was raining heavily now. Tears filled her eyes. She was cold and wet, alone and disappointed.

She should have turned away, gone home, but she didn't. Tears streamed down her face. Her hair was soaked, but she couldn't move. She stood in the rain for what seemed like hours, until James and the girl left the restaurant. James held his coat over the girl's head with one hand and hailed a cab with the other. A hackney pulled up and James opened the door. He motioned to the girl to get in. Instead she reached up, put her arms around James' neck, and spoke into his ear. James laughed and allowed the girl to pull him into the cab.

As the hackney pulled away from the kerb and into the traffic Bess could see through the rear window James and the girl locked in each other's arms, kissing.

She took the small white business card from her pocket and dropped it in the gutter.

CHAPTER FOUR

Written beneath the words "Teaching Certificate" were the words "Passed with Distinction."

'I've done it, I've done it!' Bess shouted, running into Nora's room. 'Nora, I've-- Sorry, I should have knocked.'

Nora was sitting on the edge of the bed. 'It's all right, come in.'

'I just wanted to tell you I've got my teaching certificate.' Bess was waving the manila envelope above her head when she noticed an identical envelope – which had to be from The De La Salle Teaching College – lying on the bed next to Nora, unopened.

'Congratulations, Bess. If anyone deserves to pass you do,' she said, tears filling her eyes.

'What's the matter? Why haven't you opened your letter?'

'It'll be bad news, I know it will.'

'Don't be silly, you can't know! And, even if it is, which I'm sure it isn't …' Bess searched for the right words, 'wouldn't it be better to know?'

Nora shrugged, and with the back of her hand swept her tears into her hair.

Bess picked up the envelope and sat down next to her. 'Here,' she said. 'You'll have to open it eventually, so you might as well do it now.' She wondered whether she was the best person to be with her friend if the envelope contained bad news, but there wasn't anyone else.

Breathing in slowly, Nora took the envelope from Bess, made her mouth into an O, and exhaled. 'Right! Here goes,' she said, tearing it open.

Bess watched her friend's face closely, praying that the envelope she'd insisted she open contained good news. Nora closed her eyes. 'Thank you, God,' she whispered. 'Right "Miss",' she said, when she'd finished reading. 'You can't tell me what to do, because I'm a "Miss" too. I've passed, Bess! I've passed!' she squealed, waving the certificate in the air.

Both women leapt from the bed. With their arms around each other, they jumped up and down, shouting out their congratulations.

'Lord knows what the rest of the house is thinking,' Bess said, 'with the racket we're making.'

'Nothing,' Nora said, catching her breath. 'Molly's at the flicks and Miss Armstrong's up west at a show. There's no one to hear us. So,' she said, pretending to be sad, 'there's no one to tell.'

'We could tell Mrs Mac. She might get the sherry out,' Bess said, grinning.

Nora jumped up. 'Yes! She might! Come on then, what are we waiting for?'

They descended the stairs slowly, singing "Apple for the Teacher", and by the time they reached their landlady's sitting room, she was standing in the doorway brandishing a bottle of sherry.

The following morning Nora knocked on Bess's door. 'Are you up?'

'Yes. I'm sorting through some papers. Come in. Did you sleep well?' Bess asked when Nora flung herself onto the bed.

'Not a wink. I was too excited. You?'

'Not much,' Bess said, laughing at her friend who was lying spread-eagled across her bed. 'I suppose I was excited too,' she said, pulling the crumpled papers that she'd carefully compiled from under Nora's head.

'Some of the lads from Arthur's college are going to trawl the Kings Road – find a place that's not too expensive, where we can celebrate the end of college. A kind of last supper before we go our separate ways,' she said, laughing. 'Any preferences?'

'No. But anyway, I don't think I'll be going,' Bess replied.

'But you've got to. For me. I mean, me getting a teaching certificate really is something to celebrate. I knew you'd sail through the exams, but me?' Nora laughed. 'Please say you'll come.'

Bess sat on the bed next to her friend. 'I haven't been out for ages. I haven't even been to see Natalie and Anton Goldman,' she said, sorry now that she hadn't made the effort to go to the West End and see her friends at their theatre, especially as they'd been so kind to her. 'All right, I'll come. I don't care where we go as long as there's lots to eat and lots to drink.'

Bess and Nora arrived at La Casa Romani on the Kings Road in Chelsea just before eight o'clock.

'There's a table booked in the name of The De La Salle Teaching College,' Nora announced to the young waiter who met them at the door.

'This way, Signorina,' he said to Nora, leading the way to what looked like several tables pushed together to make one long one on the far side of the room. Handing Nora a wine menu, he said, 'While you wait,' nodded and left.

'If I hadn't got my Arthur,' Nora said, pretending to drool over the waiter. Bess dug her in the ribs and they both laughed. 'Here they are. Over here!' Nora shouted as Arthur and his chums, and a couple of friends of Bess's and Nora's from the teaching college, entered the restaurant noisily.

As they ate bowls of spicy minced meat in long strands of spaghetti and drank fizzy white wine they talked and laughed about their time at college and what fun it had been living in London. They told each other about their hopes and dreams for the future; of becoming teachers, or whatever it was the boys had chosen as careers, but no one mentioned the war. The possibility of it, the fear of it, was at the forefront of everyone's mind. But they had all agreed before sitting down to eat that tonight was about celebrating and having fun.

When it was time to leave Nora's boyfriend, Arthur, egged on by his college chums, knelt down on one knee and asked Nora to marry him.

Nora's response to his proposal was an unreserved 'Yes!' Her squeals of delight were almost inaudible above the cheers of their friends.

The following morning, as she was coming downstairs, Bess heard Arthur's motorbike roar to a halt. By the time she reached the hall, she could see him through the dimpled glass in the top of the front door. She opened it and let him in.

'Is she ready?' he beamed. Before Bess could answer Nora came running into the hall and gave Arthur a kiss. 'You're early,' she scolded playfully. 'Go and get my things, there's a love, while I say goodbye to Bess.'

'I didn't think you'd be leaving this early,' Bess said.

'Nor did I. But maybe it's as well. I hate goodbyes--'

'Me too.'

'And it's not as if we're never going to see each other again, is it?'

Bess shook her head. Before she had time to answer, Arthur returned with Nora's cases, followed by Mrs McAllister and Molly. She threw her arms around her friend. 'You've got my address at Foxden, so keep in touch.'

'I will. And you've got mine. Let me know when you get a job and where you'll be,' Nora said, as Arthur opened the door. While he tied the cases onto the back of the motorbike the small crush of people in the hall nudged Nora out. 'And I'll let you know when I get a job, and where I'll be-- Where me and Arthur will be,' Nora said, grinning. Putting her satchel over her head, she climbed onto the pillion-seat of her fiancé's motorbike and put her arms around his waist.

'Hold on,' Arthur shouted over his shoulder, and started the motorbike. After kicking the steel parking stand from under the bike, it jolted forwards. 'Bye, folks,' he called, pulling away from the kerb, steering with one hand and waving with the other.

'See you at the wedding,' Nora called.

'Goodbye,' everyone shouted.

'Drive safely,' Mrs McAllister added.

The small group waved until the motorbike was out of sight and then they returned to the house and the breakfast table.

'Now you sit down,' Mrs McAllister said to Bess, and disappeared into the kitchen. When she returned she was holding a plate of eggs and bacon with a tea towel. 'Careful, the plate's hot,' she said, putting it down in front of Bess. 'You need something substantial inside you before you travel. Come on now, tuck in.'

Bess felt too sad to eat, but she didn't want to offend Mrs Mac so she ate most of it, and drank two cups of tea. When she'd finished she went upstairs and fetched her bags.

'Well, dear,' Mrs McAllister said as Bess entered the sitting room for the last time. 'You know where we are if you want to come back to us. I won't let your room until the start of the next college term, so if you get a teaching job in London, on this side of the river, all you have to do is telephone and your room will be ready.'

'Thank you, Mrs McAllister,' Bess said, hugging her now ex-landlady. 'I wouldn't want to stay anywhere else.'

Mrs McAllister was clearly moved and turned away to blow her nose.

'You will write, won't you, Bess?' Molly asked, tears welling up in her big blue eyes.

'Of course I will, Molly. And you must write to me too. Keep me up to date with your career.'

'Oh, I will,' Molly said, brightening at the thought of having a career. 'But what shall I do without you to help me learn my speeches?' she wailed. 'I shan't understand half of them.'

'You'll be fine, Molly. Mrs McAllister and Miss Armstrong will help you.'

'Oh, that reminds me,' Mrs Mac said. 'Miss Armstrong asked me to give you this.'

Bess opened the prettily wrapped package to discover a beautiful turquoise and green silk scarf and a small card wishing her luck and happiness in the future.

'It's beautiful,' Molly said, taking the scarf and putting it round Bess's neck. 'It suits you a treat, Bess, really it does,' she beamed.

'Does it, Molly?' Bess lifted the scarf to her face and felt its silky softness on her cheek. 'I'll write to Miss Armstrong when I get home. In the meantime will you thank her for me? Tell her I have never had such a beautiful scarf.'

At the front door, Mrs McAllister said again, 'Don't forget, dear, you'll always be welcome at number seventy-nine Arcadia Avenue.'

'And I'll write,' Molly said through black mascara tears.

Bess ran for the shelter of the bus stop with her satchel over her shoulder, her suitcase and handbag in her left hand, and holding the Daily Mail above her head with her right. The sudden downpour had taken everyone by surprise.

The queue for the bus going into town seemed endless. The hardy, or foolhardy, were getting soaked as they jostled to keep their place. Some people took shelter beneath the awnings of nearby shops while others huddled together in doorways.

'Excuse me, do you have the right time?' Bess asked an elderly man who had stopped next to her to let someone pass.

'Yes. If you'll bear with me?' he said, lifting his left arm and looking over the top of his glasses. 'It's just turned eleven.'

'Thank you.' She looked along the road. If she didn't catch a bus within the next fifteen minutes she was going to miss the train to Rugby.

'You'll have a long wait for a bus, Miss,' the man said, giving Bess shelter beneath his umbrella. 'Hyde Park Corner's flooded. I was on the last bus to come through. They'll close the road soon, I shouldn't wonder.'

'Will they? Oh dear. I need to catch a train at Euston.'

'You'd best get a cab, then!'

As her elderly adviser went on his way, Bess began to hail a cab. 'Taxi! Taxi!' she called as one black hackney cab after another flew past her. Every taxi heading down Kensington High Street was either taken or someone beat her to it. She had decided to walk to the nearest Underground station and catch a later train when a cab pulled up on the opposite side of the road. This was her last chance to get to Euston in time to catch her train, so she made a bolt for it.

She dragged her suitcase through the oncoming traffic to the other side of the road and waited while the cab's elderly occupant picked through her change for the correct fare. At last, drenched and out of breath, Bess collapsed into the back of the taxi and asked the cabbie to find an alternative route to Euston – as quickly as he could. She sat back on the big black leather seat. Her clothes were soaked – a small price to pay to be on her way home.

After what seemed like an age of crawling along in bumper-to-bumper traffic, the taxi turned off the main road and into a side street. Bess looked out of the window. The street was unfamiliar.

'How far are we from Euston?' she asked.

'About ten minutes.'

Bess looked at her wristwatch. 'My train leaves in fifteen.'

'Hold on!' the taxi driver shouted, yanking the steering wheel to the left. The taxi mounted the pavement and Bess gasped. She gasped again a few seconds later when the taxi cut across a traffic jam of hooting vehicles and red faced drivers making fists. 'I know a short cut!'

And he did. Bess was about to ask again if they were nearly there when she saw the sign for Euston Station. She had five minutes to buy a ticket and board the train. She jumped out of the taxi, thanked and paid the driver, grabbed her luggage and ran.

The attendant in the ticket booth put his hand up. 'I'm sorry, Miss, the train's about to depart.' Bess pretended she hadn't heard him and ran onto the platform.

'Stop!' he shouted and, abandoning his booth, he gave chase.

Bess reached the last carriage as the ticket attendant reached the buffers. Somewhere in the distance she heard a whistle blow and the train began to move. Without thinking she opened the nearest door, threw her bags in and leapt in after them. As the door swung shut,

Bess looked out of the window. The ticket collector was standing with his hands on his hips, shaking his head. She turned back to the train's interior and sighed with relief. The train was gathering speed and was almost out of the station.

'Goodness knows what all the fuss is about,' she said to her fellow passengers as she entered the compartment. She looked for somewhere to stow her case. It was too heavy to lift onto the overhead rack, so she stood it on its hinges and pushed it flush against the vacant seat in the middle of the row. She put her satchel on the seat behind the case but held on tightly to her handbag.

There were two passengers in the compartment, both women. The older of the two was a smart, tweedy, middle-aged woman with a pinched face and steel grey hair cut in the style of a man's short back and sides. The other woman was younger, probably in her late twenties, and by the look of her thick stockings, sensible shoes, and the triangle of starched white pinafore that showed beneath her navy blue belted mackintosh, she was a nurse.

Neither woman acknowledged Bess's whirlwind arrival with more than a cursory nod before returning to their respective reading material – Country Life and Woman Magazine. Bess's newspaper had long since disintegrated because she had used it as an umbrella, so to occupy herself she looked out of the window. What a dark and dreary day it was turning out to be. London was usually warmer than Lowarth, but it was duller, seemed to rain more, and was often foggy. Too many chimneys puffing out too much smoke, so the air was never fresh. The air at Foxden was always fresh. The sky was clear and the only fog, other than on exceptionally cold winter mornings, was just mist hovering above the marshes.

Bess was looking forward to spending the summer at home in the country, to spending time with her family and to riding Sable out every morning. Butterflies began to stir in her stomach when she thought of James. She had hoped to see him, but now … In Tom's last letter, he'd said that both he and Ena would be home for her twenty-first birthday, but he hadn't mentioned James. He'd also said some of her old school friends were hoping to see her while she was home for the summer. Most of her friends were courting or engaged, a couple were married – and they all still lived locally. Nothing wrong with that, if that's what you want. She'd have been living locally herself, if she'd married Frank Donnelly. She smiled, remembering how fond she'd been of Frank. He went to secondary school with Tom and was by far the best looking of all his friends.

'Will you marry me, Bess?' he blurted out some years later, while walking her home from Lowarth Picture House. 'I've asked your father--'

'You've done what?' She was outraged.

'Asked your father, for your hand... I know it's a bit old fashioned these days, but I thought with you and him being so close--'

'Who I marry is nothing to do with my dad, Frank.'

'That's what he said. He said he'd be pleased to have me as a son-in-law, but didn't think you were ready.'

'He was right! I'm not ready!' She had already won a scholarship to attend teacher training college and nothing was going to stop her. 'I'm not ready to marry you or anyone else, Frank. I'm going to college in London.'

'I'll wait for you.'

'For three years? I couldn't ask you to do that. Besides, I don't want to be tied. I'm going to be a school teacher when I finish college, and I have no idea where I'll be working. I'm sorry, Frank, but it's what I've dreamed of for as long as I can remember.'

Frank's handsome face crumpled and they walked the rest of the way in silence. Bess kissed him goodnight at the front door and said again, 'I'm sorry, Frank.'

'Me too,' Frank said. And with a hangdog look, he walked down the path to the gate. Once through it, he turned and said, 'Good luck, Bess. Knock'em dead in London.'

Bess shook her head. Recalling how generous Frank had been when she turned him down made her feel guilty.

Her second beau was Henry Green – although their relationship was more like brother and sister than boyfriend and girlfriend. Henry was a painter, an artist. He was also very clever, winning a scholarship to Oxford and ending up with a first in mathematics. While he was there he met a young man, a hopeful artist like himself, and he didn't pursue an academic career; instead he moved to live with his friend in a small village near Northampton.

As the train pulled out of Bletchley station, Bess remembered that the last letter she'd received from Henry had a Bletchley postmark. He hadn't said much other than he had moved temporarily because of a job, and to write to him care of Bletchley post office for the time being. It must be a good job, Bess thought, to entice him away from his idyllic life with his friend in the country. But if it was only temporary, he probably wouldn't be there long. She'd write to him after her birthday, she decided, and ask him why he'd moved.

James Foxden was the first boy Bess had had a crush on. From being the hoity-toity boy from the Hall, who never had holes in his shoes and wore real swimming trunks instead of someone's hand-me-down short trousers, he became her "knight in shining armour". And there hadn't been anyone since to take his place. Bess felt the colour rise in her cheeks as she remembered the first time she'd seen James. Everywhere Tom went during the summer of 1924, while their mother was nursing their new baby sister, Ena, he had been made to take her. Their mother thought

Bess, at the age of six, was old enough to go with her big brother while Margaret and Claire, four and two, stayed at home. Bess didn't realise at the time how much of a sacrifice Tom had made that summer. She bit her lip and stifled a giggle as the memories of those days, of the trouble she got into, came flooding back.

Tom was about twelve, and had asked his mother if he could go to the River Swift with some of the boys from the village. His mother had said yes, on condition he took Bess with him. 'But don't let her out of your sight, and don't let her go near the water. If anything happens to her, Tom, you'll be for it!' she threatened.

Bess remembered clearly, sitting on the crossbar of Tom's old bicycle while he cycled along the main Lowarth Road, and how her bony little bottom had hurt every time he steered the bike into a pothole. Instead of getting off the bike and pushing it up Shaft Hill, which he did whenever he gave someone a croggy, he stood on the pedals and forced his skinny legs to keep pushing down so the wheels kept turning. Bess, not daring to complain, gripped the centre of the handlebars until her knuckles were white while Tom moaned and groaned his way to the top of the hill.

It was a scorching hot day. To cool down the boys were jumping into the river at Bonn's Hole, and then swimming across to the other side.

'You can go and play with the boys if you want, Tom. I'll be good, honest I will,' Bess promised. Tom's reply was to turn his head very slowly and glare at her. 'I'll sit here like a good girl and watch you,' she said angelically.

Ignoring his sister, Tom bent down and picked up a small flat stone. He hurled it at such an angle that it skimmed the surface of the river, bouncing several times before disappearing beneath a circle of ripples.

'I'll collect some stones for you, shall I?'

Tom didn't answer. He didn't even look at her. He was watching his friends having fun. The sun was directly overhead and Bess could see bobbles of sweat on Tom's forehead. His face was so red, she thought he would explode. 'If I go for a swim, do you swear on your life you'll stay here and not wander off?'

Bess nodded. 'Cross my heart and hope to die.'

Unable to resist the cool water any longer, Tom took off his shirt and trousers and ran to the high bank above the river at Bonn's Hole, discarding his shoes along the way. When he reached the edge he launched himself into the air, tucked his knees under his chin, and plunged into the river with such force he drenched the boys who were watching. Bess clapped as he swam to join his friends and squealed with excitement when several other boys followed suit. For a time she had been content to sit and watch the boys dive-bombing each other, but the fun was theirs,

96

not hers, and it wasn't long before she was bored.

She had been good, very good. She had been sitting quietly for ages getting hotter and hotter while the cool river flowed inches from her feet. It wasn't fair that the boys were allowed to play in the river and she wasn't. She stood up and waved to Tom, but he was having so much fun he didn't see her. "What you don't see can't hurt you" was one of her mam's favourite sayings, so she kicked off her old play shoes, sat on the grassy bank and dipped her toes into the river. The cold water flowing against her hot feet took her breath away.

Sitting by the river dangling her feet in the water was wonderful, but it wasn't enough. Surely it couldn't hurt if she paddled. After all, she'd promised Tom she'd collect some stones for him and the smoothest, roundest, flattest stones were in the river. Having decided that as long as she stayed in the shallows, within grabbing distance of the riverbank, she'd be safe – and as no one was looking – she slowly slid into the water.

It was fun collecting stones for Tom. The small pretty ones she put safely in the skirt of her dress, holding it tightly with her left hand so she could collect more stones with her right. The big, less attractive ones she put back in the river, throwing them up in the air first so they plopped and splashed when they hit the water. Bess was having so much fun she hadn't noticed how far downstream she'd drifted, or how deep the water had become. It wasn't until she tried to pick up a large stone that was stuck on the river bed that she realised she couldn't bend down because the river was up to her waist. She tried to turn, to walk back to the riverbank, but the current was too strong.

She didn't know what to do. Her feet were numb from being in the cold water for so long, and her legs felt like jelly. She was frightened but she knew she mustn't panic, or she might fall over. The stones in her skirt were heavy and made her arms ache, so she let go of her skirt. She watched the shiny treasures fall to her feet, but she was no better off. Without the weight of the stones the current swept her forward. She lost her balance and fell headfirst into the river.

Boys on the bank opposite had seen Bess fall but they were too far away to help so they shouted to Tom, who was already in the water. Tom began to swim towards her but it was James Foxden, having just arrived at Bonn's Hole, who jumped into the river and pulled Bess out.

'Ouch!' she yelled, as the boy from the Hall dragged her out of the river and set her down on the bank with a thump.

'You little fool!' Tom shouted, scrambling out of the river some minutes later. 'You could have drowned. What do you think you were playing at?'

'I didn't mean to fall over,' Bess protested. 'It wasn't my fault--'

'You promised to be good. You promised me you wouldn't go near the water. Now look at you! Your clothes are soaking and you're half-drowned. Mam'll kill me.'

A crowd gathered. Someone threw Tom a towel, which he used to dry Bess's hair. He rubbed her head so hard she thought it would come off her shoulders, but for the life of her she daren't complain. Huge involuntary tears welled up in her eyes and she began to cry – not because she had almost drowned, or because she was being stared at by a crowd of older kids who were tutting and sniggering, but because Tom was angry with her, again. And he had every right to be, Bess thought, because Mam would be furious with him. She didn't care about herself – she expected a spanking from her mother – but Tom would be in trouble too, and that meant her mother wouldn't let her go anywhere with him for the rest of the summer holiday. She would have to stay at home with a squawking baby, which wasn't Bess's idea of fun. 'I'm sorry, Tom,' she sobbed. 'I wanted to please you, to collect some stones for you. I didn't mean for you to get into trouble, honest I didn't.'

'All right,' Tom said, 'but for God's sake shut up and stop bawling!'

Bess forced herself to stop crying and said nothing more until Tom ordered her to go behind a bush, which was in clear view of the onlookers, and take off her wet dress.

'I will not!' Bess said, but changed her mind when she saw the look of fury on Tom's face. 'Sorry,' she whispered, and she ran to the far side of the bush. It wasn't easy to get undressed behind a small bush and an even smaller towel, which Tom was holding up in front of her. Eventually she wriggled out of her wet dress and stood shivering, with embarrassment more than with the cold, in her knickers.

Tom threw her dress over the bush to dry and picked up his shirt. 'Here, put this on, or you'll catch your death.'

Bess slipped her arms through the short sleeves of her brother's old shirt and pulled it down, before drawing the front edges of the shirt across her thin body and folding her arms to hold it in place.

'Thanks, James,' Tom said, handing the wet towel back to the boy who had been first to Bess's rescue and who Bess now recognised as the boy from Foxden Hall. 'You probably saved the little idiot's life.'

'I'm not an idiot,' Bess said under her breath as she watched the bruises on her arms turn from red to purple.

It was James Foxden who, several years later, picked Bess out of a thistle patch when the horse she was riding threw her because she'd hesitated before jumping a fence. There had been an obvious age difference then. James was studying at university and Bess was still a grammar school girl. There was no age difference now. Not now Bess was grown up and a qualified teacher.

Bess felt the colour rise in her cheeks and looked out of the window. To her surprise she could see the pylons of Rugby's wireless station in the distance. The journey had gone quickly. As the suburbs came into view she felt the pull of the train's breaks. Next stop Rugby.

She couldn't wait to see Tom, because if James was home he and Tom were bound to go to the pub for a drink and James might tell Tom about the girl from his office. Bess wanted to know if James was still seeing her – and if so, if he was serious about her. The memory of the night she saw James in Fleet Street with the girl made Bess feel miserable. However, kissing another girl probably meant he was no longer walking out with Annabel Hadleigh, which made her feel happy. Unless …

Nodding to her fellow passengers, Bess left the compartment. She dragged her suitcase to the door, pulled down the window and hung out. 'Tom?' she shouted above the hiss of the train's brakes. She could see her brother walking along the platform, chatting to the old ticket collector. 'Tom?' she shouted again and this time he heard her.

CHAPTER FIVE

Bess kicked off her shoes, picked them up by the straps at the ankle and ran barefoot across the peacock lawn to the lake. Sitting on the grassy bank at the water's edge she watched a mother duck teaching her ducklings how to dive. The downy bundles did their best, but as soon as they dipped their heads under the water their buoyant little bodies forced them to bob back up again. Finally, wiggling their tail feathers and shaking their heads, they fell into formation behind their proud mother and paddled for all they were worth to the far side of the lake, leaving a V-shaped swell on what was otherwise still water.

With the sun warm on her face, Bess watched the raft of ducks circle a bed of water lilies before disappearing between clumps of bulrushes in the foreground of Mysterton Church. The church spire, like a shepherd's dial, cast its long afternoon shadow across Foxden's manicured lawn, reminding Bess it was time to go.

'I feel as if I've never been away,' she said, while her sister Ena tied a green ribbon round her hair before letting her unruly curls fall onto her shoulders.

'Sit still!' Ena said, flicking Bess with her comb when she leant sideways to look in the mirror. 'If you look before I've finished you'll spoil the surprise. I just have to...' Ena, forcing the last of Bess's pre-Raphaelite tresses round the fingers of her left hand, made an elegant bun and then anchored it with Kirby grips. 'There! Now you can look,' she said proudly, taking a couple of steps back to admire her handiwork.

'It looks lovely, Ena. You are clever with hair,' Bess said, admiring her young sister's talent. Bess had always felt guilty because as an academic she had been given a scholarship to pursue her ambition of becoming a teacher, but there was no such help for Ena. To be a hairdresser you had to do a three-year apprenticeship and contribute substantially to the cost of the training, as well as pay for your equipment. 'I'm sorry Mam and Dad can't afford to let you do hairdressing,' Bess said. 'Perhaps when I'm working, when I'm earning...'

'Wouldn't it be wonderful if I was a real hairdresser?' Ena said, strutting round the bedroom, comb in one hand and hairbrush in the other. 'Do come this way, Modom. Pleeeeese take a seat, Miss Dudley will be with you in a moment,' Ena announced before dropping on the bed and laughing. Her laughter was infectious and Bess laughed with her, until she realised Ena had become over-excited and was near to hysterics. Putting her arms around her sister, she held her until she calmed down. When she had recovered Ena said, 'There's no need for wave-grippers and setting lotions when you're running round after two little children every day.'

'Poor Ena, are the children very hard work?' Bess asked, aware that Ena was little more than a child herself.

'Yes they are, but it's not the hard work that bothers me. I like the kids and I like being a nanny – well, compared to being a housemaid I do. It's just that I never have any time to myself. I get Sunday afternoons off, but there's nothing to do on a Sunday afternoon except go to the pictures. I take the children if it's a suitable flick. I might as well, there's no one of my own age to go with. The other thing that gets me down is not being able to come home. Leamington's too far away. I can't come home for a Sunday afternoon, can I? And even if it was possible, Mrs Asher would find a reason to make me stay. She hasn't said I can come home for Margaret's wedding yet.'

'What? Is Margaret getting married?' Bess shrieked with surprise.

'Shush, keep your voice down,' Ena whispered. 'I've been sworn to secrecy. Margaret wants to tell you herself.'

'Don't worry, my lips are sealed,' Bess said, stepping into the green satin dress that she'd bought in the sale at Mademoiselle Modes. 'This was a model gown and even with my friend Miss Armstrong's discount it cost me every penny I had left. So,' Bess said, stepping back from the mirror, 'what do you think?'

'You look lovely,' Ena said.

'Thank you. So do you. Turn round and I'll tie your bow.'

'Do it tight, so I've got a waist like a film star,' she said, sucking in her stomach and holding her breath.

'Don't be silly, Ena! Breathe normally or I won't tie it at all. You can't spend the whole evening holding your breath.'

Ena expelled a lungful of air, purposely forcing it to reverberate between her lips so it made a rude noise, and giggled.

Bess pulled and prettified the bow at her young sister's waist and then put her arm round her shoulder. 'If I were you, Ena Dudley, I would keep breathing or you might faint. Worse still, if your bow's too tight you won't be able to eat any of my birthday cake,' Bess said, laughing.

Ena caught sight of herself in the mirror, puffed out her cheeks, hunched up her shoulders and, with her knees bent and her arms swinging at her side, lumbered out of the room like a monkey, chattering, 'Ooh oohhh aaaah aaahhhh, I want cake.' Still laughing, Bess slipped her feet into her shoes and followed her sister downstairs.

As she entered the living room the family stood and sang, "Happy Birthday to You" followed by "Twenty-one Today". Tom led them in a chorus of three cheers and afterwards threatened to give Bess the bumps. Bess's father called for hush and ordered everyone to the table.

Her mother had baked a ham, which she had sliced and placed round a large plate, each slice overlapping the one before. There were cheese and beetroot and tinned salmon and cucumber sandwiches, dishes of tomatoes, radishes, celery, pickled onions and piccalilli, as well as a large bowl of sherry trifle and an iced birthday cake.

'What a wonderful spread. This table wouldn't look out of place up at the Hall, Mam,' Bess said.

'Not every day your oldest daughter turns twenty-one. Got to mark the occasion!' Lily Dudley didn't take compliments well.

When they had finished eating, everyone helped to clear the table, except Bess. Bess followed her father into the living room and told him about her last term at college, and her hopes of getting a teaching post in London. In return her father brought her up to date with the Estate's news, the farms, the horses – and, in particular, Sable.

When the washing up was done, Tom, Margaret, Claire and Ena joined Bess and her father, followed a little later by their mother, who was carrying two small packages and a dozen birthday cards that she had hidden from the inquisitive eyes of Ena and Claire beneath a pile of ironing in the scullery. Ironing! Scullery! Neither girl would dream of looking there.

The first present was from her parents. It was in a square box covered in cream leather. Bess opened the box and caught her breath.

Between the vertical pleats of cream satin in the lid of the box and the cushion in the bottom was a gold wristwatch.

'Thank you,' she said, kissing each of her parents in turn. She laid the watch across her wrist, lifted the small square link that dangled from one end of the bracelet to meet the equally small square clasp that dangled from the other, hooked the first through the second and pressed them together. Then she held the watch at arm's length to admire its small oval face and delicately fashioned bracelet of gold leaves. 'It is beautiful, really beautiful,' she said.

'Open ours now, Bess,' Margaret said, pushing a gift of similar shape and size towards her. Eagerly she removed the shiny red wrapping paper to discover a red box. Nestling between folds of red satin was a gold locket on a chain.

'It's a good one,' Margaret said. 'Me and Tom chose it. We bought it from a jewellery shop in Coventry.'

'It's beautiful, thank you all,' Bess said, concerned because she knew how much a necklace as lovely as this one would have cost.

'Don't worry, Bess,' Ena said. 'Our Tom paid for it.'

'Shush, Ena. It doesn't matter who paid for it,' Tom said. 'The important thing is we give Bess something for her birthday, as well as for passing her exams, that she can keep. We're all very proud of you, Bess.'

'I think that calls for a toast,' their father said.

While Bess's father poured the sherry, Bess opened her cards and read each one aloud before placing it on the mantelshelf. Most of the cards were from friends who lived locally and had been delivered by hand, but five had come by post during the week. Two cards were postmarked London. The first was from Mrs McAllister and Molly, and the second was from Miss Armstrong. The third card was from Birmingham, from Nora and Arthur, and the fourth was from Bess's friend Henry Green, which made Ena and Claire giggle. Ignoring her sisters, Bess ran her finger along the flap of the remaining envelope. It was addressed to Miss Elizabeth Dudley, C/O The Post Office, Woodcote, but it didn't have a postmark.

'I wonder who this is from,' she said, more to herself than to anyone else as she pulled the cream card with the number twenty-one embossed in gold from the envelope. The message was simple and read, "Many happy returns of the day, James". Bess's blushes went unnoticed as she placed the card alongside those of her friends and family. The letter, which only she had seen, she left in the envelope and dropped into her handbag.

That night, when everyone was asleep, Bess tiptoed from the bedroom she shared with her sisters and went downstairs. In the sitting room she lit a candle and by its pale glow read James's letter. "Dear Bess, I hope this note finds you well. I'm sorry I missed you when you telephoned the office. I wasn't given your message until the following morning when I went in to clear my desk. Because I believe it's only a matter of time before England goes to war with Germany, I've left the practice and joined the RAF. I'm training at a secret location and have no idea when I'll be home next. Think of me sometimes when you ride across the Acres. Best wishes, James."

So James didn't know she'd telephoned that afternoon. The girl hadn't told him because she wanted him for herself. She got him too, Bess thought, for one night. Bess read the letter again. If James had joined the RAF the fling, or whatever it was with the girl in the office, was probably over. And, since he wouldn't have been unfaithful to Annabel, if he'd been walking out with her- Bess's heart leapt with joy. James was free.

Bess folded the letter, put it back in its envelope and returned to the bedroom. Ena was still asleep and didn't stir as she crept into bed beside her. She put James's letter under her pillow and lay thinking. Excitement and fear raced side by side. What would war mean to her family? Her father wouldn't be called up - he was too old - but Tom would volunteer; he'd said as much at New Year. Margaret, with a bit of luck, would be married by then and escape the first draft, perhaps the entire war if it didn't last long. Claire would join up as soon as she could. She had romantic notions about saving the world in a glamorous uniform. Ena, thank God, was too young.

Bess stared at the ceiling, unable to ignore the niggling thoughts that crept into her mind about her own future. If there was a war she would be called up. Her teaching career would be over before it began and all the hard work, the studying, would have been for nothing. Bess turned over and closed her eyes, but she couldn't sleep. She thought about her friends Natalie and Anton Goldman, and wondered how a war with Germany would affect them. They were persecuted in Germany because they were Jewish. If England went to war with Germany, Bess feared they would be persecuted in England because they were German. She pulled the bedclothes up to her chin and closed her eyes again. It didn't bear thinking about.

Bess finally slipped into a fretful sleep, only to be woken minutes later by the cawing of crows flying overhead. Leaving her sisters to sleep, she got up and went downstairs. She made a pot of tea and, armed with a large cup, sat at the living room table and wrote a letter to Natalie Goldman.

CHAPTER SIX

The BBC forecast glorious sunshine for July and predicted that the record-breaking hot weather would continue throughout the summer of 1939. July 1st, the day Bess's sister Margaret was to marry her sweetheart Bill Burrell at Mysterton Church, was no exception.

After taking Sable for an early morning trot along the river – it was too hot to exercise her properly – Bess dismounted and walked her back through the park which, in contrast to the open fields and meadows, was dark and cool. Sheltered by giant oak trees with huge exposed roots, it was a playground for squirrels and other small creatures. A dry twig snapped beneath Bess's boot, halting the tap, tap, tap of a woodpecker that had been pecking for grubs on the bark of a dead tree. Bess stood still and waited for the bird to resume its search for food.

If I moved to live in London I would miss all this, she thought. I would miss the peace and the privacy. For as long as she could remember, if she had something on her mind, she would come to the park and in no time the solution would come to her. The reason she had taken a detour today was not only to walk Sable in the shade, but because she wanted to be alone. And being alone in a house with six or more people was impossible, especially on the day of your sister's wedding. But here, for a few minutes, she could enjoy the peace and quiet of the woods – and she could think.

She took the letter that she'd received earlier in the week from her pocket and read it again. Christchurch Secondary School, Clapham, South London was a good school with a good reputation. The position of English Mistress was what she had worked so hard for and, because it was her first job after finishing college, the salary was much more than she had expected. So why was she hesitating? Was it because London would be a dangerous place to live and work if there was a war, or was it because James was no longer there? At the end of the letter the headmaster stipulated that, if Bess declined his offer, she should let him know in writing before July 9th. That would give him time to offer the job to his second choice.

The woodpecker resumed its tapping and Bess put the letter back in her pocket. She could think of a dozen reasons to stay at Foxden but none came with a salary, let alone a salary to match the one she'd been offered in London.

Bess was determined to find a way to stay close to her beloved Acres. 'You don't want me to leave, do you, old girl?' she said, walking Sable on. She didn't know what to do for the best, but she had a week to make up her mind, so she decided to forget about the job until after Margaret's wedding.

It was always hectic when the Dudley girls were home at the same time, but today it was like being in a very crowded nightmare. Everyone was rushing around with slices of toast and cups of tea in their hands: "breakfast on the hoof", Tom called it. People were arriving every five minutes, or so it seemed. The woman in charge of the catering at Woodcote Village Hall came to discuss the wedding cake, the florist from Lowarth arrived with the bouquets and two baskets of flowers, and several neighbours popped in for… who knew what!

Tom was first to arrive downstairs, dressed in his best suit, followed closely by his father. 'I'm going outside for a smoke,' Bess's father said, dodging a three year old boy wielding a sticky bun.

'Come here, Archie!' demanded the child's mother, who was the best dressmaker Lowarth had to offer, and who had called in case there were any last minute alterations to Margaret's dress. 'I thought I told you to sit still,' she scolded, dragging the child from the kitchen to the living room by the scruff of his neck and leaving a trail of crumbs in his wake.

'I'm taking the flowers to the church, Mam,' Bess shouted, picking up the two baskets of flowers that should have been delivered hours ago. Her mother, busy making tea for the dressmaker, florist and neighbours, didn't reply. 'It's a madhouse,' she shouted to Tom as she left.

Walking to the church, Bess made mental notes of what she had to do before Margaret's wedding. As chief bridesmaid, it was her job to make sure Ena and Claire were in their bridesmaid dresses, before helping Margaret into her wedding dress. Only when everyone else was dressed – and the bathroom was finally free – could she get ready. 'Phew!' she said, 'it's hot.'

In contrast to the heat and the humidity outside, the interior of the ancient Cotswold stone church felt pleasantly cool. The stained glass windows in the clerestory, high above in the aisle roof, let in shafts of soft pink and gold dust-speckled light, and the fragrance of lavender furniture polish and vanilla candles filled the building with a rich and calming fragrance.

Bess walked down the aisle carrying a bunch of pink and white roses as if it were a bridal bouquet, humming, "Here Comes The Bride". It might have been me getting married today if I'd accepted my old sweetheart's proposal - if I'd have cared for Frank Donnelly in the way he'd cared for me, Bess thought. She stood at the foot of the altar steps and tried to imagine herself in a bridal gown, but she couldn't. Maybe one day, she thought, smiling. Her mother had said she was stupid passing up an opportunity to marry a nice chap like Frank. 'Our Bess has always had ideas above her station. College indeed!' she'd said when Bess told her why she'd turned Frank down, which made Bess even more determined to go.

The roses stretched to two vases, both shaped like a fan. Columbine trailed from the centre of one; from the other, sorrel. The first arrangement she placed on a table beneath the pulpit, the second on an ornate piece of wood that acted as a lid to protect the font when it wasn't in use. Before she left she tied white ribbon round bunches of sweet peas and hung one on the end of each pew.

As she opened the front door Bess could hear Ena and Claire arguing.

'You've swapped the gloves,' Ena said.

'Haven't!' Claire replied nonchalantly.

'Yes, you have. Look, the tips of the fingers are grubby. Mine were clean,' Ena said, picking up a pair of gloves on Claire's side of the bedroom. 'It's not fair that you've dirtied them and I've got to wear them!'

'It's not fair that your flowers are prettier than mine, but--'

'No they're not! They're exactly the same, stupid!'

'Right. I'm not helping you do your hair for saying that!'

'What? After all the time I spent on your mousey, pump-water--'

'If you two don't stop arguing I'll come up there and bang your heads together,' their father shouted from the bottom of the stairs.

'It's not my fault, Dad, it's our Claire's,' Ena shouted.

'No it's not, Dad, Ena started it.'

'And I'm going to finish it!' Bess said. 'Put your dresses on, now!'

Angry with Bess instead of each other, Claire and Ena dressed without saying another word and went downstairs to sit with their father.

Claire and Ena's constant bickering had driven Margaret into her parents' bedroom. Bess opened the door to find her sister lying on the bed with her eyes shut and her head hanging over a pillow that had been tied in the middle like a sausage, so it didn't squash her hair.

Bess tiptoed over to the window and opened the curtains. When she turned round, Margaret was sitting up with her hands in front of her eyes, looking at Bess through splayed fingers, the way Bela Lugosi had done in the film, "Dracula", which the Dudley sisters had seen earlier in the week at Lowarth Picture House. Feigning surprise at seeing Bess, Margaret whimpered, 'I thought you'd forgotten me.' Margaret brought a sense of the dramatic to every occasion, but today who could blame her? She was getting married in less than an hour and she was the only person in the house, apart from Bess, who wasn't dressed.

Bess was not in the mood to play games, but there was only one way to coax Margaret out of her "poor me" mood and that was to give her the attention that, on this occasion, she deserved. 'Forget you on your wedding day?' Bess looked fittingly horrified at the idea. 'This is the most important day in the Dudley family calendar and you, my lady, are the most important person.'

After spreading a clean sheet on the floor, Bess took Margaret's wedding dress from its hanger, lifted it as high as she could and let it fall onto the sheet like a parachute. Then Bess helped the barefoot bride to step into the dress, making sure she cleared the small opening at the waist. Finally, in one fluid movement, Bess pulled up the bodice of the dress and Margaret slipped her arms into the sleeves.

While Margaret admired herself in the mirror, Bess fastened the buttons at the back of the dress. Each tiny round button – and there were dozens of them – had been covered in white satin to match the dress and had to be gently teased through buttonholes that were only fractionally bigger than the buttons.

'Stand still, Margaret, I'm nearly done,' Bess said, persevering until every button had been pushed through its corresponding buttonhole. She then placed a veil of fine net on her sister's head, followed by a garland of tiny pink rosebuds – to keep the veil in place – and held her hand while she stepped into her new white shoes.

Moving away, but not taking her eyes off her sister, Bess shook her head and sighed. 'I don't think I've ever seen a bride look so radiant. You look beautiful, Margaret.'

'Do I, Bess?' Margaret said, her eyes sparkling with emotion.

'Yes, but don't you dare cry, you'll spoil your make-up. Stay there and don't move,' Bess ordered. 'I'm going down to get Dad.'

'Bess is right, you do look beautiful, Margaret.' Her father stood for a long minute, his eyes moist. 'Come on then,' he said, after clearing his throat. 'Let's get you to the church.'

It was the perfect day for a wedding. The sun was shining, the warm fruity scent of wild honeysuckle pinked the air and the lane leading from Woodcote to Mysterton Church, was lined with people waiting to see the bride.

Tom and his mother were first to arrive, followed by Claire and Ena. Margaret and her father were five minutes late, not because being five minutes late was the tradition, but because they had to wait for Bess, the chief bridesmaid, to get there before them.

'Give us a whirl, Margaret,' someone in the crowd shouted, and Margaret complied. Halfway along the path leading to the church she stopped and gave the onlookers a twirl. Everyone clapped and Margaret smiled like a film star. As the organ began to play "Here Comes the Bride" she turned to her father, rested her hand on his arm and allowed him to guide her into the church and down the aisle to her future husband.

The old church was full to the rafters. Margaret spoke clearly and although she had said many times during that week that she would be too nervous to sing, she sang beautifully and every bit as loud as she did at choir practice. Bess took the bouquet at the right time, and when Margaret and Bill said, 'I do,' there was a flourish of handkerchiefs and the customary dabbing of eyes and blowing of noses.

After the service the local chemist, the nearest thing Lowarth had to a photographer, took photographs of Margaret and Bill in traditional bride and groom poses, gradually adding other members of the wedding party. First the best man and the bridesmaids, followed by the bride and groom's parents. Finally it was time for the group photograph, which took so long to set up some of the guests began to drift off, lured away by the promise of cold fruit punch and ham and cheese sandwiches in Woodcote Village Hall.

Guests that had driven to the church drove down to the reception. Those who lived in the village and had walked the half-mile to the church walked back, but the newly married Mr and Mrs Burrell travelled in style – transported from the church to the reception in the hansom cab that Bill's mother and father had hired for the occasion.

The day Margaret and Bill returned from their honeymoon was the day Bess needed to write to the headmaster of Christchurch Secondary School in South London if she was not going to accept the job as English teacher. She was sitting at the living room table reading the letter when her father came in.

'Decided what you're going to do yet, Bess?' her father asked, pulling out a chair and sitting next to her.

'No!'

'Do you want to talk it through? It might help.'

Bess laid her head on her father's shoulder. She wished she could tell him how she felt about James. Instead she said, 'I'm not sure I want to go to London.'

'Then don't. Stay here. Get a job in Lowarth or Rugby.'

'If only it was that easy. The chances of finding full-time employment this near to the start of the autumn term are very slim.'

'Why don't you have a word with the headmistress at Woodcote Junior School? She might be able to suggest something.'

'I already have. She was very nice, but the only work she can give me during the coming school year is on an ad-hoc basis, to fill in if any of her staff are off. She suggested I gave private lessons. She said there are often children who need extra tuition. Some fall behind through illness, especially in the winter. And some are grammar school hopefuls, children of local businessmen and wealthy farmers whose parents are prepared to pay to get them through the eleven plus.'

'There you are then!' When Bess didn't answer, he said, 'So what else is bothering you?'

Lifting her head and looking seriously at her father, she said, 'It's time I contributed to the family financially. I won't be able to do that if I stay here, but I will if I go to London to work.'

'Is that what this is about?'

'It's not the only reason, but yes, I'm twenty-one, it's time--'

'Life isn't just about money, Bess. You need to follow your heart too.'

'I know,' she said. If only she could tell her father what was in her heart - but she couldn't. She looked into his kind, tired face and smiled. She knew he didn't earn much working as second horseman, but she would rather die than say anything to embarrass him. 'I just think that if I was earning I'd be able to help Ena and Claire. Girls of their age--'

'But you have helped them-- do help them. Your sisters wouldn't have done half as well at school if they hadn't had you to look up to.'

'But being at college all this time and not bringing in any money, when Tom contributes and Margaret's been working in the factory and paying for her keep - it makes me think I should take the job in London. At least then I won't be a drain--'

'A drain? On who? You've always won scholarships, been awarded grants to pay for your education – you've never been a drain.

Forcing herself not to cry, Bess said, 'But you work so hard and--'

'I might not earn a big wage, but being a groom is what I chose to do, Bess. When I left school working with horses, exercising them and training them was all I wanted to do. It was my dream. If you want my advice do what *you* want to do, what'll make *you* happy, not what you think you should do. There is one thing …'

'Go on, what is it?'

'If there's a war--'

'London will be a dangerous place!'

Her father's eyes, a combination of worried and serious, grew moist. 'Yes.'

'I thought about that too, but London's only a few hours away by train. I can always come home.' Laughing, she said, 'I'm more worried about what Mam will say if I go back to London than I am about the Germans attacking.'

Smiling, her father said, 'Whatever you decide, your mother and I will be behind you all the way.'

Bess rolled her eyes and bit her lip, in an over-exaggerated way, making her father laugh.

Still laughing, he got up and kissed Bess on top of her head. 'You leave your mother to me,' he said, and left.

Living in London, earning decent money, would mean she could afford to go out, which she hadn't been able to do while she was at college. On the other hand, living at home would mean she'd be with her family, be able to exercise Sable every day, and be here when James returned from training with the RAF. She ached to see him, to be close to him, to talk to him. She took his letter from her pocket, read it again, and decided to write to the headmaster of Christchurch School and say that it was with regret that she was unable to accept the post of English Mistress. If she wrote the letter now, she could take the short cut across the fields to Woodcote and catch the last post.

Holding the letter tightly, Bess skirted the woods on the south side of the lake, leapt over the three-step stile, and ran along the overgrown footpath that led to the main road on the far side of a small thicket south of the bend on Shaft Hill. As she ran into the road she felt the sharp stabbing pain of a stitch in her side. Instinctively she stopped, put her hands on her knees, and began to breathe deeply and slowly. She neither saw nor heard Lady Foxden's car, which had turned the corner at exactly the same time. Luckily, Lady Foxden had seen her and had hit the brakes before she hit Bess.

Lady Foxden leapt out of the car and, for what seemed like an eternity, the two women stood and stared at each other in disbelief. 'Are you alright, Elizabeth?' her Ladyship asked across the highly polished black bonnet of her motorcar. 'I'm sorry, I didn't see you until I turned the bend.'

'It's not your fault, your Ladyship, it's mine. I wasn't looking,' Bess said, trembling and out of breath. 'I should have looked before I ran into the road. I'm fine, thank you.'

'Well, as long as there's no harm done. Are you going to Woodcote?'

'Yes, to the post office.' Bess waved the envelope in the air as if it was some sort of justification for almost getting herself killed.

'You'd better hop in dear, there's only five minutes until the last collection.'

Still trembling, Bess lowered herself onto the soft cream leather passenger seat of the Rover motorcar and closed the door. Lady Foxden, having regained her composure, got back into the car, put her foot on the accelerator, and cautiously drove down the hill.

'Congratulations on passing your exams, Elizabeth,' Lady Foxden said. 'Your father tells me you've been offered a teaching post in London.' But before Bess could reply her Ladyship had moved the conversation on to her son. 'James was in London, you know, for several years. He isn't there now, I'm pleased to say. I mean,' she continued without pausing for breath, 'if there is a war, London would be …'

Lady Foxden chattered on, and Bess knew the drill. She and her sisters had had it drummed into them from a very early age that they were not to speak unless they were spoken to, especially in the presence of Lord and Lady Foxden. Listen and learn, their father would say, listen and learn. And that was what Bess was doing now; she was listening and learning about James – the same James who, as a boy, had gone scrumping

124

apples with her brother Tom. The same James who had saved her from drowning when she was a child and who, only a few months ago, Bess had beaten in a race across the Foxden Estate.

Bess was eager to hear anything and everything about James, whether it was his work in London or more recently his training with the RAF.

'It's top secret, very hush-hush!' Lady Foxden whispered, pausing just long enough for Bess to acknowledge the importance of her son's work. 'The poor boy,' she went on, 'has been working so terribly hard. I don't know what he'd have done without the Hadleighs. I was so relieved when my friend Lady Eleanor wrote to tell me that James was a regular visitor at Hadleigh Hall.'

'Hadleigh?' Bess heard herself say.

'Yes, James is training at an RAF camp in Kent. And according to Eleanor, James and her daughter Annabel have become inseparable. They've always been close, so it is no surprise ....'

Bess didn't want to hear about James and Annabel becoming inseparable and tried to think of a way to change the subject without being rude. 'Is it all right if I open the window, I'm feeling--?'

'And,' Lady Foxden whispered, leaning towards Bess as if she was sharing top secret information with her, 'Eleanor hopes – well, we both do – that in the not too distant future James and Annabel will announce their engagement. And, if there is a wretched war, there could be wedding bells sooner rather than later.'

The car was unbearably hot and stuffy. Bess inhaled deeply, but the combined smell of petrol and warm leather made her feel sick. The sun was reflecting off the walnut dashboard, blinding her and stinging her eyes. Unable to see for the glare, Bess lowered her head. She felt a searing pain spread across her forehead, and the shiny dashboard turned black.

'Elizabeth, are you all right, dear?' Bess was aware that someone was speaking to her but she couldn't make out who they were or what they were saying because they were so far away. Then the sharp repugnant smell of bitter chemicals powered its way into her consciousness and she opened her eyes.

She lifted her head to see Lady Foxden kneeling on the grass next to the open passenger door with a bottle of smelling salts in her hand. 'You're burning up, child,' she said, pressing the back of her hand against Bess's cheek. 'It's no wonder, running in this heat, it's not good for you,' she scolded.

'Yes, it must be the heat. I'd better go home,' Bess said, still in shock after hearing about James's forthcoming engagement to Annabel Hadleigh.

'But your letter? Would you like me to post it for you?'

'No. Thank you.'

The following day Bess posted a letter to the headmaster of Christchurch Secondary School in Clapham, South London, accepting the job of English teacher.

CHAPTER SEVEN

'Have you all got your gas masks?'

'Yes, Miss Dudley,' was the collective reply from the pupils of 1B as the home bell echoed through the freshly painted corridors of Christchurch School.

'Off you go, then. See you on Monday,' Bess shouted above the noise of desk lids slamming, chairs being scraped along the hard wooden floor and the chatter of twenty-five excited eleven year olds who, like Bess, had come to the end of their first week at a new school. 'Walk in single file, please!' she reminded them as each child pushed to be first in line to leave the classroom. 'And go straight home!'

Life as a teacher in a London school was better than Bess had thought it would be. She got on with her fellow teachers and she had gained the respect of her pupils rather more quickly than expected when she calmly evicted a mouse from her desk. No doubt the boys responsible for putting the mouse in there had hoped to see Miss scream, and perhaps a different personality would have, but not Bess. Bess had lived in the country for most of her life and was not afraid of animals, large or small. Besides, this particular little rodent was tame.

Bess asked if anyone in the class was willing to give the mouse a home and immediately the hand of a young tearaway named Fredrick Jenkins shot up.

'Lucky for the mouse you had a box handy, Fred,' Bess whispered into the boy's unwashed ear as she handed him the tiny creature.

'Yes, miss,' Fred mumbled, dropping the mouse into a box ventilated with holes the exact circumference of his pencil.

Bess liked the children in her class, she liked her colleagues and she liked South London. It was only a ten minute bus ride from the school to where she lived, on Clapham Common's East Side, but she preferred to walk. Walking across the Common reminded her of the park at Foxden, and James. Although she would put him out of her mind immediately.

Making a detour to the drapers on the High Road on her way home, Bess bought a yard of blackout material and later that evening made a small curtain for the window in her front door. Satisfied that the curtain covered the window fully on the inside, Bess went outside to make sure the curtain didn't allow any light to escape.

She pulled her cardigan across her chest and folded her arms. It had been a warm day, an Indian summer sort of day, but now the sun had paled. What had been a refreshing breeze had turned into a cold wind. She stood for some time on top of the wrought iron staircase outside her apartment and watched three boys try to control the erratic flight of a large triangular kite. The kite, a black dragon breathing red fire on a white background, took a swirling nosedive. Before it hit the ground a gust of wind swept it up again and drove it deep into a horse chestnut tree. The boys pulled and tugged at the kite's guide rope, but the more they tugged the faster the kite stuck. Eventually the rope snapped and the dragon's tail snaked to earth, leaving the angry dragon blowing fire at the fading sun.

The three boys left the Common as the sun began its descent behind the rooftops on Clapham Common's west side. The clouds, earlier ribbed with crimson, had turned to grey and suddenly, as if someone had thrown the switch on the world's lights, it was dark. Satisfied that the light in her hall did not show through the blackout curtain, Bess went inside.

Her apartment was above the garage of a large Victorian house, owned by the headmaster of Christchurch School's elderly aunt. The aunt was abroad and had asked her nephew to find someone suitable to live on the premises while she was away, as a burglar deterrent. It was Bess's good fortune that she had accepted the job at Christchurch School while the headmaster was looking for a tenant. In more affluent times the apartment would have been the living quarters of the chauffeur. Today it was a school teacher's sanctuary.

The main room was L-shaped, and was both living room and bedroom, with the bed tucked neatly behind a decorative wooden screen in the foot of the L. The living room had a bay window that overlooked the Common, a drop-leaf table, two high-back chairs, and a cottage style settee and chair on either side of a small fire. The other rooms in the apartment, the galley-style kitchen on the left of the entrance hall and the bathroom and toilet on the right, were considerably smaller, but well-designed and functional.

Bess loved the peace and quiet of her small apartment, especially after a day teaching noisy, sometimes naughty, and always energetic children. As the oldest girl in the family it had fallen to her to help her mother look after her younger sisters. It wasn't until she went to the grammar school that her sister Margaret was made to share the responsibility. Even so, Bess rarely went anywhere without taking at least one of her siblings with her – usually Ena – which was probably why she and Ena were so close. As she looked around her small neat home an involuntary smile crept across her face. Bess had never had a bed of her own, let alone a bedroom. Now she had a whole apartment to herself and she loved it.

Bess styled her hair in a fashionable bun, dabbed rouge on her cheeks to add colour to her pale complexion, and patted it down with face powder before applying burnt-orange lipstick and dabbing Goya Gardenia perfume on her neck and wrists. Not bad, she thought when she caught her reflection in the mirror. Not bad at all.

Happy with what she saw, she put on a pair of fully-fashioned stockings, taking care not to snag them with her nails. After checking there were no wrinkles, she fastened the metal garter hooks of her girdle over the small rubber buttons to hold her stockings in place. Satisfied that the seams were straight, Bess stepped into the green dress she wore on her twenty-first birthday and then her shoes, before putting on her hat.

Her hair made the hat sit at a jaunty angle, which Bess thought looked rather chic. She looked fine. She looked better than fine, but if she didn't leave now she was going to be late. Quickly putting on her coat, Bess picked up her handbag and left the flat. After locking the door, she made her way to the Underground station at Clapham South where, after a short journey, she would see her friends Natalie and Anton Goldman at the Prince Albert Theatre on the Strand.

Bess had written to Natalie from Foxden during the summer but she hadn't seen her since she'd been back in London. She hadn't seen any of her friends and she'd turned down several invitations to go out with her work colleagues, but she wasn't going to turn down any more offers to go out.

She left the train at Waterloo station and walked across the bridge, stopping briefly to take in Big Ben and The Houses of Parliament on her left and a few minutes later, St. Paul's

Cathedral and the docks on her right. At Lancaster Place she turned into the Strand and crossed the road to the Prince Albert Theatre.

'I'm here to see Mr and Mrs Goldman. My name is Bess Dudley,' she said to the young man in the Box Office.

'If you'd like to take a seat, Miss,' he said, pointing to a maroon-coloured seat on the opposite wall, 'I'll phone through and tell them you're here.'

Bess thanked the young man, walked over to the seat and sat down. The seat matched the heavy drapes at the windows and doors. The floor was marble. It reminded her of Foxden – and for a moment she thought of James and the night of the New Year's Eve party. The floor also reminded her of her childhood. When her mother cleaned for Lady Foxden she would often take Bess with her and sit her in the corner of the hall while she and another estate worker's wife scrubbed the marble floor on their hands and knees. Her mother's knees were swollen for weeks afterwards and her hands were red raw from using strong detergent. She was sorry that her mother had to do that kind of work - and grateful that she didn't.

She was miles away when she heard Natalie Goldman calling her. 'Bess, how good to see you, and looking so well.' Natalie kissed Bess on both cheeks. 'Come, Anton is looking forward to seeing you and to finally giving you a guided tour of the theatre.'

Natalie thanked the young man in the Box Office and, taking Bess by the hand, led her through a set of doors marked "Private".

Anton Goldman was as charming and kind as Bess remembered him to be, and he whisked her off on a guided tour of his theatre. He introduced her to the front of house manageress, Miss Lesley, and to Bert, the stage doorman. He took her to the workshops in the dock where the carpenters were making final adjustments to the scenery, and the scene shifters were playing cards, because they weren't needed until the show began.

Upstairs Anton introduced her to Miss Horton, the Wardrobe Mistress, who took her to the costume storeroom, where there were rows and rows of exotic gowns made of fine silks and satins, crepes and muslins. Next they went to the room of hats. At one end, Indian turbans, 19th century bonnets and the enormous hats of the early 1900s – decorated with flowers, feathers, ribbons and tulle – sat on mannequins' heads with featureless faces, next to the modern cloches and berets of the 20th century. At the other end of the room, there were as many different styles and colours of wigs, feather and beaded headdresses, crowns and coronets. Glass cabinets displayed diamond and ruby and emerald and pearl necklaces, bracelets and rings. And beneath them were drawers of belts and gloves, and racks of shoes. Bess shook her head in amazement.

'We're not done yet,' Miss Horton said, leading the way to a room crammed full of men's costumes. In wardrobes the size of small rooms, decorative coats, evening jackets and waistcoats made of brocade and velvet hung above trousers, breeches, leggings and shirts. Below them, rows of boots and shoes stood next to racks of walking sticks, canes, riding crops and umbrellas.

'Enjoying yourself, Bess?' Miss Horton asked.

'Yes, I am,' she said, following the Wardrobe Mistress along the corridor and into what she thought was the most exciting room of them all. 'A dressing room,' she gasped, 'where the artists put on their costumes and make-up.' She looked around like an excited child, taking in the long bench-style dressing table with make-up boxes, brushes and combs, perfume bottles and jewellery. Above it were square mirrors surrounded by light bulbs and below, chairs with artists' names on them.

'Thank you so much,' Bess said, following Miss Horton down several flights of stairs and along half a dozen passages to Anton Goldman. 'No wonder they call backstage the rabbit warren,' she said as Anton lead her down a flight of narrow steps, through a pass-door and into the auditorium where Natalie was waiting for them.

'That's our box, Bess. That's where we'll be sitting to watch the show tonight,' Anton said, pointing to a large box on the left of the auditorium. 'You are coming to the show, aren't you?'

'And you will stay for the party afterwards? Oh, do say you will, Bess. First night parties are such fun,' Natalie added.

'I'd love to, but I need to get home at a reasonable time. I have the exercise books of twenty-seven young Einsteins to mark before Monday, as well as next week's lessons to prepare.' Natalie looked disappointed by Bess's excuse. And it was an excuse; the excuse she made to avoid going anywhere. She was never going to celebrate James marrying Annabel Hadleigh. But since she could do nothing to stop it, it was time she accepted it and got on with her life. 'Thank you,' she said. 'I'd love to see the show tonight. And yes, I will come to the party afterwards. It's time I had some fun.'

Natalie clapped wildly. 'Are you hungry, Bess?' She didn't wait for Bess to reply. 'We will have lunch next door, at the Fleur Jardin Café, and afterwards walk to Oxford Street and do some window shopping. Don't worry my darling,' she said, kissing her husband on the cheek, 'we will be back long before the show opens tonight. Come, Bess,' she said, taking Bess by the hand and playfully dragging her out of the theatre.

The Fleur Jardin Café attracted a bohemian clientele. Beneath its blue and white striped awning young writers, poets and artists sat at wooden tables drinking strong coffee and talking excitedly about literature, art and music. They made grand gestures with their hands and laughed loudly. Bess envied them their carefree lifestyle and wondered, if there was a war, how long it would be before their lives changed.

The inviting aroma of freshly ground coffee and aromatic herbs met Bess and Natalie when they stepped through the door, as did a young waiter. 'Bonjour, Madame Goldman, Mademoiselle,' he said, smiling. Then to Natalie, 'Your usual table, Madame?'

'Yes, thank you, Eric,' Natalie replied, following him to a table by the window, where he pulled out Natalie's chair and then Bess's. When they were seated, he handed them each a menu.

'I would like onion soup to start, followed by Carré d'agneau. What about you, Bess? I'm having the lamb. I can recommend it.'

'It all looks delicious but I'll have the lamb too. Thank you,' she said, handing the menu back to the waiter.

'And we'll have two glasses of claret, please,' Natalie said, smiling at Bess.

'Merci, Madame,' the waiter said, and left.

'Are you enjoying being a teacher, Bess?' Natalie asked while they ate their meal.

'Yes I am, very much. Some of the children in my class are a little rough around the edges, but most of them are eager to learn.'

'And what about your apartment? Is it comfortable?'

'Yes, it's lovely. I can't believe my luck. I pinch myself sometimes to make sure I'm not dreaming.'

Natalie laughed. 'So you have a job you enjoy and a lovely home, but what about a social life; a young man to take you dancing?

'I'm too busy for dancing,' she said, dismissing the question.

'That's a shame, Bess. You need fun in your life as well as work. What about the young man who gave you his card? I thought you were fond of him?'

'I am-- was. But he isn't free. The last I heard he was getting engaged. He joined the RAF and I haven't seen him since.'

Laying her hand on Bess's, Natalie said, 'You'll meet a wonderful man one day. A man who deserves you, Bess.'

Bess was desperate to tell Natalie how wonderful James was and how much she loved him when the waiter appeared with the bill on a small round silver dish, which he placed on the table beside her. Natalie covered it with a pound note, nodded and said, 'Thank you, Eric.' Her way of saying keep the change, Bess thought.

Smiling, Eric said, 'Merci, Madame.' Then he turned, nodded to Bess and left. And the moment to tell Natalie about James had gone.

After using the Ladies', the two friends set off to Oxford Street via Covent Garden. Taking a short cut through the market they walked briskly past the Royal Opera House and the Coliseum, and zigzagged their way through the side streets to Shaftsbury Avenue, where they read reviews in glass frames outside some of the West End's most famous theatres: "Fantastic and Funny", and a little further down the Avenue, "Another Hit for Noel Coward." But the best notices were "Flanagan and Allen At Their Best" and "Flanagan and Allen – The Best Show in Town."

Natalie whispered, 'The critics are in tonight. I do hope they like the show, for Anton and the company's sake. They have all worked so hard.'

'I'm sure they will. By tomorrow night, the walls of the Prince Albert Theatre will be covered in wonderful reviews.'

Squeezing Bess's arm, Natalie said, 'Thank you.'

The windows of the shops in Oxford Street were dressed with "New Season" autumn and winter fashions. By the time Bess had seen the coming season's coats, must-have shoes, and dresses for "that special occasion" she had spent an imaginary fortune.

'I need a drink,' Natalie said. 'Shall we go to Lyons Corner House for tea?'

'Yes, I haven't been to the new one yet,' Bess said. She was parched and her feet ached from walking so far in high heels.

In no time at all, Berwick Street market and the exotic shops of Soho were behind them and they were entering Piccadilly's newly refurbished Lyons Corner House.

'This,' Natalie said, 'is the most fashionable place to take tea in, in London, they say.'

'And the most modern,' Bess added, 'Look at those marble counters and the mirrors on the walls behind them. They must be six feet tall,' she marvelled.

Sitting in the tea bar area the two friends kicked off their shoes and giggled like teenagers.

'Tea for two?' Natalie trilled, when a pot of tea, cups and saucers, a plate of sandwiches and two iced buns with cherries on top arrived.

'Sounds like you're about to burst into song,' Bess said, laughing.

'Don't dare me or I will,' she warned, before tucking into a salmon and cucumber sandwich.

When Natalie and Bess eventually left the Lyons Corner House, they walked down Haymarket to Trafalgar Square. Under the watchful gaze of Admiral Lord Nelson they fed the pigeons before walking the short distance along the Strand to the Prince Albert Theatre and the first night of "Seven Wonders of The World".

CHAPTER EIGHT

Anton escorted Bess and Natalie to the Goldman's private box where four high-backed chairs had been placed in a row. On the seat of the chair nearest to the stage was a corsage of three pink orchids.

Natalie's face lit up. 'Thank you, darling,' she said, handing the corsage and its small pin to her husband, who attached it to her dress. He then took a similar corsage in cream from the seat on his right and gave it to Bess. She had never worn orchids before. Her sister Claire had a young admirer who sometimes gave her an orchid. He was an apprentice gardener in a large country mansion and when he worked in the orchid-house he was allowed to take the occasional less than perfect flower home, as a perk of the job. Bess turned to Anton and Natalie and said, 'Thank you, they are beautiful.'

The audience was seated and the usherettes, who had been checking the tickets and showing people to their seats, had themselves sat down. Bess laid her orchids on the empty chair beside her and took her seat next to Anton. If things had been different James might have been sitting there, after he had pinned the orchids on her dress. His parting words came flooding back. 'We could meet in town, see a show and have a bite of supper.' Before the tears that were already threatening began to fall, Bess shook James's words from her mind. She would ask Natalie to pin the orchids on her dress in the interval.

As the lights began to fade a hush swept through the audience like a giant wave. The safety iron began to rise, the maroon and gold fringed stage curtains began to open, and the orchestra's string section began to play. And when the curtains were fully open, the stage lights came up on the Great Pyramid of Giza.

Bronze, muscular male dancers, dressed as Egyptian slaves, pulled huge boulders across the stage, climbed onto them and struck masculine poses. Two ballerinas, one dressed as a black cat and the other as a golden eagle, led the Pharaoh and his Queen onto the stage. Handmaidens waited-on, nymphs danced attendance, and eunuchs – slim boys wearing extravagant face make-up – fanned the royal couple with reeds.

As the scene came to an end a juggler dressed as an Egyptian merchant kept four golden spheres in the air at the same time, while a snake-charmer played a rhythmic flute to lure not a snake but a slender bejewelled belly-dancer out of an Ali Baba basket. Free of her wicker confinement, the belly-dancer clapped her hands sharply once and the lights went out.

To set the scene for the second Wonder of the World a magician waved a magic wand over a top hat and produced two doves. The doves circled the auditorium, and when the curtains opened flew up to the fly-deck high

142

above the stage. As the doves disappeared into the darkness two trapeze artists appeared out of it, and the lights came up on the Hanging Gardens of Babylon.

The trapeze artists, in white costumes trimmed with feathers, turned to each other at exactly the same time and began to slide from their seats. The audience gasped. But instead of falling the human doves bent their knees, hooked them over the bars they'd been sitting on, and swung towards each other with outstretched hands. Their fingers almost touched. But not quite. They swung towards each other again. This time they were closer, but not close enough. Then the female trapeze artist straightened her legs and was suddenly falling through the air. The audience gasped again, louder this time. But before the lady dove plunged to her death her partner thrust his powerful body towards her and caught her by the ankles, and the audience went wild, cheering and applauding.

As the act drew to its close a rope ladder appeared out of the flies and the female artist swung her slender legs towards it, catching it between her feet. Followed by her partner, she climbed down the ladder to a standing ovation. As the lights began to fade, the trapezes disappeared into the flies as quickly as the doves had done.

At the end of each tableau comedians told jokes, singers sang songs, acrobats stood on each other's shoulders and tumbled to the ground, and magicians pulled rabbits out of hats.

At the interval a waiter arrived with a bottle of champagne and while Natalie pinned Bess's orchids onto her dress, Anton poured each of them a glass. As they sipped their champagne, Bess and Natalie chatted about the set, which Natalie had designed. Bess could tell by her friend's relaxed manner that the show was all she'd hoped it would be. Anton, apart from agreeing with Bess that his wife was a talented designer, said nothing.

The second act began with the Temple of Artemis and the Statue of Zeus. The stage was set with gold pillars and silver statuettes. Mighty Zeus, with his golden eagle and beloved Victory at his side, was guarded by four of the tallest men Bess had ever seen. Lesser Gods bowed before him as drum rolls emulated thunder and lights flashed in time to the clash of cymbals.

Taking place on a giant chess board, the next Wonder was a choreographed battle between the Centaurs and the Lapiths, and the Greeks and the Amazons. An army of female warriors marched on stage to the sound of heavy artillery, took their places, and the battle began. As the chess pieces toppled the lights dimmed until the stage was flooded with a red wash. When the battle was over a dense ground fog licked the bodies of the fallen chess pieces and the lights faded to black.

Before the last Wonder, the Prince Albert's leading lady Nancy Jewel, dressed in an old fashioned sailor suit, led the Doris Henshaw All Women's Band onto the stage singing "The Fleet's In Port Again". As the song came to an end the curtains opened on the Colossus of Rhodes and the Lighthouse at Alexandria.

A huge painting of the lighthouse hung on the up-stage flat. Statues of Tritons standing at its four corners looked down on Poseidon. Dancers dressed as mariners weaved banners of blue and green silk in and out and over and under to make the sea, lifting them up and down to create the illusion of waves, while others hoisted the sails on a tall ship.

At the curtain call comedians took their bows by performing a sand-dance and bumping into each other. Jugglers came on stage juggling and the high-wire artists took their bows from their trapezes high in the air. The last artists to take a curtain call were the Prince Albert Theatre's resident company of dancers and singers who had played the Pharaohs, Gods, Goddesses, Kings and Queens, warriors, slaves and maidens. The company ran on stage to rapturous applause and joined the Doris Henshaw All Women's Band who, with the orchestra, played "God Save The King" to an audience already on its feet.

Anton, Natalie and Bess stayed in the box to finish the champagne, and to give the audience time to clear the theatre. 'You must come to all our first nights,' Anton said, when Bess told him how much she had enjoyed the show. 'We're trying to book the Crazy Gang for the winter. I saw them at the London Palladium. Not only was theirs the funniest show I've ever seen, but it was a sell-out.'

'I thought you put on musicals and plays at the Albert?'

'We do. We were going to open with Ever Green, followed by a Coward, and at Christmas we'd planned to do Mr Cinders, but the advanced bookings were almost non-existent. People are frightened to come into town because, if there is a war, London will be targeted. So we need an act that will bring the audience in. The Crazy Gang will do that.'

'Anton is going to take a leaf out of the Windmill's book and put on a season of variety shows and revues, which will be cheaper and easier to stage,' Natalie said.

'But the Windmill Theatre put on shows with nudity!' Bess said.

'Yes, tableaux vivants, the living picture – and they pack the houses. Don't worry,' Anton said, laughing, 'nudity isn't our style. We prefer our artists to keep their costumes on – however skimpy they are. Mrs Henderson's right though, London theatres must change.' Anton laughed again. 'The last time we spoke she said, "War or no war, the Windmill will never close its doors." Time will tell. But,' he said thoughtfully, 'we're living in a time of uncertainty. Variety is the

146

way forward for London theatres, and the way to bring audiences into the West End is with comedy shows and comedians like Flannigan and Allen and the Crazy Gang.'

It was pandemonium backstage, on every floor, on every stairway and in every room. Half-naked dancers ran in and out of each other's dressing rooms, dodging wardrobe assistants pushing metal clothes racks and assistant stage managers laden with props. And as if all that didn't clog up the rabbit warren sufficiently, local delivery boys who had delivered first night flowers hung around on the stairs and landings hoping to get a glimpse of a scantily clad dancer, or the autograph of a famous comedian.

The first night party was in full swing by the time Bess, Natalie and Anton arrived.

'Sorry!' a young man shouted, after twirling one of the showgirls off the dance floor straight into Bess's path.

'That's all right,' she shouted back.

'Thank God Pamela Lesley had the foresight to put a reserved card on this table,' Natalie said, sitting down and motioning Bess to sit next to her.

'Pamela's going to fetch us at midnight,' Anton said.

'To mingle,' Natalie explained.

'We say complimentary things to the critics in the hope that they say complimentary things about the show when they write their reviews,' Anton added.

'But we've got ages yet. Come on. Let's get something to eat while Anton pours the champagne,' Natalie said, taking Bess by the hand.

The buffet, on a long table at the side of the dance area, was a selection of hot and cold dishes. Bess helped herself to breast of chicken and new potatoes.

At midnight Miss Lesley, the front of house manager, came over to the table and reminded Natalie it was time to 'mingle.'

'Will you be all right, Bess? We won't be long,' Natalie said.

'I'll be fine. Go and mingle. And,' Bess said, putting her hand to her mouth so only Natalie could hear, 'be nice to the theatre critics.'

Laughing, Natalie said, 'I will, don't worry.'

Bess watched Natalie and Anton move effortlessly between different groups of people, greeting some formally and kissing others. They talked, listened, and laughed with performers, directors and critics – and, like good hosts, seemed genuinely interested in what their guests had to say.

'More champagne?'

Bess turned to see a good looking man standing by her side. 'Oh! Yes, thank you. Didn't I see you dancing with one of the showgirls earlier?'

'Yes. I danced with her until I saw you,' he said, filling Bess's glass to almost overflowing.

Bess laughed. 'Charmer!' Still laughing, she pushed her chair back and, leaning forward, sipped the fizzy wine until she had consumed enough to lift the glass. 'Oh no,' she gasped, 'that was a mistake.' As the effervescent liquid hit the back of her throat she began to choke.

The young man handed her a clean handkerchief. 'May I?' he said, motioning to the chair next to hers.

'Yes, of course. Thank you,' she said, taking the handkerchief and dabbing her eyes. 'I'm out of practice. I've been a student for three years. Grants and scholarships don't run to ginger wine, let alone champagne.'

'I thought you were a dancer in the show,' he said, peeling the gold foil from the top of another bottle of champagne, twisting and loosening the fine wire that held the cork in place.

'I'm afraid not,' Bess said as the cork shot out of the bottle with a pop.

'My name's Dave.'

'Pleased to meet you, Dave. My name's Bess,' she said, lifting her glass. 'Cheers!'

'I'm pleased to meet you too, Bess. Here, let me refill your glass.'

For the first time since she'd learned that James was going to marry Annabel, Bess was enjoying herself. And why not, she thought; she was young, single and free. Free, and having fun with a good looking man.

Dave raised his glass. 'To you!'

Bess returned the gesture. 'To you!' The bubbles tickled the back of her throat and she began to giggle again.

'So if you're not a dancer, what are you? How do you know this lot?'

'I'm a teacher – and it's a long story.'

'I'm not going anywhere,' Dave said.

'I had my handbag stolen,' Bess said at last, 'and Natalie and Anton Goldman, the owners of the Prince Albert, took me to their home, looked after me, and made sure I got to my lodgings safely.' Bess told Dave about her upbringing, her job, her time at college in London, Foxden and her brother Tom. 'I'm worried about Tom,' she said. 'He joined the Army and--.' She shivered.

'I'm in the Army too. Well, not the Regular Army,' he said. 'I'm an officer in a highly specialised training unit with the bomb disposal squad. Tonight could be my last night in civvy-street for a while. Or perhaps in any street.' He picked up his glass and stared into it, as if something dark and terrible was hiding in the bubbles. 'Here's to whatever tomorrow brings,' he said, before downing his drink.

Dave recovered from his short-lived black mood and made several more toasts. He raised his glass to life, friendship, and to meeting Bess. He filled Bess's glass again and said, 'Here's to the most beautiful girl in the room.'

Bess giggled. 'Champagne takes away your inhibitions! I read that somewhere,' she said. 'I haven't drenk, I mean drunk a lot of champagne in the past. I don't drink at all as a rule, but tonight is a special occasion.'

'You're special,' Dave said. 'I'll always remember you.'

'Why thank you, kind sir. So are you,' Bess said, draining her drink. 'I'll always remember you too, Dave.'

'I'm sure you will,' he said, filling Bess's glass again. 'Let's celebrate,' he shouted.

'Yes, let's… ' Bess agreed. She lifted her glass but wasn't able to hold it up long enough to clink it against Dave's. 'Let's celebrate,' she slurred. 'Tonight we'll have fun and tomorrow… Well, what's the worst that can happen? I don't prepare next week's lessons for the little darlings I teach? I'll blame it on the bubbles. I'm young and free and… Oh dear,' she said. 'I feel dizzy. I think I'd better go to the Ladies'.' Bess stood up, but the room began to spin so she sat down again.

Dave helped her out of her chair and across the room to the foyer. 'C'mon. I know what you need.'

'Where are we going? The Ladies' cloakroom is over there.' Bess pointed to the clearly marked door, but Dave hurried her to the main entrance.

'You don't want people to see you in this state. You don't want to embarrass your friends the Goldmans, do you?'

Bess stopped. Leaning back, she squinted. 'No, I don't want to embarrass my friends.

Thank you, Dave. Thank you for looking after me. You're very kind.'

Dave strong-armed Bess out of the club. The doorman – helping two showgirls into the back of a taxi – shot Dave a glance.

'Too much champagne,' Dave shrugged.

'She looks like the showgirl you were dancing with earlier,' Bess said, pointing to the girl with blonde hair. 'Look.' The taxi pulled out into the traffic on Long Acre. 'She's making a fist at us. She's jealous …'

CHAPTER NINE

Bess's eyes had adjusted to the darkness in the narrow alley – and what she saw she didn't like. To her right there was a metal door with "Kitchen" in white lettering. Next to the door, a little further along on the ground, she could see a wooden trapdoor – probably the door to a cellar, she thought.

The kitchen door stood slightly open, and a shaft of light spilled out into the alley. Bess could hear the clatter of pots and pans, and waiters calling for this food or that, for this bottle of champagne or that bottle of wine. She felt a waft of warm air as Dave hurried her past. She shivered. She wasn't wearing a coat and she was cold.

Just visible at the far end of the alley, Bess could see two iron staircases. The one on the right must lead to and from the upper floors of the Prince Albert, the one on the left to the Albert's neighbour, the Club Royal. The alley was dark and disturbing, full of shadows and littered with rubbish. Bess tripped over a crate, sending half a dozen empty bottles spinning like skittles. It was a filthy, disgusting place and it stank of urine.

'I'm going back. The smell is making me feel sick.' Bess turned to leave, but Dave put his arms around her waist and pulled her to him. 'Stop it, Dave. Let me go. I want to go back to the club, it's freezing out here.'

Dave loosened his hold on her long enough to light a cigarette, then he flicked the burning match into a mound of newspapers. 'It's always the way isn't it?' he said, bending down, his eyes level with Bess's eyes, his nose level with her nose. He drew deeply on his cigarette and blew the smoke out of the corner of his mouth in one long stream. 'I don't know, you try to help some people and all you get is rejection. Here, have a drag,' he said, offering Bess his cigarette.

The acrid stench of urine in the alley, combined with cigarette smoke and Dave's stale breath, made Bess retch. 'No thank you, I don't smoke.' Trembling, she pushed Dave's hand and the cigarette away. 'I'm going inside, I'm cold.'

'All right, let me finish my fag and I'll take you back.' Dave took off his jacket, put it round Bess's shoulders and pulled her closer to him. 'There, that's better, isn't it?' He didn't wait for a reply. 'You might be the last girl I hold in my arms. Still, if one of those little buggers at the Army's Bomb Disposal Centre does blow me up tomorrow, I'll die happy.'

'Don't talk like that,' Bess said. 'Besides, you said you were going to the training centre, so you won't be in danger of being blown up, will you?'

'Won't I? Not even with Special Ops Command? Well, that's all right then!' he added sarcastically. 'It's all in my

154

imagination, is it? Or perhaps you're calling me a liar?'

Dave relaxed his hold on her again, and looked into the mid distance. His eyes lost focus, as they had done when he stared into the champagne at the party. 'Of course I'm not calling you a liar.' Bess felt ashamed for implying that he was. She looked up at him and smiled. He was a big man, well over six feet tall, but he looked like a hurt child. 'Poor Dave.' Standing on tiptoe, Bess kissed him on his cheek. 'There,' she said, 'friends? I didn't mean to doubt you, honestly. And you're right; I didn't want anyone to see me drunk and I didn't want to embarrass my friends, but I am cold and I do want to go back inside now.'

He tightened his grip on Bess's shoulder, bent down, and kissed her with such force that his teeth bit into her lips. She pushed him away and let out a cry.

Dave stepped back, open-mouthed. He looked like a big dough-faced child, wide eyed and bewildered. 'What are you doing?' he asked.

'No, Dave, what are *you* doing?' Bess retaliated.

'I'm kissing my girl, who I might never see again. Come here,' he said, grinning, and forced Bess to accept his slobbering mouth for a second time.

Bess knew she was in trouble but she couldn't think straight. She didn't know what to do. She was sobering up, but not fast

155

enough. Her sight was blurred and her head was swimming. She wondered whether she would be able to fight Dave off, but the odds were against her. He was twice her size and weight, and probably three times stronger. There was no way she could stop him from hurting her by force, if that was his intention. But she might be able to talk him out of it – if she could persuade him to stop slobbering over her long enough.

'Dave, wait a minute, I want to talk to you,' she said, taking his hand in hers and stepping back so she was able to look into his eyes.

'You started it, you kissed me first,' he taunted, as a thirteen year old schoolboy might have done after a fumble behind the bike sheds. 'Or were you being a tease? Were you leading me on?'

'I kissed you, yes. As a friend. I didn't mean for this…'

'This?' He sneered. 'What do you mean, this?' Dave stamped his foot and shook his head from side to side like an angry bull. In a matter of seconds his personality had changed from a teasing schoolboy to a wild animal – and Bess was frightened. 'I disgust you, don't I? You're disgusted by the idea of doing it with me, aren't you?'

'Doing it?' The realisation of why Dave had brought her to the filthy alley hit her. She needed to think and think fast. 'Of course you don't disgust me. It's the alley that disgusts me. I don't want to do it in this filthy alley--'

'It's not good enough for you, aye? It's good enough for me, but then I'm probably not good enough for you either? I'm good enough to fight a war for you. Risk my life for you. Probably get killed for you. But I'm not good enough to kiss you, or touch you.' He grabbed her round the waist again and jerked her closer.

Dave was being awkward, spoiling for an argument. One minute he was a boy, a child, needing to be loved and understood. The next he was a nasty, manipulating bully, exerting power in the only way he knew, by brute force. Bess realised there was nothing she could do or say to talk him round, because he wasn't being rational. She had two choices. Give in to him, which she wasn't going to do without a fight, or try and get away. She chose the latter.

'Of course you're good enough for me. You're good enough for any girl – that wasn't what I meant. And I'm not a tease.' Bess kept talking. 'I didn't mean to lead you on and if you think I did, I'm sorry.'

Dave let go of her and Bess took off his jacket. 'Here, put it on and we'll go back to the party. We'll have another drink and a nice talk; get to know each other properly.'

Smiling, Bess held Dave's jacket up, keeping eye contact with him until he turned round. He lifted his left arm and slid it into the left sleeve. Before he had time to put his arm all the way down, Bess lifted the right side of the jacket. Encouraged by this, Dave put his right arm into the right sleeve. With both arms halfway down their respective sleeves, and disabled behind Dave's back, Bess pushed him as hard as she could. As his drunken bulk hit the wall, she ran for the street.

As she neared the kitchen door she heard voices. At first they were distant, no more than a mumble. Soon they grew louder, sounded nearer. A few more steps. She was almost there. She opened her mouth to shout for help, slipped and fell. She scrambled frantically to her feet. But it was too late. Dave grabbed her from behind. With one hand over her mouth, the other round her throat, he dragged her into the shadows beneath the fire escape.

The voices Bess had heard belonged to two men dressed in kitchen whites. The younger of the two took a packet of cigarettes from his pocket. He gave one to the older man, and then took one for himself. After lighting both, he flicked the match into the air in the same way that Dave had done earlier. Rotating his shoulders as if they were stiff, the younger man walked across the alley to check the match was out. On his return he lifted his head and exhaled a smoke ring, and the older man shouted, 'Bravo!'

Dave's hand was clamped hard over Bess's mouth. She could hardly breathe. She watched helplessly as the two men prepared to return to the kitchen. The older man drew on his cigarette. He inhaled deeply before crushing the stub beneath his boot. He coughed, cleared his throat, and spat. The younger man took a couple of extra pulls on his cigarette, extinguished it in the same way, and then followed him inside and shut the door.

When he was sure the two men were not going to re-appear, Dave took his hand from Bess's mouth.

'You're hurting me, Dave. Please take your hand from my throat ... Please Dave...' Bess rasped. Her voice was hoarse and barely audible. Her head throbbed from the pressure on her neck. She tried to concentrate on the bricks in the wall. She struggled to focus, as consciousness began to slip away.

'Do you promise to behave yourself?'

Hardly able to stand, or speak, she managed to whisper, 'Yes, I promise. Please-- I can't breathe.'

Dave took his hand from her throat and turned her round. Thick saliva had collected in the corners of his mouth. As he tried to kiss her, dry spittle snapped like rotten string. Bess gagged. She made fists and lashed out, but Dave was too quick. He caught hold of her arms and forced them behind her back. Now it was her turn to be disabled.

With a sickening grin he bent down and kissed her again. He straddled her and, holding her wrists tightly with one hand, he forced the other between her legs. Incensed by his actions Bess lifted her knee and drove it hard into his groin. But it wasn't hard enough. He doubled over in pain and took his hand from between her legs. But instead of falling to the ground, as Bess had hoped he would, he straightened and slapped her across the face.

'Now look what you made me do. Why did you make me do that? Why do you want me to hurt you?' he asked.

'I'm sorry! I don't want you to hurt me.' Her cheek was smarting, and her jaw ached from the impact of Dave's plate-like hand. 'Look, I've stopped struggling.' Bess knew the only way to survive what was fast becoming inevitable was to stop fighting. 'If you promise not to hurt me, I promise not to struggle,' she said.

'Why would I hurt you?' He was the boy again. 'You're my girl; I don't want to hurt you, I want to make you happy.'

'Of course you do. I know that now,' Bess lied. 'I'm sorry.' Bess shuddered as she forced herself to smile at her vile abuser. Then she closed her eyes. She had to endure him, but she did not have to look at him.

She could smell his sour breath on her neck as he slurred drunkenly into her ear. He said words that Bess had hoped one day to hear from the man she loved. The man she would marry. Struggling to undo the buttons on his trousers, he cursed and mumbled one inarticulate profanity after another. Then he began to talk dirty. He said things that were degrading and humiliating, but Bess showed no emotion. She knew she mustn't react to anything he did or said if she was going to survive.

Holding her wrists behind her back with his left hand, he pulled her pants down with his right. 'Lift your feet,' he ordered. Bess did as she was told and he pulled her knickers off. 'Now lift this leg up. Higher.'

Bess thought she would die of shame. She lifted her left leg as high as she could and he put his right hand under her buttocks and pulled her closer. Her right foot was barely on the ground. As he forced himself into her, she began to plan the lessons for the coming week at school.

'You all right?' he asked, in a frantic stilted whisper.

Bess wanted to scream, *No, you vile and disgusting creature, you're hurting me!* But she was paralysed with fear.

'Are you all right?' he shouted. He was angry, agitated and breathless. He began to pant like a rabid dog.

'Yes!' Bess shouted back at him. 'Yes, I'm all right.'

Whatever it was that this monster needed from Bess's submissive agreement he got, because a second later he gave one final thrust, let out a sickening moan, and stopped.

What would happen now? Bess wondered. Would he let her go? Or would he take her again? He dropped her leg and relaxed his grip on her wrists, but he didn't take his eyes off her. He was waiting for a reaction. Bess didn't react. She wouldn't give him the satisfaction. Her legs hurt. Her left leg hurt at the top, where he'd held it for so long in an unnatural position, and the muscles in her right leg ached from having taken his weight, as well as her own. But it was over and she had survived.

While he was bending down, groping round his ankles for his trousers, Bess thought about trying to escape again. But she knew she wouldn't be able to run fast enough, because she hurt too much. Besides, if he caught her he might kill her this time. After what seemed like an age of fumbling he stood up and buttoned his trousers. Then, as if to reward himself, he took a box of cigarettes from his jacket pocket, lit up and inhaled deeply. 'Turn around.'

'What?'

'Turn round and face the wall.'

'Why, what are you going to do?'

'Nothing if you do as you're told. I don't want to hurt you, but if you don't turn round you'll make me angry. And you know what happens when I get angry,' the boy in him pleaded. 'So do as I say. Turn round and face the wall!'

As she turned, Bess heard what sounded like dry leaves rustling beneath a pile of newspapers under the fire escape.

'What was that?'

Bess shook her head. 'I don't know.'

Dave took a drag of his cigarette, threw it on top of the newspapers and laughed. 'Oh dear,' he said, 'I'd better make sure my fag's out or it might set fire to that pile of old rubbish.' Still laughing, he went over to the mound of newspapers and kicked into it as hard as he could.

Bess turned her face to the wall and held her breath. She heard him walking up the alley, whistling a tune she didn't recognise and hoped she would never hear again. As the sound of his footsteps grew fainter so did the whistling – until there was silence.

After two or three minutes, Bess slowly turned round. She wondered how long she'd been in the alley and, hoping there would be enough light to see what the time was, she lifted her arm to look at her wristwatch. It had gone. The loss of her watch was the last straw. Exhausted and in pain, she slid down the wall to the ground, hugged her knees, and cried.

'I'm sorry,' she heard someone say. 'I'm so sorry.'

Bess looked at the mound of rubbish under the fire escape as an elderly man crawled out of a makeshift bed of cardboard and newspapers. He had a broken nose and red veined cheeks from years of living rough. He held Bess's wristwatch in trembling hands and looked at her with sad rheumy eyes. 'It came off when he…'

'Thank you. It was my twenty-first birthday present from my parents. I thought it had gone forever.' As she took the watch from the old man she touched his hand and he winced. That monster hadn't stamped on the cigarette. He had stamped on the old man's hand.

'You should go to the hospital,' Bess said.

'So should you,' the old man replied.

Bess nodded in agreement but she knew, as he did, that neither of them would. 'I don't know how I can ever thank you. If you hadn't been there ... if you hadn't made a noise, I think he would have hurt me again.'

'I wish I could have stopped him from hurting you the first time,' the old man said. 'I would have done, a few years ago--'

'Shush...' Bess raised her right hand and put her forefinger to her lips. 'There's someone in the alley.'

CHAPTER TEN

Unable to look at her naked reflection in the bathroom mirror, Bess switched off the light. She knew another bath wouldn't make her feel any cleaner but she ran one anyway. She dipped her toes into the water, but it was too hot, so she turned on the cold tap. When the water was cool enough, she stepped into it and lay back until she was completely submerged. She couldn't bear to touch herself with her hands, so she took a flannel, lathered it with soap, and scrubbed at her body until she was raw. But she still didn't feel clean.

It was five o'clock in the morning. The water was stone cold, and so was Bess. She hauled herself out of the bath. Wrapping a large towel round her body, and a smaller one about her head, she went into the kitchen and made a cup of cocoa. The last cup hadn't helped her to sleep, so this time she added a cap of brandy. If nothing else, it might take the edge off. It didn't.

Sunday morning, Bess forced herself to go out. Putting on a brave face, she walked to the station to buy a newspaper. The newspaper vendor, who was German by birth and Jewish by religion – but had lived in South London for many years – was having his fate decided by a group of ill-informed vigilantes.

'He's a spy,' the first man in the queue said.

'A Nazi,' the second one shouted.

'They ought to lock him up and throw away the key.'

'No, we'd have to keep him then. Send him back to his Nazi mates in Germany.'

'No!' the newspaper vendor protested. 'I am not a Nazi, I am a Jew. I came here to escape the Nazis. You know that is true,' he said to the man standing in front of Bess. The man ignored him. 'I am your neighbour. Please, my friend, you have known me for ten years. Your children play with my children. Our wives are friends. We are friends.'

'Not any more, we're not!' The man swiped a paper from the top of the pile, threw a handful of change on the ground, and kicked over the advertising board before walking away.

Tears rolled down the newspaper vendor's cheeks. 'Please, my friend,' he called after him, but the man kept walking. 'Please believe me,' he said to the others as, one by one, they turned their backs on him and left. 'Please …'

Bess had known the newspaper seller for as long as she'd lived in South London and felt ashamed that she hadn't gone to his defence. But she was too frightened. The humiliation she'd suffered the night before had destroyed her confidence. She no longer felt strong enough to speak out, let alone confront a crowd of angry men. She lifted the advertising board to an upright position and paid for her newspaper. 'I'm sorry,' she whispered, and left.

Shaking, Bess filled the kettle and put it on the stove before going into the living room. She began to read the newspaper. The headlines running across the top of the front page read, "September 1st Germany Invades Poland." And below, in letters a little bolder, "September 3rd Prime Minister To Talk To The Nation." She turned on the wireless in readiness and turned the dial to the Home Service. While she waited she took writing paper and a pen from the desk drawer and wrote a letter to Natalie Goldman. She thanked her first for her discretion in putting her in a taxi the night before, telling her – without being too explicit – what had happened in the alley. She ended with "P.S. I will telephone soon". She then replied to Mrs McAllister who, in her last letter, had expressed concern about the health of her young friend Molly. Accepting an invitation to tea, she asked her old landlady to let her know which Sunday would be most convenient.

When Big Ben struck the first chime of eleven, Bess had just started a letter to her mother. She stopped writing and put down her pen. 'This is London,' the newscaster said 'You will now hear a statement from the Prime Minister.' She sat transfixed, listening to the strained voice of Neville Chamberlain as he told the nation about the invasion of

Poland and that Britain had asked for an undertaking from Hitler to withdraw his troops. 'I have to tell you now that no such undertaking has been received and that consequently this country is at war with Germany.'

Bess felt sick. She wondered how her father had taken the news. Her brother Tom believed going to war with Germany was the only way to stop Hitler and his Nazis from dominating Europe – and by all accounts he was right. Her father, having fought on the front line in the Great War from 1914 until three months before it ended in 1918, said there ought never to be another war.

Bess turned off the wireless, flung open the window, and caught her breath in panic. There was not a soul in sight. There were no cars, no buses, no cyclists and no people. The newspaper vendor had abandoned his pitch. The tennis courts on the Common, always busy on a Sunday morning, were empty. Beneath the horse chestnut tree a lone dog barked at the flapping kite. But there were no little boys tugging on the guide rope. The area was deserted.

She wanted to walk across the Common, feel earth beneath her feet. Instead the air raid siren wailed through the apartment, so she closed the window, grabbed her gas mask and handbag and ran outside. As she turned to lock the door, she heard the kettle whistling. She rushed back into the flat. The kitchen was filled with steam. Not daring to think what would have happened if she hadn't gone back, she turned off the gas. Then, after checking the other knobs on the stove were in the 'off' position, she left again.

The Anderson shelter was in the garden of the main house. There were three in a row, dug into the lawn. As she approached them, Bess thought how small they were. If a bomb landed nearby, exactly how much protection would half a dozen sheets of corrugated iron give, she wondered.

'Quick as you can, Miss,' the Home Guard man shouted, pointing to the door of the middle shelter. 'And mind the steps.'

'Thank you,' she said, by which time he was chasing two little boys who were running around with outstretched arms like aeroplanes, screaming, 'Errrrrr…Boom!' and, 'Bang! Gotcha!'

Bess stepped down the first of three steps leading into the shelter, and froze. It was dark inside, and the damp, musty smell reminded her of the alley the night before. Fear pulsed through her. She couldn't get her breath and began to shake uncontrollably. She wanted to run, but she was unable to move. She grabbed the doorframe and clung to it until the feeling of panic subsided. Eventually, her eyes adjusted to the semi-darkness. She cautiously entered the shelter, crossed the earth floor, and settled on a small bench. Above it was a shelf with an oil lamp and a box of Swan Vesta matches. In case we're still here tonight, Bess thought. She didn't relish the idea. Opening the box, she found the red phosphorus match-heads were damp and stuck together. She made a mental note to buy a box of matches. Sitting on the hard wooden bench, Bess opened her handbag. She had forgotten her book. As soon as she got home she would put a cushion, a book and a box of matches by the front door in readiness for the next air raid. Suddenly the siren stopped wailing. A second or so later it started up again.

She ran up the steps and poked her head out of the door. The two children from the neighbouring shelter were running behind the man from the Home Guard. 'What's going on?' she shouted, above the rise-and-fall of the siren.

'That's the all clear. Appears there wasn't an air raid after all. It was a false alarm. Never mind, it's good practice for when the bombs do start falling,' he shouted.

'I suppose so,' Bess said, wondering how the Home Guard knew the difference between the two sirens. They sounded the same to her. Gathering her belongings, she made another mental note to add a blanket to the things she was putting by the door. It wasn't only damp inside the shelter, it was cold.

Bess stretched, inhaled the cool air, and looked up at the late afternoon sky. There wasn't a cloud in sight. She felt exhausted from not having slept the night before and shaken after the air raid, even though it didn't actually happen. Sitting in the small shelter was not only frightening, it was claustrophobic. So while it was still light, she did what she had wanted to do earlier. She went for a walk.

On Sunday evenings during the summer a jazz band played on Clapham Common. It attracted people of all ages and from all walks of life. Some sang along with the songs, others danced, and many brought picnics. But most people just sat on the grass and listened to the music. Tonight, because of the blackout, there was no band and no people.

Bess began to tremble. What was she thinking, walking across the Common on her own? Anything could have happened. Could still happen. She crouched down at the side of the steps leading up to the bandstand and made herself as small as she could.

'Hello there. Are you all right?'

Bess lifted her head, surprised to see a young woman, perhaps a little younger than herself, in trousers and a Fair Isle jumper standing next to her. 'I am now,' she said. 'It sounds silly, but I panicked when I realised I was alone on the Common and it was getting dark ....'

'Well, you're not alone anymore,' the young woman said, offering Bess her hand. 'And soon we'll have light.'

'What do you mean, light?'

'Look over there,' she said, pointing to a small crowd of people walking towards them carrying lighted candles. 'We're protesting against the war. Come and join us.'

A musician took a saxophone from its case and after a verse of "The Last Time I Saw Paris" he played Jack Hylton's theme song, "Why Did She Fall for the Leader of The Band." In no time, everyone was singing and dancing to "The Lambeth Walk" and "Roll Out The Barrel".

Bess stood in the shadow of the bandstand for a while before joining the girl in the Fair Isle jumper and her friends. The girl gave Bess a lighted candle and moved to make room on the grass next to her. Nodding her thanks, Bess sat down and joined in with the singing.

As evening turned into night the mood became more serious, and songs like "Harbour Lights" and "I'll Be Seeing You" replaced "Champagne Charlie" and "You're Driving Me Crazy." The last song was "There'll Always be an England."

The girl in the Fair Isle jumper stood up when the saxophonist finished playing. 'It's time to go,' she said, as her friends began to drift off. 'Before the authorities hear about our little picnic and nick us. '

'It was nice meeting you,' Bess said.

'Likewise. Will you be okay getting home?' the girl asked, 'only I could walk with you some of the way. Until you're off the Common, at least.'

'Thank you, but I'll be fine. There are lots of people going my way.'

'Bye then,' the girl said. 'Take care, won't you?'

Bess nodded, and the girl ran off and caught up with her friends.

Walking home, Bess was overwhelmed by a feeling of camaraderie. She decided that not only was she strong enough to cope with what had happened to her the night before in the alley, she was strong enough to deal with anything life threw at her.

The staff meeting took place during the morning break, when Bess was on playground duty, so she only caught the tail end of what the Headmaster was saying. '…the pupils of Christchurch Secondary School will be among the first in South London to be evacuated. At the end of this month the school will close and the children will be taken by train to Dorset, where they will stay for the duration of the war. The schools in the West Country will need extra teaching staff, so I shall be asking for volunteers at the end of this week. Thank you!'

Several members of staff wanted to know what would happen to them if they didn't want to go to the country. Others protested that they should have been consulted first.

'I am sorry, ladies and gentlemen, but the decision is out of my hands,' the Headmaster said, before turning and leaving the room.

Bess didn't want to lose her job, but she wasn't keen on moving to the West Country either. On the other hand, a different environment might be a good thing. But did she really want to be that far away from her family and Foxden?

It seemed everyone was on the move. Tom had joined the Army. He was stationed in Kent while James, her mother said in a recent letter, was training to be a bomber pilot at Bitteswell Aerodrome, near Foxden. She was worried for Tom - and tried not to think about James.

There was a knock on the door. 'Damn,' Bess mumbled. She was rinsing her hair. Her eyes were shut, so she didn't get shampoo in them.

'Just a minute!' she called. Until ten minutes ago she'd looked decent. Now she was dressed in old slacks and a shirt. She felt around for a towel, found it and dabbed her eyes. Able to see again, she wrapped the towel round her head like a turban, left the bathroom and made her way along the passage. As she reached the door there was a second knock.

'Hang on a second.' She turned off the hall light and pulled back the blackout curtain. She didn't open the door to anyone unless she knew them, not even in daylight. Peering through the small window she saw her late visitor was wearing an RAF cap. She waited until he lifted his head. When he did, she recognised him straight away. 'James!' she gasped, opening the door. 'Whatever are you doing here?'

'Hello, Bess. May I come in?'

'Yes, of course,' she said, moving out of the way so James could enter.

Leading the way to the small sitting room, Bess thought her heart would explode with excitement.

'Sorry to call so late. I telephoned the school but there was no reply.'

'No, there wouldn't have been, the school's closed. The children have been evacuated to Dorset. Would you like some tea?' she asked, taking James's coat and cap and at the same time trying to balance the towel on her head.

'Yes, thank you. It's quite a journey from Foxden.'

She left James warming his hands by the fire while she went to the kitchen and made a pot of tea. She took a deep breath to steady her nerves. 'I haven't much in the way of food, but I could scramble a couple of eggs if you're hungry,' she said on her return.

'No thank you, tea will be fine. I'm meeting some of my old colleagues later. There's a restaurant a couple of doors down from my old chambers and one of the chaps has reserved a table.'

Bess looked away, embarrassed by the memory of the night she followed James and the girl from his chambers to that restaurant. She put the tray of cups and saucers, plates, and a slab of Madeira cake on the writing table in front of the bay window and wondered if the girl was "one of the chaps."

'I'd rather you dried your hair, I don't want to be responsible for you catching your death from pneumonia.'

Grateful for the suggestion, Bess withdrew to the bathroom where she replaced the damp shirt she'd been wearing with a jumper. She usually dried her hair by hanging her head upside down in front of the fire, but as James was sitting next to it she couldn't do that tonight so she brushed it back and tied a ribbon round it in a loose version of a pony-tail. It was supposed to keep her curls away from her face, but her hair was still wet and the ribbon slipped off. Tying it again, this time tighter, the knot held and she returned to the living room.

Aware that James was watching her, Bess crossed the room to the table beneath the window. As she poured the tea her hair once again escaped its restraints, tumbling onto her shoulders in loose curls.

James leapt from his seat. 'The skinny kid sister of my old friend Tom has certainly grown up,' he said, picking up the ribbon and handing it to her with a smile.

'Thank you,' she said, her heart throbbing. Blushing, she put the ribbon into the pocket of her skirt. 'Sugar?'

'No, thank you, I'm sweet enough.' Then, laughing, he said, 'Sorry, that was terrible, wasn't it?'

'Yes. And it's been said before.'

'More than a few times.'

Laughing, Bess poured milk into both cups of tea and handed one to James.

'Thank you,' he said, still smiling.

Sitting down opposite him, Bess took a sip of her tea. Damn, it was hot. She put the cup down heavily and it clinked loudly in the saucer. 'How are things at Foxden?' she asked. Her cheeks flamed again.

'That's why I'm here,' he said. 'The grooms, most of the stable lads and farm labourers have joined up. Some are waiting for their papers; some have already left.'

'If the stable lads have gone, who's looking after the horses?'

'They've gone too, I'm afraid, except for the carthorses and mother's pit ponies.' James put down his tea. 'There's no easy way of telling you, Bess, but Father had to sell them. Sultan wasn't sold, he belongs to me; he was a gift from the Hadleighs.'

Damn the Hadleighs. Bess didn't care about the Hadleighs. 'What about Sable? Did he sell Sable?'

'No, the old girl was reprieved at the eleventh hour, because your father said if Sable was still there, you might consider coming back.'

'Come back? To Foxden?' A few months ago she'd have given anything to hear James ask her to come back to Foxden. She had wanted to be close to him for as long as she could remember – and to work with him on his beloved estate…

'Life at Foxden will have to change,' he continued. 'We've had orders from the Ministry of Agriculture to turn the estate into arable land.'

'When?'

'Immediately! The directive said we need to have the land cultivated and be producing root crops by the spring and cereals by the summer. It sounds impossible, I know, but they're sending us half a dozen fully trained women from the agricultural centre in Nottinghamshire. The thing is, because Father spends most of his time at the MOD here in London, and I'm at Bitteswell Aerodrome, we were hoping you'd come back and organise things. It's asking a lot of you, Bess. There's a huge amount of work involved, but your father agrees that you're the best person for the job.'

'It's a lot to take in,' Bess said, trying to absorb what James had told her and understand what would be required of her in terms of work and commitment if she were to return to Foxden. She needed time to think, to come to terms with the fact that her teaching career would be over for the duration of the war if she accepted James's offer, as well as be sure in her mind that she had the knowledge to succeed if she took on the job. She also needed to be sure that she had the willpower to cope with seeing James regularly.

'... I'll leave you to think it over, Bess. Thanks for the tea.'

Bess wondered why he hadn't mentioned Annabel. He could easily have mentioned the engagement when he said Sultan was a gift from her parents. Bess momentarily pondered if James was waiting for her to congratulate him. If so, he'd be waiting a long time. James headed for the door.

'I'll see you out,' she said, following him.

'I hope you'll come back to Foxden, Bess,' he said, putting on his Air Force overcoat. 'It would be a real challenge. An adventure.'

Bess switched off the hall light as James opened the door. She watched him walk down the wrought-iron staircase. At his car he opened the door and jumped in. 'Oh, Bess?' he called from behind the steering wheel. 'Dorset or Foxden? I know which I'd choose.' Smiling, he wound up the window of his small sports car and a second later he was gone.

Mrs McAllister opened the door before she had time to knock. 'Hello dear, what a wonderful surprise,' she said loudly, putting her forefinger to her lips when Bess opened her mouth to greet her. 'Don't let Molly know I asked you to come,' she mouthed.

Nodding that she understood, Bess stepped into the hall. 'Hello, Mrs McAllister.'

'Take your coat off and go through,' Mrs McAllister said, dragging Bess's coat from her back. 'Look who's here, Molly!' she called, following Bess to her private sitting room, but not entering. 'You go in to Molly and sit down now, and I'll make a nice pot of tea,' she said, and disappeared into the kitchen.

Bess entered the room to find Molly gazing out of the window into the back garden. 'Hello, Molly. How are you?' she asked.

Molly turned and blinked back tears. 'I'm all right. I've got a bit of a cold, that's all,' she sniffed.

'I bet Mrs Mac's spoiling you. You were always her favourite,' Bess teased.

'She's been ever so kind, Bess. She's been like a mother to me these last few weeks. I wish my real mum was here,' she cried.

Bess sat down next to her young friend and put her arms around her. Molly wept like a child. When there were no tears left, she took a shuddering breath and went limp. She was exhausted.

As if on cue, Mrs Mac brought in the tea. 'I'm ready for a cuppa. Aren't you, girls?' she said, pouring the tea and heaping two teaspoonfuls of sugar in Molly's cup, but none in her own. 'A nice cup of tea will do you the world of good,' she said, handing Molly the cup, which she accepted gratefully. 'And I've made these especially. They were Bess's favourites, if I remember right,' she said, putting a plate of six sponge fancies on the side table next to Molly.

Bess smiled to herself. The cakes were Molly's favourites. Mrs Mac would have known that.

During tea the three women chatted light-heartedly. Mrs McAllister voiced her disapproval of tinned food and rationing. Molly complained that there were no pretty clothes in the shops. And Bess broke the news that she was going back to Foxden to oversee a team of land girls and turn the Estate into arable land.

Mrs McAllister was full of reservations about Bess giving up teaching after all her hard work at college. However, when she explained the importance of the work, Mrs McAllister conceded that if women had to do that sort of work, which she was not at all sure was necessary; the country was the place to do it.

When Mrs McAllister left the room to refresh the teapot, Molly smiled. 'Dear Mrs Mac, she's a love, isn't she?'

It was the first time Bess had seen Molly smile since she had arrived, but it didn't last. Within a few seconds Molly had reverted to being a frightened child, and was staring into space.

'What's the matter, Moll?' she asked. 'Do you want to talk about it? Sometimes it helps.'

Molly nodded. She took a breath, but before she could formulate the words, she burst into tears. 'Oh Bess, what am I to do?'

'If you tell me what's upsetting you, Molly, I might be able to help.'

'I can't tell you. You'll think I'm a bad girl. You'll be ashamed of me. You'll think I'm wicked and common and….' Molly began sobbing again. She rocked backwards and forwards, banging her head on the back of the settee.

'Molly, stop!' Bess said sharply. 'Stop it! You'll hurt yourself.'

Molly stopped instantly. She looked at Bess, her eyes wild and sparkling. 'I don't care if I hurt myself!' she screamed. 'It's no more than I deserve!'

'What do you mean, sweetheart? What on earth is the matter?'

Molly looked at Bess for some time before she said, 'I'm expecting, Bess. I'm going to have a baby.'

Bess had always looked on Molly as a child. Now the child was going to have a child. 'I didn't know you had a boyfriend. Is he going to stand by you?'

'He doesn't know. It was the night before he left to join his regiment. I didn't want to, Bess, but he said I was his girl and he loved me. He said it would be all right. But it's not all right! I'm so frightened.' Molly burst into tears again.

'Have you told your uncle? Will he help?'

'He said he was ashamed of me. That I was a trollop. He said he doesn't want anything more to do with me. Oh, Bess, what am I going to do?'

Bess was desperate to help her young friend. She understood a little of what Molly was going through. It was only luck that she wasn't pregnant. She shuddered at the thought. 'Come with me to Foxden. You can say your husband's away in the Army, which is true in a way. Well? What do you think?'

'I don't want to be a burden.'

'You won't be a burden, far from it. I need all the help I can get. Besides, moving to the country and working with lots of other young women will be fun. And once you're there you'll have plenty of time to work out what you're going to do when the baby's born.'

'There won't be any need for Molly to go to the country, Bess. She'll be quite all right with me and Miss Armstrong,' Mrs McAllister said, standing in the doorway with a freshly brewed pot of tea in her hand.

Molly looked at Mrs McAllister, her eyes wide and questioning. 'You and Miss Armstrong knew I was …?'

'No dear, we didn't know. But we wondered.'

'Why didn't you say anything?' Molly cried.

'We were waiting for you to tell us,' Mrs McAllister said, taking a handkerchief from her pocket and gently wiping the tears from Molly's eyes.

'Thank you,' Molly whispered. Turning to Bess she said, 'Thank you, Bess, but I'd like to stay here with Mrs McAllister. If you don't mind?'

'Of course I don't mind, Molly. As long as it's what you want.'

'It is,' Molly said. 'This is my home.'

The last hour of her visit was as heartening as the first had been worrying. As she reached the end of the avenue Bess turned and waved a final goodbye. Mrs McAllister had a protective arm round Molly, who appeared at last to be dry-eyed. Saddened to be leaving her friends, Bess consoled herself with the thought of seeing them again when Molly's baby was born.

CHAPTER ELEVEN

'Mavis Holloway? Polly Jennings? Laura Salisbury? Iris Taylor?'

Mr Porter called out each name as if he was conducting a military roll call. Each young woman, recently arrived at Lowarth station from Nottingham, took a step forward and answered, 'Here.' When it was Sylvia Muir's turn she stood to attention, saluted and replied with military clarity, 'Here, Sir!'

'We were expecting seven young ladies. Has anyone seen a Miss Katherine Woodcock or a Miss Myfanwy Jones?' Mr Porter shouted above the chatter of the five women who stood before him.

Kitty Woodcock, in a skintight red pencil skirt, red high heels and matching lipstick, accompanied by Fanny Jones in a contrasting grey coat and flat brown brogues, materialised from the ladies' toilet.

Mr Porter stood open-mouthed as the vision of peroxide curls and red lips that was Kitty Woodcock sashayed towards him singing, 'We're here.'

Ticking off the last two names on his list, Mr Porter directed the young women to the vehicles that were waiting to transport them the short distance to Foxden Hall.

Having never learned to drive, Bess had booked Mr Crane's taxi for the return journey to Foxden. Laura, Iris and Mavis settled themselves in the back of the black Austin, while Bess sat in the front next to Mr Crane. Mr Porter drove the farm pick-up truck with Kitty and Fanny in the front next to him, and Sylvia and Polly astride bales of hay in the back.

Mr Porter had changed since she'd been back. He still enjoyed a good grumble and almost always compared the old farming ways to the "new-fangled" ones, but he appeared to be more content. Bess had even seen him smile when he thought no one was looking.

On the day she returned to Foxden Mrs Hartley, the housekeeper and cook, was in tears. 'I'm so glad you got here in time, Bess,' her old friend said. 'You've got to do something.'

'Do something?'

'Yes. You've got to stop him,' Mrs Hartley said. 'You've got to stop him!'

'Stop who?'

'Mr Porter, of course. Stop Mr Porter from leaving. He's all packed, look,' Mrs Hartley said, pointing to a large leather trunk and two suitcases standing in the middle of the kitchen. 'Crane's taxi is picking him up at ten to take him to the station.'

'Why is he leaving? Is it because of me, because I've come back?'

'No... Yes... Oh, I don't know. I don't think it's because of you personally. Well, it might be a bit because of you. Oh dear,' she said, lowering her ample body onto a chair at the kitchen table.

Sitting down beside her, Bess said, 'Tell me exactly what he said, Mrs Hartley.'

'Well,' she said, 'Ernest has got it into his head that there won't be a place for him at Foxden now you're in charge of things. He said an old stick like him would be in the way when young women are running the Estate. He's never been very good around women as you know, especially young ones, and I don't think he can face the changes.'

Mrs Hartley took a handkerchief from her pinafore pocket and rubbed her eyes. 'Ernest hasn't had a happy life,' she said. 'His parents were estate farmers for his Lordship's father and when they died, Ernest was sent to live on the Suffolk Estate. There were no women at Suffolk. No one to show him affection, poor little mite. But he did well at school and when he grew up, he became a jockey. In his heyday he won cups at Towcester and Cheltenham,' she said proudly. Mrs Hartley's mood darkened. 'Until a big stallion was stung in the ear by a wasp and went mad. The horse trampled Ernest almost to death. His left leg and shoulder were broken in so many places.' She paused briefly. 'He never raced again.'

Bess understood Ernest Porter better now. He was an excellent horseman. His knowledge of horses, and all that ailed them, made him indispensable. Now the stables, which for the last thirty years had housed more than twenty horses and had buzzed with lads and grooms, were empty except for Sable and Sultan, two ponies, and a pair of Suffolk Punches. No wonder he felt his life had become meaningless.

Walking across the courtyard, Bess caught sight of Mr Porter sitting alone in the stables. He'd aged. His shoulders seemed narrower. His hair, which had been thick and salt-and-pepper in colour, was thin and almost white. But the most obvious change was in his face. His former bronzed complexion, from years of working outside, was now sallow. The old man no longer looked weather-beaten. He just looked beaten.

Turning quickly, before he'd seen her, Bess walked silently back across the courtyard and approached the stables again, this time with heavier footsteps. And by the time she entered Mr Porter was on his feet. 'Mr Porter, it's good to see you.'

'Miss Dudley,' he replied solemnly, as if he was expecting to hear bad news.

'Mr Porter, I'm so sorry you're not happy with the situation. If it's any consolation, nor am I,' Bess said. 'When I agreed to come back to Foxden, I thought you and my father would be here to help me. Turns out it's not to be.'

Mr Porter didn't say anything.

'The thing is, Mr Porter.' Bess hesitated, choosing her words carefully. 'I'm not going to be able to do the work that's required of me on my own. I could handle the young women who are coming to work on the land well enough. I've had experience with young people. But as for turning the Foxden Estate into arable land – I don't have the knowledge or experience to do that without help! I need someone to work with me who does have the knowledge and experience. Someone who knows the Estate farms and farmers. Someone who not only knows the land, but knows the Foxden Estate. In short, Mr Porter, I need you.

'Would you consider staying and working with me, Mr Porter?' Bess said, leading the way to the servant's kitchen, where Mrs Hartley, freshly baked scones, homemade jam, and a large pot of tea awaited them. They ate in silence and when Mr Porter had finished, Bess said, 'Will you stay, Mr Porter? Will you help me turn the Foxden Estate into arable land?'

The old man took a packet of cigarettes and a box of matches from his pocket and said, 'Yes, miss. Now, if you don't mind, I'll take my leave and go outside for a smoke.'

'And then you can take these cases out of my kitchen,' Mrs Hartley said, winking at Bess.

There was no need for Mr Porter to go outside to smoke his cigarette but Bess didn't object. She guessed he wanted to be alone. It was quite something for him to accept Bess as his equal. She knew he did because when he said, 'Yes, miss.' there was no emphasis on the word "miss."

Mrs Hartley waited until Mr Porter had closed the kitchen door before putting her arms around Bess. 'Thank you, Bess. It hasn't been easy for him, watching the lads go off to war,' she said. 'It's the guilt, you see.'

'Why should he feel guilty? His generation did their bit in the last war.'

'That's the problem, Bess. Ernest didn't go to war. He volunteered time and time again, but the Army wouldn't have him because of his damaged leg.'

'He's certainly had his share of heartache over the years,' Bess said. 'Well, we can't change what has happened to Mr Porter in the past, but we can make sure he feels needed and worthwhile in the future.'

Standing in the doorway of the groom's old sleeping quarters, Bess marvelled at the transformation. She had only been inside the dormitories once before, with her father, and remembered them to be plain and bare. Now, instead of a row of wooden bunks, the room was divided by tall screens into seven spacious areas, with a bed, chest of drawers and a chair in each. Blue curtains hung at the windows and behind them were small squares of black fabric with a small brass ring at each corner. During the day the blackout curtains couldn't be seen but at night, when it was dark, the black squares would be hooked up behind the curtains and held in place by four small nails so the lights in the dormitory couldn't be seen from the outside.

'Good idea, Mr Porter, to have blackout curtains behind the blue ones.'

'That was Mrs Hartley's doing,' he said, proudly. 'She made the curtains, and those screens.'

'Gives the young ladies some privacy,' Mrs Hartley said, suddenly at Bess's side.

Looking again, and taking in the whole space, Bess said, 'I would never have believed the lads' old sleeping quarters could look like this. These are terrific billets, Mrs Hartley.'

Bess sat at the scrubbed table in Mrs Hartley's warm kitchen reading the agricultural college reports on the women and drinking coffee. She savoured every mouthful. When the coffee she had brought from London had gone, she'd have to resort to drinking Camp, with its sickly sweet aftertaste.

The estate farmers and their wives arrived at four o'clock, the land girls fifteen minutes later. Laura, a physical education teacher before the war who had been made redundant when the children she taught were evacuated, was the first of the land girls to arrive, followed by Polly, who was as petite and dark as Laura was tall and fair. Iris, Mavis and Sylvia came in next. Iris, in her late twenties, was the oldest of the girls and the only one wearing a wedding ring. Mavis, dressed in a pretty floral dress, was the youngest, and Sylvia, in government issue khaki shirt and trousers, green pullover, brown riding boots, and hair cropped like a boy, was the only one who looked like a land girl.

The last girls to arrive were Myfanwy and Kitty. Myfanwy, or Fanny, as she preferred to be called, was from North Wales. She wore an old-fashioned grey pinafore dress and flat brown shoes. Kitty, a typical cockney sparrow, was outgoing, loud and funny, with permanently waved bleached blonde hair. She'd changed out of the tight fitting skirt and blouse that she arrived in, into an equally tight fitting dress with a sweetheart neckline. She was still wearing red high heels. Kitty, at nineteen, was younger than Fanny by two years but unlike Fanny, who was shy, Kitty exuded confidence. When Kitty entered the room everyone turned to look at her, which delighted her but embarrassed Fanny, whose cheeks were now the colour of Kitty's lipstick.

Having visited the Estate farms, Mr Porter knew what each of them required to cope with the extra workload. Charity and High Fields Farm needed two land girls, but Low Farm only needed one, leaving two girls to work with Bess and himself at Foxden. And each farm needed girls with different skills. Except for a couple of dozen laying hens, Low Farm's meadows and pastures were going to be turned into arable land. Charity Farm and High Fields Farm had the same directive, with the proviso that Charity would keep a small flock of sheep and a dozen pigs, and High Fields a dairy herd. High Fields also needed domestic help because the farmer's wife, Annie Baylis, had been ill. Whoever worked at High Fields would be expected to help Annie in the house occasionally, and spend time with her as a companion.

The wishes of the land girls were important too. They not only needed to be trained for and suited to the work they would be doing, but it had to be the kind of work they enjoyed. It was also important that they get on with the people they were going to be working with. What they earned and how many hours they worked was standard. They would be billeted together in the dormitories above the stables and eat their main meals - breakfast and supper - in the servants' kitchen at the Hall. The farmers would provide lunch and any other refreshments that the girls wanted during working hours.

Getting to and from work was easy. All three farms were within walking distance of the Hall, but if transport was needed each farm had some sort of vehicle, and every farmer's wife owned a bicycle.

Finally, time off. Everyone agreed that the girls would have their evenings, after dinner, to themselves and their day off would be Sunday. If they had to work on Sunday for any reason – like in the lambing season, or bringing in the harvest – the girls would be given time off in lieu. The only exception to having all day off on Sunday would be at High Fields Farm. High Fields had a dairy herd so whoever chose to work there would have to alternate their day off, so there was always someone to help with the milking.

Bess was delighted when Laura and Sylvia said they wanted to work with her on the Estate. Laura could not only drive a motorcar, she could also drive the new Fordson. At the agricultural college she'd been top of her group for ploughing with a horse and a tractor. She'd be an asset. Sylvia would be invaluable too. She had been part of an all-girl threshing gang and knew how to thatch. She knew how to stook wheat sheaves, fork hay and build hayricks and offered to teach those who didn't when the time came. An advocate of traditional farming, Sylvia preferred ploughing with a pair of Suffolk Punches, which was handy because the Estate only owned one tractor. Polly was a good all-rounder and said she didn't mind where she worked, which suited Bess because she needed someone who was flexible enough to work at Low Farm and Foxden.

Iris and Mavis said they'd like to work with the sheep at Charity Farm, and Fanny and Kitty had worked together in the dairy at agricultural college. 'I came top of my group,' Kitty said. 'The teacher said I was one of the best milkmaids they'd ever had.'

Everyone applauded Kitty, which made her blush. She enjoyed shocking people by wearing lots of make-up and high heels, but she took her work as a land girl seriously and was proud to receive a compliment from her teacher at college. Probably the only sincere compliment the girl has had, Bess thought.

By the time tea was finished each of the women of Foxden's Land Army knew where she would be working and what her responsibilities were.

CHAPTER TWELVE

Bess wasn't able to see any light, not even a chink, through the blackout blinds at the windows of the new dormitory. It didn't mean the girls were asleep, but if they weren't they soon would be. It had been a long day and tomorrow was going to be longer. She looked at her watch. The job of turning the Estate into arable land was going to begin in a few hours.

She crossed the courtyard to the stables. Whatever the weather, making sure the horses were safe and settled for the night was the last thing Bess did before going to bed. When she rubbed Sable's nose, the horse lowered her head and gently butted her until Bess said, 'All right, girl, I know what you want.' Laughing, Bess took two carrots from her pocket, which she did most nights even though there was a food shortage, and flat-handed both animals a treat. Sable shook her head from side to side, flaring her nostrils and exhaling warm breath.

Looking up at the full moon in the clear sky reminded Bess of New Year's Eve, and James. She hadn't seen James since she'd been back, which was probably a good thing. Whatever happens, James must never know her feelings for him were more than those of a friend. For the most part, she had put what happened in the filthy alley in London behind her. Even so, loving James, or anyone else for

196

that matter, could never happen now. Bess had made a decision before coming back to Foxden that James would never know she loved him – had loved him – and why she no longer could. Perhaps it's not such a bad thing that James has Annabel Hadleigh, she thought. Closing the stable door, Bess wiped tears from her eyes.

It was the tradition that on Sunday afternoons, after tea, the Dudley family gathered round the fire to tell each other their news. Everyone had something to say, but it was Margaret who took centre stage. 'I'm going to live in London with Bill.'

You could have heard the proverbial pin drop. It was her mother, Lily, who broke the silence. 'Being the capital, it'll be the first place the Germans bomb. You're not going to London. It's not safe!'

'It's safe where Bill's staying, Mam, in north west London. There aren't any Army or Air Force bases; there isn't even a factory for miles. It's the suburbs and it's a long way from the centre of London – it's as far away as Lowarth is to Rugby,' Margaret explained. 'Honestly, Mam, there's nothing to worry about.'

'If Bill wants to live in London that's up to him, but--'

'He's not there by choice. He's there because he failed his medical!' Margaret said indignantly. 'He wants to do his bit for the country.'

'That's as maybe, but he doesn't have to go to London to do it. There's plenty he could do for his country up here.'

'He's transporting top secret documents from the Ministry of Defence in Whitehall to-- well, I can't say where, because it's top secret. But it's a very important job!'

'What about *your* job?' her father asked.

'I've handed in my notice. I'll get another job when I get to London. The Goldmans are in business. I might be able to work for them.'

'Ha! The Goldmans, is it? I might have known our Bess had something to do with it.' Their mother glared at her, but Bess said nothing. Margaret's news was as big a shock to her as it was to everyone else. 'So what kind of business are these Goldman people in?'

'All sorts,' Margaret said, looking at Bess. 'They own a theatre. And a smart club. They're bound to need book-keepers and clerks and things.'

She needs me to back her up, Bess thought, and opened her mouth to speak.

'Sounds to me as if you've made up your mind,' her father said.

'I suppose I have,' Margaret admitted.

'In that case,' her mother snapped, 'there's nothing more to be said! You're your husband's responsibility now.' With that, she turned on her heels and stormed out of the room.

'It might only be for a few months,' Margaret called after her mother, 'until Bill finishes his training. I miss him. Mam!'

From somewhere a door slammed shut.

'What next?' their father said.

'I've joined the WAAF,' Claire announced.

'What?' He turned and looked at her sternly. 'When did this happen?'

'A few weeks ago. I'll be training up in Morecambe, in Lancashire.'

'But--'

'I'm coming home, Dad,' Ena said. 'I've got a job at the Rover munitions factory in Lowarth. Not as exciting or heroic as Margaret and Claire's work-'

'Did you know about this, Bess?' their father asked.

Smiling apologetically at Ena, Bess shook her head. Then, turning her attention to her father, she said, 'No. And for the record, I didn't know Margaret was going to London either.'

Feeling sorry for Ena, because her homecoming had been overshadowed by Margaret and Claire's shocking news, Bess put her arm around her youngest sister's shoulder. She listened to the rest of the family's domestic dramas, giving her opinion only when asked. She was more concerned with the bigger drama that was taking place across the Channel, in which her brother Tom was playing a part.

CHAPTER THIRTEEN

Bess shivered. The air was damp as well as cold. It was only four o'clock in the afternoon, but the winter sun was fading fast. She looked up and waved to Polly, who had attracted her attention by blowing a piercing whistle. 'Look, no hands,' Polly shouted, waving her hands above her head and freewheeling down the lane towards them on Mrs Hartley's bicycle. Laura, who had been checking a crop of winter cabbage in a neighbouring field, was standing on the bottom rung of the five-bar gate that separated the two fields pointing at her wristwatch with exaggerated actions. Bess looked up at the darkening sky. If they were going to get back to the Hall before dusk they'd have to leave soon.

Putting her foot down, she drove the tractor along the track that separated Swallow's Field from Larks Meadow to where Polly had joined Laura and was opening the gate. Bess drove through and stopped. 'What's that noise?'

'Sounds like thunder. We'd better make a move or we'll be caught in one hell of a storm by the sound of it,' Polly said.

'That isn't thunder,' Bess said, jumping down from the tractor. 'It's a plane. It must be on its way to Bitteswell or Bruntingthorpe.

Laura nodded. 'It sounds as if it's flying a bit low, doesn't it?'

The three women looked to the south where the noise was coming from and saw the plane.

'Sounds like a light bomber,' Bess shouted. 'And it *is* flying low, dangerously low.' Then, as quickly as the plane appeared, it disappeared.

'It's heading for the Hall!' Polly screamed. 'It's going to crash into it! What if it's carrying bombs?'

'It won't be. It's coming home. It'll have offloaded.' Seconds later Bess spotted a Blenheim flying through a break in the clouds. 'It's missed the Hall.'

But before Laura had time to reply the plane made a loud cranking noise, as if someone was trying to start a heavy artillery truck with a starting handle. Then the engine began to splutter. 'Oh my God!' The colour drained from Laura's face. 'It's coming down! And it's heading this way!'

The Blenheim vanished behind a small copse on the far side of Larks Meadow and for what seemed like an age the women braced themselves for the crash. Instead they heard a succession of heavy bumps, followed by a loud scraping sound, and finally a dull thud. For a moment there was an eerie silence.

'Polly, go to the Hall. Telephone the aerodrome. Tell them a Blenheim's come down on the Estate. And tell them we don't know how many it's carrying. Then phone the fire brigade. Laura, you come with me,' Bess said.

Polly set off at such speed that the front wheel of her cycle skidded and she nearly came off. She put her foot down and regained her balance. 'Be careful!' Bess shouted, before running across the field to the aircraft.

Landing on its belly, the Blenheim had churned up everything in its path, but because the meadow was flat and it had been raining heavily for several days the plane had remained upright and in one piece. By the time Bess and Laura reached the plane's cockpit the hatch was sliding back.

Bess's father and the ARP wardens were first on the scene. They'd seen the plane come down from their watch point on the Rugby Road, and arrived within minutes of it crashing.

'Get these boys out of here, Bess,' her father shouted. 'Keep the civilians as far away from the plane as you can,' he called to one of the other ARP men.

'Out!' Bess shouted, beckoning the plane's passengers. 'Come on! Get out!'

Half a dozen dazed and disorientated servicemen scrambled out of the plane. The pilot and first officer were wearing RAF uniforms. The other men were dressed in belted overcoats with the silver wings of the Polish Air Force on their shoulders.

Bess and Laura pulled, pushed, mimed and shouted until they had dragged every man out of the ditched plane and handed them over to

Bess's father. Military vehicles and RAF personnel arrived by the dozen, along with the emergency services, the police, the fire brigade and ambulance. Sirens wailed and bells clanged. But they were too late. Suddenly the plane's fuel tanks exploded.

The power of the blast knocked Bess and Laura off their feet. Fragments of burning metal flew into the air, showering them with red hot splinters. People who had been knocked down stayed down, and those that had been left standing threw themselves to the ground and covered their heads with their arms for protection.

Bess's father appeared at her side. 'Don't move!' he ordered. 'Your coat's on fire.

An ARP warden threw a wet blanket on top of her. 'Stay down and roll over!' he urged. Fear drove her to roll over and over in the grass and mud. When he was satisfied that she wasn't going to burst into flames, her father hauled her to her feet to inspect her coat.

'Everyone on your feet,' he bellowed, 'we've got to extinguish the burning plane.'

'What happened to the airmen?' Bess asked.

'Garth Davis has taken them up to the hall--'

'Buckets!' an ARP man shouted above the kerfuffle.

'Spades!' called another.

'Form a line!' shouted a third.

News of the crash spread quickly. Within half an hour most the residents of Woodcote village arrived carrying buckets, bowls, large pots and pans, spades, and even watering cans.

The ARP organised two human chains, one to pass buckets filled with water from the River Swift up the hill to the plane, the other to pass the empty buckets down again. Local youths stood knee-deep in the freezing river, filling whatever receptacle came their way.

'The barn! Look! The wind's blowing the flames in the direction of the barn!' Bess shouted. Seconds later her voice was drowned out by the noise of shattering glass as the cockpit exploded, showering the countryside once more with razor-sharp shards of burning glass. 'We've got to douse the barn before the flames reach it!'

Her father shook his head. 'It's too late. It's already caught.'

Bess turned towards the barn, but her father caught hold of the sleeve of her coat. 'It's too dangerous, Bess!'

Swirls of smoke had started to drift into the night sky from a small chimney on the barn's roof. 'We've got to try to save it, Dad,' Bess pleaded. 'The winter feed for Charity Farm's sheep and High Fields' cattle is in there. We can't afford to lose it.'

Her father nodded and let her go. 'All right. Form two groups,' he hollered. 'Get some spades over here as quick as you can.

And someone get a fireman. Tell him to bring a ladder.'

Bess split the people at the top of the chain into two groups. One group stayed in the water chain and doused the walls and door of the barn, while the other group – half a dozen people – dug a trench to stop the flames from travelling along the ground to the hedge, which was next to the barn and as dry as tinder. Mr Porter arrived with a fireman who climbed onto the roof of the barn and poured buckets of water down the chimney until the smoke abated.

'It'll be all right now,' her father said, 'it's stopped smoking.'

'Thank God for that!' Bess left the barn and ran to Laura, who had been on the hot end of the plane chain. 'Laura,' she called. 'The fire's out. The plane's--' but before she could finish the sentence someone shouted, 'Stop!'

'It's raining!' someone else shouted. 'It's raining,' they called again, and everyone cheered. The fine drizzle that had been in the air for most of the day had turned into rain and was heavy enough to douse the surrounding foliage and stop any rogue fires from igniting.

People at the beginning of the chain who had been standing for hours in freezing water or mud staggered about as if they were drunk, exhausted from hours of bending down and lifting heavy buckets of water. The firemen, military personnel and ARP who had worked alongside the villagers stood in silence, too numb with cold to speak. Some people fell to the ground, others wandered round in a daze and some marched on the spot blowing hot breath into their cupped hands in an attempt to stimulate circulation.

When the RAF crash unit arrived Bess and Laura left the field. At the gate both women turned and looked back. Smoke drifted eerily across the Foxden Acres like a legion of ghosts. The once powerful aeroplane was a burnt-out shell, silhouetted against the night sky.

Covered from head to toe in soot and ash, their faces striped with tears from the dense smoke, Bess and Laura were the last of the women to arrive back at the Hall. There was no sign of the RAF officers, Polish airmen or any land girls, which was not surprising considering how late it was. The girls would be asleep by now and the airmen would be at one or other of the nearby aerodromes.

Bess and Laura entered the warm, welcoming kitchen in silence. On the table a fat church candle illuminated a plate of spam and mustard, and cheese and pickle sandwiches under a thin muslin cloth. On the far side of the room there were two tin baths in front of the fire, separated by a clothes-horse with two large towels draped across it, and in the brick alcove next to the fire Mrs Hartley's linen copper was letting off steam.

Laughing from exhaustion more than anything else, the girls took off their smoke-stained clothes, filled the baths with boiling water, and while the water cooled, sat in their underwear and devoured their supper as if they hadn't eaten for a week.

After a much needed bath Laura, sitting by the fire in just her towel, started to laugh.

'What?' Bess asked. She was so tired that Laura's laughter became contagious and she began to laugh too.

'I was wondering,' Laura said, hardly able to get the words out, 'whether to go back to the dormitory in my towel, or my underwear? Which do you think?'

'Definitely the towel – it's too cold to go out in your underwear,' Bess said. 'And it's raining, so when you get there you can dry yourself if you go in the towel.'

Laura laughed. 'Dry myself off with a wet towel?'

'I know,' Bess said, 'I'll fetch Mr Porter's old umbrella and you can sing "Stormy Weather" as you cross the yard.'

'If that's your only suggestion, I'm staying here by the fire. Good night,' Laura said sleepily, pretending to fall asleep.

Still laughing, Bess ran upstairs to her room. She and Laura were about the same size so she took a pair of slacks and a jumper from her wardrobe. She hadn't been upstairs long but when she returned to the kitchen Laura really was asleep. Bess thought about leaving her. If she'd fallen asleep in a comfortable chair, she might have done, but not in a wooden rocker. 'Laura,' Bess whispered. 'Wake up, time to go to bed.'

Laura opened her eyes and yawned.

'I'm sorry, I'd have left you in front of the fire, but I think you'd have a very stiff neck in the morning if you spent the night in that old chair.'

'I think you're right,' Laura said. 'So what is it to be, towel or knickers?'

Both women laughed again before Laura put on Bess's clothes.

Bess watched her friend cross the courtyard and enter the dormitory. Then she locked the door, blew out the candle and went to bed.

Bess opened her eyes. Her body ached, but she forced herself to sit up. She looked out of the bedroom window and watched a magpie hop from one branch of an old beech tree to another. Every time the bird landed on a different branch a russet-coloured leaf floated to the ground.

It had rained continuously throughout October. The River Swift had burst its banks. The lowlands had turned into a bog, and the marshes had edged their way, day by very wet day, as far as the bridle path that linked Foxden with Lowarth, making it impossible for anyone to walk or ride the route. In contrast, November was turning into one of the coldest months. If the cold snap kept up the earth would soon be too hard to farm. Bess smiled. A fraction of her beloved

Foxden Acres would remain uncultivated for a while longer.

She watched the magpie fly off and considered staying in her warm bed. Instead she forced herself to get up and dress. It was a bright morning, so after breakfast she saddled Sable and took her for a gentle trot along Buffton to Woodcote. Sable needed the exercise but Bess, painfully aware of every cobble along Chapel Street, wasn't sure she did.

Woodcote's shop and post office was the heart of the village, the place where people met for a chat or to gossip while they bought a pint of milk, loaf of bread, or quarter of tea. It was mandatory that, as food coupons were handed over the counter, local news was passed back. If Mrs Moore had had the foresight to put tables and chairs in the shop and serve pots of tea while the ladies waited for their pensions, she would have made a fortune.

Bess walked Sable through the village and dismounted outside the post office. Almost immediately, like a gaggle of excited geese, a posse of elderly ladies surrounded her demanding to know who was in the aeroplane. And, if they were foreigners, would the ladies of Woodcote be safe in their beds at night?

'Ladies, ladies, if you'll let me speak!' Bess waited until they had quietened. 'Firstly, let me assure you that you are quite safe. Apart from the pilot and co-pilot – both RAF officers – the other servicemen were Polish airmen who had escaped the German occupation.'

'They didn't look like Poles,' one old lady said.

'No,' said another, 'they looked like Germans.'

Bess couldn't help but smile. How the old ducks had come to that conclusion, not having seen the men in the aeroplane, or anyone from Germany or Poland for that matter, she didn't ask. 'You can take my word for it. The passengers in the plane were Polish!' she said, and left them to it.

By the end of the week Bitteswell Aerodrome's engineers had dismantled the burnt-out plane, a structural and forensic examination had been carried out and the plane's passengers had been discharged from the Walsgrave hospital in Coventry, where they had been taken the day after the crash with a variety of broken bones, cuts and bruises.

RAF Bitteswell and Bruntingthorpe were Commonwealth aerodromes and when construction finished they would be home to air force personnel from every country in the Commonwealth while they trained with the Royal Air Force. The Polish flyers would be based at Bitteswell eventually, but as the living quarters were not yet ready the Squadron Leader asked Bess's father, as a member of the local ARP, if he could find each of them a room with a family in Woodcote. And, so the families didn't suffer any shortages, the RAF would provide the airmen's food along with extra rations of cigarettes, coffee and chocolate. The residents of Woodcote were queuing up to take a paying guest – whatever their nationality.

It was a young pilot named Franciszek, shortened to Franek because no one in the family could pronounce his name, who stayed with Bess's parents.

Franek spent his days with Claire, who had joined the WAAF and was waiting for her papers. Franek wanted to learn English, so Claire agreed to teach him if he taught her Polish. Claire described photographs in magazines and books in English, and Franek repeated what she said. Then Franek described them in Polish and Claire repeated what he'd said. Claire had an ear for languages and learned the rudiments of the Polish language as quickly as Franek learned English.

A couple of weeks after he'd left his temporary billet with the Dudley family and was living permanently on the aerodrome at Bitteswell, Franek returned for his English lesson.

'Hello, lad. Come in,' Bess heard her father say. 'If it's Claire you've come to see, you've missed her. Her papers came yesterday; she left for Lancashire first thing this morning, but Bess is here. Bess, it's Franek. Look after him, will you?' her father shouted. 'Sorry I can't stop, I'm on ARP duty tonight,' he said, and left.

Bess called Franek into the living room. 'I've just made a pot of tea, would you like a cup?'

'Yes. Thank you. I would like a cup of tea.'

Bess smiled. 'Your English is very good, Franek.'

'Thank you. Claire is - was - very good teacher.'

While they were drinking their tea, Franek took an envelope from his pocket. 'My mother and father,' he said proudly, handing her a selection of small grainy photographs. 'In our garden, next to linden tree. It is a very special tree in my country. A symbol of faith and a good life.'

Franek's mother was fortyish, pretty and slim with fair hair. His father, not much taller than his wife, was some years older and had dark greying hair. 'I can see where you get your good looks, Franek. Your parents are a handsome couple.'

'Thank you, but I think you make fun, like my sister, Vanda,' he said, laughing. He pointed to the next photograph. A slender blonde girl was standing under the same tree, blowing a kiss. 'She is funny and clever. She is only twenty years, but she has very good English. Before war she studied at University of Cracow. Now I do not know where she is. I pray she is safe,' he sighed.

Franek being a long way from home and not knowing where his sister was reminded Bess that her brother was a long way from home too. She had no idea where Tom was, if he was safe, or even if he was alive. While she sipped her tea her thoughts turned to James. She didn't know where he was either. She hadn't seen him for months and wondered when he would come up to the Hall next.

CHAPTER FOURTEEN

'Penny for them?'

Bess jumped. She was miles away, thinking about the letter she'd received that morning from Mrs McAllister in London. 'James?' she gasped, turning to see the man she loved. Correction: the man she had once loved. The man she had hoped one day would love her. But that was in another life.

Standing in the doorway of the stables, Flying Officer Foxden looked as handsome and smart in his Royal Air Force uniform as Bess looked plain and untidy in her work overalls and pullover. She had tied an old scarf around her head to keep her hair from falling into her eyes while she worked, but the scarf had worn loose and strands of hair bounced before her eyes and tickled her nose. She pushed the unruly curls away, poking them under the scarf with her finger, and then worried that because she was recovering from a cold the freezing air had made her nose run. Putting her hand up and pretending to clear her throat, she touched her nose. It was dry.

'What are you doing mucking out on Christmas Eve?'

Bess didn't reply. She could hardly tell James she was working to exorcise the demons that plagued her, or because it made her feel closer to him, the man she loved but couldn't have. Ignoring the pounding in her heart, she said as casually as she was able, 'I've finished now.'

'Good. Do you think Mrs H will take pity on me and give me some breakfast?' James said.

Bess laughed. 'You know she will.'

'Well, if it isn't Mr James,' Mrs Hartley said, as Bess and James entered the kitchen. 'What a pleasure it is to see you, sir.' Mrs Hartley pulled out the chair at the head of the table next to the place she'd laid for Bess. 'Now, you sit yourself down there. How would you like a couple of fried eggs and some of my best short-back bacon? And because it's Christmas, what would you say to a hot mince pie for afters?'

'Mrs H, you spoil me,' James said as Mrs Hartley manoeuvred her ample body to the pantry quicker than Bess had thought was physically possible.

James sat down at the kitchen table as Mr Porter entered from the scullery. 'Excuse me,' Bess said, walking towards the door that Mr Porter had come through. 'I'll go and wash my hands. Shan't be a minute.'

'Use my washroom, Bess. There's some soap and a clean towel in there,' Mrs Hartley said, miming washing her face and patting her thick grey hair. 'Take your time, breakfast won't be ready afore you've *tidied* yourself up,' she added, jerking her head to the right and rolling her eyes in the direction of the washroom.

'Thank you, Mrs Hartley,' Bess said, bemused by her old friend's performance. Looking at herself in the small mirror above the sink, Bess knew immediately why Mrs Hartley had suggested she use her washroom instead of the scullery sink. From the bottom of her left ear to the tip of her nose there was a streak of mud. She felt foolish but there was nothing she could do except wash her face, which she did using Mrs Hartley's lavender-scented soap before tying her hair back with her scarf.

Mr Porter wasn't comfortable eating at the same table as James and only spoke when he was spoken to. James, however, tucked into his breakfast and talked about the Acres and the Estate farms with enthusiasm.

When they had finished eating, Mr Porter nodded his thanks to Mrs Hartley, and stood up. 'If you'll excuse me sir, I'll be getting on. Bess, if you need me I'll be in the stables,' he said, and left.

'I must go too,' James said. 'I want to see Mother before I head back to the aerodrome. I volunteered for duty over Christmas – give some of the married chaps a chance to get home to their wives and families – and I haven't told her yet.'

How strange, Bess thought, that James had volunteered for duty when he had Annabel, his fiancée, to consider. I wonder if he's told her yet?

'You work too hard, Mr James,' Mrs Hartley said, clearing the table. 'I keep telling

Bess; it's not good for you young people to work all the time and never go anywhere, never have any fun. All work and no play…'

'How right you are, Mrs Hartley. There's a dance at the aerodrome tonight and as long as my sergeant knows where I am, in case there's an emergency, I don't see why I shouldn't go along and have some fun. The problem is I don't have a dance partner. I don't suppose you'd accompany me to the RAF's Christmas dance tonight, would you, Bess?

Bess hadn't been listening to what James was saying; she was thinking about Annabel. 'Sorry…?'

'The RAF's Christmas dance tonight. Would you come with me?'

'To… tonight?' she stuttered. 'Sorry, yes, I'd love to come. Thank you.' She could hardly say, 'What about Annabel?' though she wondered what she'd think.

'Good. I'm afraid I can't leave the aerodrome. But I'll send my driver--'

'No! No, there's no need to send anyone. I'll come with Ena and her friend, in Crane's taxi.

'Well, if you're sure? I'll pick you up at the main gate. Shall we say seven-thirty?'

'Seven-thirty's perfect,' Bess said, smiling.

Crane's was the only taxi in Woodcote and Ena's friend Beryl, the taxi owner's daughter, offered to work in her father's place on Christmas Eve on condition he let her stay at

217

the dance with Ena when she'd taken all the fares there. That way, she argued, she'd already be there to take the customers home. Mr Crane agreed, so Bess was able to hitch a lift as far as the aerodrome's gatehouse, where James and his driver were waiting.

The dance was in full swing by the time they arrived. Ray Walker's Band was playing "Ain't Misbehavin'" and the dance floor was heaving with bodies. Bess took off her coat and hung it up in the cloakroom. After adding a little lipstick and powder she joined James, who was standing beside a small table on the edge of the dance floor holding two glasses of fruit punch.

'You look lovely, Bess.'

'Thank you,' she said, blushing. 'Oh, thank you,' she said again, accepting the glass of punch that James was offering her.

They chinked glasses. 'Cheers,' James said.

'Cheers.' As soon as she had taken a sip, James took her glass and put it on the table next to his. 'Dance?'

Bess felt a tingling sensation in the pit of her stomach as she took James's hand, and her cheeks flushed as she moved towards him, 'I'd love to,' she said. But no sooner had she turned to lead the way to the dance floor than Franek and the other Polish airmen she had helped out of the burning aeroplane stepped between them.

Saluting James, the first one said, 'Excuse please, sir,' took Bess's hand and kissed it.

Franek and two other Polish flyers did the same, saluting and thanking Bess for getting them out of the crashed plane before singing a song in their native language, which Bess thought was probably the Polish version of "For She's A Jolly Good Fellow". When they stopped singing, and the band began to play, the first airman took Bess's hand again and said to James, 'I would dance with your beautiful partner, sir, with your permission?'

Bess looked into James's eyes, willing him to say no. Instead he raised his eyebrows and shrugged his shoulders good-heartedly, as if to say, 'What can I do?' and the young airman waltzed her onto the dance floor.

Bess danced with each of the Polish flyers in turn, looking over their shoulders constantly to where she'd left James, hoping to catch a glimpse of him, but the dance floor was too crowded. When Franek escorted her back to her seat at the interval James had gone.

'Excuse me, miss,' said the young sergeant Bess recognised as the driver who had brought James to meet her at the gate earlier. 'Flying Officer Foxden has been called away. He sends his apologies and said I was to tell you that he'll be at Foxden for the New Year. When you're ready to leave, miss, I'll be outside in the Flying Officer's car.'

'Thank you, but there's no need for you to drive me home, I'll catch a lift with my sister and her friend.'

'It's no trouble, miss.'

'You're very kind, sergeant, but I'm sure you have better things to do on Christmas Eve than hang around waiting for me.'

'But Flying Officer Foxden said--'

'But I don't want you to drive me home! Thank you!'

'I'm sorry, miss. I was only following orders. Good night.' The young airman turned on his heels and walked briskly out of the dance hall.

'Good night,' Bess called after him, but he'd gone. She hadn't meant to be rude to James's driver, but she wasn't ready to be alone with a man she didn't know, even if he was answerable to James. Just thinking about it opened floodgates of fear, and she began to drown in the memories of Dave, and the disgusting alley in London.

Tears threatened, but Bess clenched her fists and refused to cry. She hated Dave for what he did to her that night, but she hated him more for what he was still doing to her. He had taken her confidence and made her fearful of everyone and everything. He had cast a dark shadow over her life. She wondered if she would ever be free of him.

People began to leave before the end of the dance. It was snowing heavily and they were eager to get home while the roads were still clear. At eleven forty-five Beryl returned after taking her last fare home to Lowarth. 'Time to get to St Mary's,' she called. 'Shake a leg, you two.'

Normally Bess would have enjoyed Midnight Mass, but suddenly she wanted to go home. Besides, she had arranged to meet Mr Porter at seven to exercise the horses. 'Christmas or not, I'm working in the morning. Any chance of dropping me off at Foxden first?' She might as well have saved her breath because neither Ena nor Beryl would hear of her going home and frog-marched her out of the hall to the car.

So much snow had fallen during the evening that it was impossible to see where the fields ended and the road began. The car bumped the grass kerb several times while they were driving along the narrow strip of road leading to the gate.

'Stop!' Bess shouted as they approached the security gate on the main Coventry Road.

Beryl hit the brake pedal and the car skidded to a halt a few inches from a small vixen that was standing in the middle of the road. 'Why doesn't she move out of the way?'

'I don't know,' Bess said. The vixen flicked her ears and angled herself threateningly in front of the car. Then her back legs folded under her and she dropped her head until she was sitting with her muzzle in the snow.

'Do you think we should get out of the car and see if it's all right?'

'No!' Bess said. 'She could bite if she's injured. She'll move when she's ready when she realises we're not going to hurt her.'

But the vixen didn't move. She sat and stared at the car through glazed eyes.

'Poor thing, it's so cold tonight,' Ena said.

'She won't be cold. She's wearing a fur coat,' Bess joked.

Eventually the vixen lost interest in the car and its occupants and limped through the gate. They watched her as she walked feebly along the side of a boundary hedge until she found a gap in the leafless branches – and suddenly she was gone.

The church was full by the time Bess, Ena and Beryl arrived. Because of the blackout there had been no welcoming candles in the porch, nor warm light emanating from the stained glass windows, as there had been in previous years. Nor was there a choir to keep the residents of Church Street awake.

The congregation was made up of mostly young people, many of them couples. Sweethearts who would soon be parted when one, or maybe both of them, went off to war. Bess prayed for the young servicemen and women who would probably see more death than life in the coming months. She prayed for Molly and wondered how she would cope bringing up a baby without a husband, and for Mrs Mac, who would have her work cut out looking after them both. And she prayed for Miss Armstrong who, Mrs Mac had said in her last letter, was in good health now, but had suffered a breakdown after losing her job. Poor Miss Armstrong. She had missed out on marriage and motherhood to concentrate on her career. Now she had neither. Bess hoped that wasn't going to be her fate.

Her mind wandered to earlier in the evening, and James. She wondered when she'd see him again. In the New Year, his sergeant had said. Annabel would probably be at Foxden then. Feeling sad and guilty in equal parts, she cuffed a tear and shook her head. Nothing mattered as long as he was safe.

'Are you all right, Bess?' Ena whispered.

'Yes, of course.'

'You don't look it.'

'I'm fine. It's Midnight Mass. Always makes me feel a bit emotional.'

Nodding, Ena held Bess's hand.

Bess gave Ena's hand a squeeze and reflected on her own family. Her father put on a brave face when he talked of the work he did in the foundry, although he hated it, and her mother made light of Margaret living in London and Claire going up north to join the Women's Auxiliary Air Force, but Bess knew she worried for both of them. And Tom! Bess prayed for her brother's safe return – from wherever he was.

Tom had said in his last letter that his regiment would soon be on the move, so Bess's mam insisted they post Tom's Christmas box early. She had been saving her chocolate coupons and had bought two bars of Cadbury's, which she wrapped in a pair of thick woollen socks. Claire added a quarter of Mackintosh's toffees and Ena put in a small jar of Brylcreem that she'd bought from the barber in Lowarth. She didn't have enough money for a regular size jar, so she'd persuaded him to sell her the small jar from the display in the window for half the price. The Brylcreem made the parcel heavy, but Ena insisted it went in the box. Bess wrote a long letter, adding the two shiny new shillings that the bus conductor had given her in London in the New Year of 1939. She wrote a P.S. that read: "Lucky 2/- Keep them until you can let us know you're safe. Love Bess x."

Christmas morning was unusually quiet. Tom was somewhere in France, Margaret had stayed in London to be with Bill, who was working over the Christmas holiday and Claire, although she was home on leave, was up in her bedroom learning French. Franek had taught her the rudiments of the Polish language, which she had picked up quickly, as well as a smattering of German, so she had volunteered for some sort of special assignment, which meant she needed to learn several languages. She was swotting like mad because she had an exam when she returned to the base.

Ena and Bess put on their hats and coats and went out for a walk. For as far as the eye could see the world was white. Fields, tree, houses, even the roads were carpeted in snow. The two sisters walked arm in arm through Foxden's park and along Buffton to

Woodcote. By the time they returned home dinner was ready.

Staring at the roast chicken, Ena said, 'That's not Daisy or Dotty, is it, Mam?'

'No, it's a gift from his Lordship,' Thomas Dudley said, shaking his head as he sliced into the large bird.

'That's all right then! I couldn't eat one of ours, it would be like eating our Claire, but more tender,' she said, pinching the small roll of flesh that showed above the waistband of Claire's skirt.

'Ouch! That hurt,' Claire said.

'Course it didn't, you--'

'Is it too much to ask that just once a year we sit down and eat a family meal without you two ragging each other?' their father asked. 'Ena, sit down next to me. Claire, over there next to your mother.'

'Sorry, Dad,' the two sisters said in unison, looking at each other and trying not to giggle.

The food was delicious, but the atmosphere was subdued. After dinner Ena and Claire – the pinching episode forgotten – took a plate of cold chicken, a slab of fruit cake, a few nuts and sweets for the children, to their neighbour's house. The Dudley family didn't have much but their neighbour, Mrs Barnett, with a sick husband and seven small children, had next to nothing.

Bess left her mam and dad sitting by the fire listening to the wireless, went upstairs to her old bedroom and lay on the bed. She wished she'd danced with James on Christmas Eve and wondered if he would ask her out again. Third time lucky. She closed her eyes. She dreamed she was riding across Foxden Acres with James at her side. She was free and happy. She no longer cared about the past, because she had the future with James. She looked up at the sky. It was clear and blue. There wasn't a cloud in sight. Then she looked down. She felt herself falling, spiralling towards the earth. Before she hit the ground, she woke up.

CHAPTER FIFTEEN

On the morning of December 30th, while Bess was talking to Mrs Hartley in the kitchen at Foxden, her Ladyship arrived. 'Good morning, Bess,' she said, before turning her full attention to Mrs Hartley. 'As you know, Lord Foxden was needed at the war office in London over Christmas. He has just telephoned to say he'll be coming home later today.' Without waiting for a reply she turned to leave, then paused. 'Oh,' she said, turning back, 'and he's bringing Lady Hadleigh and her daughter Annabel with him.'

'But the guest rooms aren't aired, your Ladyship,' Mrs Hartley protested. 'And I don't know if there's enough meat. How long will they be staying?'

'Get Porter to light a fire in two of the guest rooms. And as far as food is concerned, we'll make do with whatever you have in your larder tonight. We'll worry about tomorrow's menu tomorrow. There's a war on here too. It's not confined to London!' she said, leaving the kitchen and closing the door to the main Hall firmly behind her.

'Well I never!' Mrs Hartley said, sitting down with a bump, as if the stuffing had been knocked out of her. 'His Lordship, bringing two guests at this short notice? Well I never!' she said again.

'I'll go and find Mr Porter and ask him to light the fires,' Bess said. She sympathised with Mrs Hartley. She wasn't happy about the imminent arrival of the Hadleighs either.

The following morning, while Mr Porter saddled Sultan, Bess tacked up Sable. It was seven o'clock and Bess wondered if history would repeat itself. Last New Year's Day she expected Tom, but James took his place. This year there was no possibility of Tom joining her. But she dared to hope James might.

'If Mr James doesn't come down this morning, Bess, I'll take Sultan out,' Mr Porter said, tightening Sultan's girth straps.

Mr Porter needn't have worried. James did come to the stables, but he wasn't alone. Annabel Hadleigh was with him. She looked radiant in a ruby-red riding habit and black fitted jacket, her dark hair held neatly in place by a black net.

James explained that because he was only at the Hall for the day, he needed to spend some time with his father. 'Perhaps Annabel could take my place and ride with you this morning, Bess?'

Never in a million years was what Bess thought, but 'Yes, of course,' was what she said.

'I'd love to see what you've done with the Acres, Bess,' Annabel said. 'James is always singing your praises, telling me how hard you've worked. You're a modern day miracle worker, according to him,' she laughed.

Bess smiled politely before leading the way out of the stables and across the cobbled courtyard to the park. After skirting the woods she led Annabel along tractor paths that bordered ploughed fields – fields that Annabel would have remembered as meadows.

'When we were children my sisters and I spent our summer holidays in these fields. And in the autumn we'd pick wild mushrooms for breakfast.

'And in the winter?' Annabel asked.

'Skating on the lake. When it was frozen, of course.' Bess paused. 'Foxden is where I learned to ride.' With James, she wanted to say, but thought better of it. 'I pestered my father to teach me to ride until eventually he asked Lord Foxden and Mr Porter if he could walk me around on one of Lady Foxden's retired pit ponies. I soon grew out of the pony. When I was eleven, and went up to the grammar school, dad thought I was old enough to ride a timid mare named Crystal. By the time I was twelve I was confident enough to ride any of the horses in Foxden's stables.' Bess laughed. 'I used to get up while it was still dark, run up to the stables, and ride out with the lads before going to school.'

'I've always loved riding too. I used to exercise my horse along the beach,' Annabel said. 'When I was a girl I had a chestnut mare called Biscuit. She loved to gallop along the wet sand when the tide was out. She would get so excited as we neared the sea. She'd lift her hoofs in anticipation and when I least expected, she'd make a bolt for it and splash about in the shallow waves.' Annabel looked suddenly sad. 'You can't do that now. The coastline is covered in landmines.'

'Are the landmines visible? Do people know where they are?' Bess asked.

'Oh yes, but it doesn't matter because the entire coastline is fenced off. There's no access from the land. The beaches are covered in miles of barbed wire. You can only get to them from the sea,' Annabel said. 'Not that anyone would want to.'

Bess was surprised how easy Annabel was to talk to. Annabel told her about the work she did for the Red Cross and the hospital in Ashford where she was a volunteer nursing assistant, and Bess told Annabel about her short career in teaching. She also told her what a wonderful horseman her father was and how her brother Tom, who Annabel had met at the beginning of 1939, bought and sold horses for Lord Foxden in Suffolk. Bess hadn't heard from Tom for several months and confided in Annabel that she was worried for his safety.

Because James was on duty over the New Year Annabel was at a loose end and asked Bess if she could help her on the Acres. Bess could hardly say no, so they exercised the horses together, fed them, groomed them and cleaned the tack room – and often before breakfast. Annabel was not like any Lady that Bess had ever met – and she'd met several. If she saw a water trough that was frozen, or a

230

fence that needed mending, Annabel would dismount and attend to it straight away. If the job couldn't be done without tools she'd go back later in the day with a pickaxe, a hammer and nails, or whatever it was she needed to do the job.

Annabel had been born into a wealthy society family, and she'd had a privileged upbringing, but she wasn't afraid of hard work or getting her hands dirty – not as a volunteer in the local hospital where she lived in Kent or on the land at Foxden. Bess thought, after spending time with her, that they had a lot in common. They both had strong views on women's role in society and neither was afraid to share them, or voice their opinion. Bess had to be more careful than Annabel - she could hardly argue women's rights or equality with Lord Foxden - but she'd had several lengthy debates with her father.

Bess admired the achievements of the women's suffrage movement and was in awe of Annabel when she learned that her godmother was a suffragette and had encouraged her from an early age to speak up for what she believed. Annabel was a mixture of traditional and modern values. She didn't look down her nose or patronise Bess. Perhaps she had done, a little, when they first met, when she found James talking to Bess during the previous New Year's Eve party, but not since. Nor did she look down on the land girls, Mr Porter or Mrs Hartley. She didn't suffer fools, she had once told Bess, and expected people to treat her as she treated them.

Annabel called on Bess one Sunday afternoon while Bess was visiting her mother and father. Bess was embarrassed, because there were clothes airing on the clothes-horse at the side of the fire and the living room could have done with a dust, but Annabel didn't seem to notice, or if she did, she didn't care. Bess's father was used to being around the upper classes - he had spent half his life riding with the gentry, accompanied Lord Foxden when he played polo and rode at Lady Foxden's side as second horseman - but Bess's mother had a tendency to fuss in the company of people like Annabel.

Annabel's visit to the cottage lasted several hours. She was fascinated by the stories Bess's father told her about the horses of the Royal Engineers in the First World War, and how he and the men of his regiment built bridges on horseback. Annabel was not only impressed by her father's knowledge of horses, she seemed to genuinely like him. And he liked her, Bess could tell.

The more time Bess spent with Annabel the more she liked her and the more she liked her, the guiltier she felt about loving James. She decided not to think about it.

As the telegram boy pushed his bicycle towards Bess she felt her body stiffen. The boy's boots pounded the cobbles but she couldn't hear them above the pounding of her heart. She put out her hand to take the small buff envelope and began to tremble. Was this the telegram that would break her mother's heart, break her heart? Who was the subject of the news? Was it Tom? Or Claire? What if it was Margaret, or Bill? Or – God forbid – James? Bess stared at the envelope.

'It's good news,' the telegram boy said, grinning.

'Good news,' a small voice in Bess's head repeated.

'Yes, miss. The Miss Parkers at Lowarth post office said as I wasn't to spoil the surprise by telling you your friend in London has had a baby, but I was to say, "It's good news" when I gave you the telegram – put your mind at ease, like.'

'Thank you,' Bess said, her voice still hardly audible as she ran her finger along the top of the envelope.

The telegram boy jumped on his bicycle and pedalled off across the cobbles. 'Enjoy your surprise,' he shouted.

A GIRL = BOTH FINE = COME SOON = LOVE ALL AT 79. Dated Friday 10th May 1940. Bess laughed with relief. It certainly was good news.

With the telegram still in her hand, Bess ran to the barn where Laura and Mr Porter were sharpening a scythe. She told them that her friend in London had had her baby and asked if they could manage without her for a few days at the end of the month. Laura

233

thought it was time she had a break anyway and Mr Porter agreed, assuring her that he and Laura would take care of things until she returned. She then ran to the kitchen and told Mrs Hartley before cycling to the post office in Woodcote to telephone Mrs McAllister.

Mrs Mac, near to tears with emotion, didn't spare Bess a single detail of Molly's lengthy labour and the baby's birth. And when Bess told her that she was coming to London to see Molly and the baby, and asked if she could stay at number seventy-nine for a few days at the beginning of June, her old landlady was overjoyed.

'I'll let you know the date as soon as I know it,' Bess said. 'Give Molly and the baby my love and give my regards to Miss Armstrong.' As she was saying goodbye to Mrs McAllister, she heard three sharp pips and the call ended.

CHAPTER SIXTEEN

Bess had been saving clothes coupons for months and at last had enough to buy something new to wear in London. The weekend before she was due to go down, she took the train from Lowarth to Leicester and bought a navy blue two-piece and a pair of court shoes for herself, and a pretty pink dress with a matching bonnet for Molly's baby.

Bess was looking forward to seeing her friends. She was also looking forward to not getting up before dawn, not working for ten hours every day, and not looking like a scarecrow. For two whole weeks she intended to look and feel like a woman.

On the morning she was due to leave Bess packed her suitcase, put on the clothes she was travelling in, and went down to breakfast. To her surprise, Lady Foxden was sitting in Mrs Hartley's kitchen when she arrived.

'Bess, dear,' Lady Foxden said, in the tone she used when she wanted Bess to do something. 'I know how much you have been looking forward to seeing your friends in London, but I'm afraid we can't spare you.'

Bess opened her mouth to protest, but Lady Foxden continued before she had a chance to speak.

'Some of the grooms and lads who were evacuated from Dunkirk will be coming to stay for a week or two. They don't have families, you see, and consider Foxden their home. We'd like to put the ground floor of the west wing, the library and the gardens at their disposal while they convalesce. And...' Lady Foxden inserted a dramatic pause before playing her ace card. 'His Lordship asked if you would personally take charge of the arrangements. The local boys from Woodcote and Lowarth are on their way home too, and they will be more than welcome to spend their days here. I don't think any of them need medical attention. It's more rest and quiet. Well, dear? Of course, if it's too much to ask...'

What Bess would give to know that Tom was safe and on his way home. She replied without a second thought. 'Of course, Lady Foxden. If I can use your telephone I'll ring my friends.'

Mrs McAllister understood completely. 'Don't worry, Bess, we know how important your work is. Come down later in the year. We'll still be here. We're not going anywhere. And you never know, by then this wretched war might be over,' she said, before handing the telephone to Molly.

'Mrs McAllister said we should get Elizabeth christened, so if we wait until you come down, would you be her godmother, Bess?'

'I'd love to, Molly. Thank you for asking me.'

'We all miss you, Bess. And Elizabeth can't wait to meet you.'

'I miss you too, Moll. See you at the christening. Give Elizabeth a hug from me.'

Miss Armstrong came on the line. 'Hello, Bess. I'm sorry we won't be seeing you today.'

'Thank you, Miss Armstrong, I'm sorry too. How are you?' Bess asked.

'I'm quite well. We all are. Molly is a devoted mother and is busy planning the christening. I'm making Elizabeth's christening gown and Mrs McAllister is saving food coupons for the christening tea. It will be wonderful, all of us together again.'

'Yes, it'll be like old times,' Bess said. 'I'll write when I have time.'

'And I'll write to you with the news from number seventy-nine. Take care, Bess. Try not to work too hard. Goodbye.'

Bess said goodbye and replaced the receiver on its cradle. Seconds later the telephone rang. She looked along the corridor expecting Mr Porter to come marching along cursing new-fangled inventions, or Annie Timpson, Lady Foxden's elderly maid, who had been brought out of retirement when the servants were called up, but there was no one in sight.

The harsh ring resonated along the corridor. Bess knew it could be heard as far away as Lord Foxden's study. But still no one came. She wondered whether she should answer it. It could be an important call for his Lordship, or James. So, after clearing her throat, she picked up the receiver. 'Lowarth 154.'

'Hello, Bess Learned to drive a car yet?'

'Tom! Where are you?' Bess cried. 'How are you? Why haven't you been in touch?'

'If you let me get a word in edgeways, I'll tell you.'

'Sorry. It's just that we've been so worried.'

'I'm fine, really. It was murder getting out of Dunkirk, but I was one of the lucky ones and got out in one piece. I tried to send a telegram.'

'I got it, but all it said was, 'Tell Mam I'm alive.' We've heard nothing since.'

'Well I'll be damned. And she didn't take the two shillings.'

'What are you talking about?'

'I gave a girl the two shillings that you sent me at Christmas and asked her to send a telegram to you, so you could tell Mam I was OK. I didn't send it directly to Mam because I knew getting a telegram would upset her. Anyway, when I woke up in hospital I still had the two shillings, so I thought the girl hadn't bothered. She must have put them into my pocket when I collapsed.'

'Hospital? Collapsed?'

'It was nothing. I'll tell you when I get home.'

'When will that be?'

'I don't know for sure, but soon. I caught a bit of a cold, so they're keeping an eye on me down here in Ashford hospital.'

'Poor you,' Bess said.

'Oh, it's not so bad. The nurses are pretty and there's the odd familiar face.'

'Familiar face?'

'I should be home in a couple of weeks, sooner if I can hitch a lift.'

'Look, Tom, we're turning the west wing into rooms where the lads and grooms who have returned from Dunkirk can stay while they convalesce. If you can persuade the hospital to let you leave we can look after you up here.'

'I'll see what I can do. Must go, there's a queue of blokes waiting to ring their wives and sweethearts, lucky saps. Give my love to Mam and Dad.'

The line went dead.

'Tom's safe, Mrs Hartley,' Bess said, running into the kitchen. 'Tom's safe,' she said again, dancing round her old friend and nearly knocking her off her feet. 'Mr Porter,' she called as the old man came into the kitchen from the scullery, 'Tom's safe. He's back from Dunkirk.'

As she left the kitchen she saw Laura and Polly. 'Tom's back from Dunkirk. I'm going down to tell Mam and Dad, shan't be long,' she shouted, running down the drive as fast as her legs would carry her.

Bess's mother, who had been emotional since the evacuation of Dunkirk, burst into tears at the news.

Still crying, not with sadness now but with joy, Lily Dudley busied herself by fetching in the washing, laying a winceyette sheet on the kitchen table, and putting the iron on the stove to get hot. Bess's mother's way of celebrating the good news was to do the ironing. Bess left her to it and went back to the Hall.

Bess renovated the ground floor of the west wing with the help of Ena and her friends from the munitions factory. They came after work in the evenings and at the weekends. They refurbished the dining room, adding more tables and chairs, and turned the ballroom into a hospital ward, scrubbing and disinfecting every inch of it. The servicemen would be vulnerable. Bess didn't want them picking up infections while they were at Foxden. They left the library in the main, taking several dozen of the most popular books down to the sitting room and putting them on shelves that had, until then, housed a collection of fine china figurines, which Bess had previously packed and stored in one of the spare bedrooms in her Ladyship's private quarters.

Halfway through the refurbishment Lady Foxden came to see her in the west wing. 'I have a message from James,' she said.

Bess's heart almost leapt from her chest. James hadn't been to Foxden for weeks. She was desperate for news of him.

'He has arranged for a dozen single beds to be delivered. They have a surplus at Bitteswell, so they are lending them to us.'

'That's wonderful,' Bess said. 'Did he mention bedding?'

'No. And I didn't think to ask him.'

'It isn't important until the beds are here, but when you speak to him next will you tell him we'll need at least two sets of bedding for each bed.'

'Will do! Oh, and he asked which day you'd like the beds delivered.'

'Saturday would be best. I'll have half a dozen extra pairs of hands here then.'

'I'll telephone him straight away,' she said.

Bess wanted desperately to know when James was next coming to Foxden. She couldn't ask her Ladyship outright so she said, casually, 'Will James be overseeing the delivery of the beds?'

'No, dear. They're preparing for a big push over Germany. He's on standby. He has to be ready to fly at a minute's notice. That's why he's living on the aerodrome. I'll ring him straight away,' she said as she left.

The delivery of twelve single beds didn't seem so wonderful to Bess now she knew James was about to see action. The Lowarth Advertiser printed the names of local service men and women who were missing or killed in action – and the list grew longer every day. Bess had stopped reading the newspaper and rarely listened to the news on the wireless. It was too upsetting, too worrying.

She was worried, too, about who was going to look after the servicemen. The land girls were too busy. There was no staff left at the Hall, except Mr Porter and Mrs Hartley, who both worked twelve hours a day, and Annie Timpson, who clung to her Ladyship like a limpet and was too frail anyway.

While Bess added the final touches – soft furnishing, rugs and cushions that she had commandeered from the guest rooms in the main house – Laura supervised the cutting of cabbages, swedes and carrots, and Mr Porter oversaw the planting of next season's potatoes, as well as looking after the horses and keeping in touch with the Estate farms. It was a busy time.

'Tom, you're here!' Bess threw her arms round her brother's neck. 'You're here,' she said again, and burst into tears.

Her handsome brother's face was ashen. His uniform hung off him and his eyes were dull with dark circles under them. 'Hey, come on, Sis. Don't cry. Look who I found in Ashford Hospital.'

'Annabel? What are you doing here?' Bess said, trying to hide the disappointment in her voice with surprise.

'Chauffeuring this chap,' she said with a wry smile. 'I couldn't believe my eyes when I saw him skiving in my local hospital. And when he told me he was discharging himself and coming up here to help you with the new wing, I thought I'd better bring him, make sure he got here in one piece. I was coming up for the summer anyway, so I just brought my visit forward. And I've had a fair amount of experience looking after servicemen and women with war injuries in Ashford so if there is anything I can do to help, let me know.'

Bess didn't want Annabel around, but she needed her. 'A couple of days ago I was out of my mind with worry, because I didn't know where I was going to find someone with nursing experience, and now you turn up.'

'Like the proverbial bad penny,' Annabel said, laughing.

Bess bit her lip, smiled, but said nothing. 'Welcome home,' she said to Tom, putting her arm round his waist. 'I've missed you so much.' The three of them walked towards Mrs Hartley, who was standing in the doorway of the kitchen, crying with happiness. Recovering her manners, Bess said, 'Welcome, Annabel. Thank you for bringing my brother home.'

Annabel's room was on the first floor of the west wing, which meant she was on hand if any of the servicemen needed her. It also meant she wasn't far away from James's rooms in his mother's apartment. For the first time since she'd been back at Foxden, Bess was pleased James was living on the aerodrome.

As each serviceman arrived, the doctor from Lowarth was called out to check or prescribe medication. A few patients needed dressings to be changed, which the District Nurse attended to on her weekly rounds. Most of the men were suffering from fatigue, shell shock, or pneumonia. Other than rest they only needed painkillers or sleeping tablets, which Annabel administered.

When servicemen wanted to be on their own, they could stroll through the Park, or go down to the lake where there were only swans and ducks for company. As their health improved, they were encouraged to walk across the fields to Lowarth or to neighbouring villages. And as they grew stronger still, they were given light jobs to do, like feeding the chickens and collecting the eggs. They could work in the walled flower garden, or tend the vegetables in Mrs Hartley's kitchen garden. There was always something for the men to do – when they were ready.

When he was first home, Tom went up to the Hall every morning. He exercised the horses with Mr Porter, groomed and fed them, and then Mrs Hartley would give him breakfast. Tom had known Mrs Hartley since he was a child. He would make her laugh by taking her in his arms and dancing with her, or singing to her, and she loved it – she loved Tom. He spent hours in the west wing with Annabel, lifting patients in and out of bed, helping with their physiotherapy, pushing them round the grounds in their wheelchairs, reading to them or playing cards. And if he wasn't in the west wing he was servicing the Estate's machinery, or Annabel's car. Bess thought he was pushing himself too hard by taking on so much.

'Where's Tom today?' Mr Porter asked Bess at breakfast.

'I thought he was with you.'

'He's probably nursing a hangover,' Laura said. 'Polly and I saw him at the Crown last night with some of the village lads.'

Polly laughed. 'He must have had a few by the time we got there.'

'What makes you say that?' Bess felt her hackles rise. She would defend Tom whatever.

'He didn't seem to know us when we first arrived.'

'That's right, Bess,' Laura said, 'and when we pulled his leg about it he overreacted.'

'What do you mean? Did he get angry?' Bess asked.

'No. He looked as if he was going to, but then he laughed and introduced us to his friends.'

'Even those we already knew,' Polly said.

'Then he bought everyone a drink to welcome us to the Crown. He'd forgotten we'd been there before.'

'I hope he didn't have too much to drink,' Bess said.

Mrs Hartley put her hand on Bess's shoulder. 'No need to worry about Tom,' she said. 'He'd know when he'd had enough.'

Bess did worry about Tom. The last time she saw him he looked pale and tired, and when she asked him if he was all right he shouted at her, saying he was fine, he just hadn't slept. He hadn't shaved for a couple of days either, and he'd let Mr Porter down by not turning up to exercise the horses. The first time Bess rode in his place, but the second time she was busy on the Estate and Mr Porter had to ride Sultan and lead Sable. Tom seemed to have lost interest in the horses, the west wing, even Annabel.

'What's wrong, Tom?' Bess asked when she called to see her mother and found Tom sitting on the ground next to his car with his head in his hands.

'Nothing a pint of Arthur Hanley's best won't put right.' Tom jumped up and brushed himself down. 'Got to go, I'm meeting some of the lads at the Crown. Don't look so worried,' he said, kissing Bess on the cheek. 'I'll see you later.'

Bess didn't see Tom later; she didn't see him until the next day when he came to the Hall wearing the same clothes he'd been out in the night before. His hair was uncombed, his shirt was grubby and his jacket looked as if it had been hung on a hedge instead of a hanger.

'Tom!' Bess shouted, as her brother approached the steps to the west wing.

Tom sauntered over to Bess with his hands in his pockets and a silly grin on his face. 'I can't stop, Sis, I promised to help Annabel with the chaps.'

'You're in no fit state to help anyone,' Bess said. 'Go home! I don't want the lads in the west wing to see you looking like that.' *She didn't want Annabel Hadleigh to see her brother looking like that. She didn't want her telling James or his mother that Tom had turned up so dishevelled--* 'Are you drunk, Tom?'

'Of course I'm not drunk!' he protested. 'I was at home last night by nine. I had a blinding headache and I was sweating. Mam thought I was coming down with the flu, but I was fine after a couple of Aspirin. The trouble was, I dropped off in the armchair and when I got to bed, I couldn't sleep. I'm tired, that's all. So if you don't mind,' he shouted, 'I'm going to see Annabel!'

Bess stepped out of the way. She was shocked by her brother's reaction. He hadn't lost his temper with her since she was a child. At the risk of making him even angrier, she called after him, 'Tom, I really think you should go home and get some rest. Come back tomorrow, or this evening, when you've had a shave and changed your clothes.'

Tom stopped and swung round. He looked downcast, not angry. 'All right, you win,' he said, but as he turned to leave Annabel came out of the Hall. 'Annabel ….'

Annabel ran down the steps. 'Tom, what's the matter? You look terrible.'

'He's got the flu,' Bess said.

Tom took a step towards Annabel, tripped, and she caught him.

'Come on,' she said. 'I'll take you--'

'Thank you, Annabel,' Bess interrupted, 'but I'll look after my brother.' Annabel was eager to help and hardworking, but she had a tendency to take over. 'I'm sure you have enough to do looking after the men in the west wing.' Bess shot Annabel a sideways look and took Tom firmly by the arm. 'Come on,' she said. 'I'm taking you home.'

Halfway down the drive, Tom said, 'She's a cracker, isn't she?'

'If you say so, but she's James Foxden's cracker, so stay away from her, Tom.'

'Lucky old James.'

Tom argued he was sober, but Bess could tell he wasn't. As they approached the front door of their parents' cottage, their father opened it. 'Put him to bed, Dad,' Bess said, shaking her head.

Her father nodded and put his arm round Tom's shoulder. 'Come on, son. Let's get you upstairs so you can sleep it off.'

CHAPTER SEVENTEEN

'There's a telephone call for you, Bess,' Mr Porter shouted. 'He won't give his name. Just said it was important.'

'Thank you.' Bess took the receiver. 'Hello, this is Bess Dudley.'

'Bess, it's Arthur Hanley, at the Crown here. Would you come and fetch Tommy? He's in a bad way.'

'Does he need a doctor, Mr Hanley?'

'Not that sort of bad way, Bess. He's had a few drinks and he's a bit shaky.' Arthur Hanley paused. 'He's been saying he killed his best mate in Dunkirk, and I'm worried he might harm himself if he's left on his own.'

'I'll be with you in ten minutes. Hang onto him until I get there, will you?'

Within a couple of minutes of Bess telling Mr Porter about the telephone call, they were speeding down the drive to Woodcote in the farm pick-up truck. The Crown was empty except for the landlord, Arthur Hanley, behind the bar and his wife, Annie, who was sitting next to Tom on the opposite side of the room.

Bess stood at the door and acknowledged Mr Hanley with a smile before speaking to her brother. 'Hello, Tom. I've come to take you home. Mr Porter is going to drive us. Are you ready?'

Frowning at Mr Porter, Tom stood up. 'What's he doing here?'

Mr Porter started towards his young friend, but Bess put her hand on his shoulder and he stopped.

'He knows!' Tom cried. His eyes, penetrating and intense, looked from Ernest Porter to Bess and back again. 'He knows,' he cried again. 'He's always in my dreams. "Go on, lad," he says, "Get out of here" And I did!' Tom began to sob. 'I did. And I left him there to die. I killed the man that made it possible for me to escape. I'm sorry.' He rubbed his eyes. 'I'm so sorry.'

Walking over to Tom, Arthur Hanley said, 'Let Bess take you home, there's a good lad.'

Tom nodded. 'I'm sorry, Arthur.'

Arthur Hanley put his arm around Tom's shoulder. 'No need to be sorry, lad. We can't imagine what you went through over there.'

'Thank you, Arthur. And thank you, Mrs Hanley, Annie. Thank you,' he said again, allowing Arthur to guide him across the room.

Bess put her arms around her brother. It broke her heart to see Tom drunk and confused. He let her hold him for some time and then he pulled away and said, 'Will you take me home, Sis?'

Bess made a pot of very strong coffee and poured two cups, adding milk to hers. 'Drink your coffee, Tom.' Tom tried, but was violently sick. 'You've poisoned your system with too much alcohol. Here, drink some water instead.' Tom took several sips of water and was sick again. She encouraged him to drink the black coffee and the water alternately until he stopped being sick and stopped blaming himself for the death of his friend.

As the alcohol began to leave his system, he began to shiver. His legs twitched, as if they were trying to keep up with a fast beat. Bess put the back of her hand on his forehead. It felt hot and sticky, but his hands were cold, so she fetched a blanket. Folding it double, she put it over his legs and wrapped her arms around him. 'How are you feeling now?' she asked when he eventually stopped shivering.

'I don't feel as sick anymore, or cold, I just feel tired. I expect it's because I haven't slept properly since I got back. Every time I close my eyes, I see the pier at Dunkirk going up in flames. I look for my mate Jock but I can't see him. I can only see bits of dead soldiers: arms and legs floating in the sea. I call for Jock over and over, but he can't hear me above the screaming.' Tom lowered his head and shook it gently. 'I don't help them, I just scream louder to drown out their screams. I have the same nightmare night after night... I think I'm going mad.'

Bess held him tight. 'You're not going mad, Tom. You've experienced something that is so terrible, so horrific, that you can't cope with it. And unfortunately you're reliving it in your sleep.' Bess paused, and when Tom didn't reply she said, 'Have you talked to anyone about Dunkirk? What you went through when you escaped?'

251

Tom shook his head. 'No.'

'Perhaps it would help if you did,' she said. 'What do you think?'

It was three in the morning, but Bess was past being tired. She had decided to stay with Tom all night if necessary. He needed to talk about what had happened in Dunkirk. Exorcise the ghosts, or he'd never be able to get on with his life. There was no guarantee he'd ever get over it, but Bess was determined to do everything in her power to help him try.

'We got the order to retreat on June 1st,' Tom said suddenly. 'We'd only been in France a few months.' He shook his head. 'It was so bloody unfair.'

'What was unfair?'

'Leaving us behind when the rest of the division retreated. I was put in charge of the men. Jock, a big redheaded Scotsman. His real name was Angus McPherson. Jock was my mate. George Higgins, the youngest of the group who we called Geordie, because he came from Newcastle, and Archie Middleton, a Cockney barrow boy.' Tom smiled briefly. 'Archie used to say he could steal your umbrella at one end of Borough Market and sell it back to you at the other.' He took a shuddering breath and carried on. 'Our job was to clear the campsite. Destroy all evidence that the British Expeditionary Forces had been there.

'We spread out and slowly walked to the camp's perimeter, scanning the ground for anything that looked out of place in the woods. Then we turned around and did it again, and again, until we were sure that every piece of paper, cigarette end, or nail clipping had been picked up. Jock and I scored the undergrowth and roughed up the grass with a couple of old forks we'd found in a deserted barn a few miles down the road. Geordie filled in the latrines and Archie ripped the paperwork up – including letters from home. If the Division was captured on the way to Dunkirk they wouldn't have anything on them that'd tell the Germans who they were or where they'd come from.

'Jock and I found a place to bury what was left of the camp that couldn't be seen from the road, where the weeds and brambles were dense and the ground was so wet that any roots we disturbed would take hold again quickly. Jock took off his jacket and shirt and began to dig. He was a big bloke, and strong. He threw the spade at the ground, using his weight to force it into the earth until he heard the roots of the weeds and brambles snap. Then he lifted the spade and did the same again, and again, until he had loosened several square feet of earth and vegetation. He was sweating. It was only half past seven in the morning, but it was already hot.

'I lifted the patches of sodden earth, making sure the roots stayed attached, and laid them to one side. Then I left Jock to dig a hole and went to find Archie. He was sitting on the ground bawling his eyes out. He said some fella's mother had written to him saying his wife had been killed in a bombing raid.

'I didn't know what to say. We'd been ordered not to read anything, but I couldn't tick him off, he was upset enough. "Come on, mate," I said, and slung a sack over my shoulder.

'"We should have burned it, it's not right it rotting, not the letters anyway," he said.

'"The smoke would alert Gerry. Come on, pick your sack up and let's get it to Jock."

'It was like being at a funeral. We upended the sacks into the hole, Jock shovelled soil on top until the hole was full, and I replaced the squares of earth, making sure they fitted as neatly as possible. Then we scattered weeds and nettles on top. One good downpour and any unattached roots would start to grow – and what was beneath them would disintegrate, destroying all evidence that the 48th had been in France.

'We took the spade and forks back to the derelict barn and put them back where we'd found them. We had a wash in a nearby river, and set off to walk the hundred or so kilometres to Dunkirk. We stuck to the fields and woods during the day to avoid any rogue gangs of German soldiers. They stalked the main routes to Dunkirk, and used British soldiers as target practice. We did our serious walking at night under cover of darkness.'

'How long did it take to get to Dunkirk?' Bess asked.

'Three days. We arrived on the fourth exhausted and dehydrated.' Tom took a sip of water and carried on. 'In no way were we prepared for what was to come. From the top of the cliff overlooking the beach we saw thousands of British soldiers. Some were crawling along the burning sand. Others were dragging injured comrades up the beach to the dunes to get out of the sun. And some were so badly injured they just lay where they'd fallen, surrounded by dead comrades.' Tom stopped and caught his breath.

'Do you want to take a break?' Bess asked.

'No, I'm all right.' He took another drink of water before carrying on. 'I knew if we were going to be rescued we needed to be on the beach, and to get there we'd have to go down the cliff. "It's the only way," I said. "And we'll have to move quickly, we'll stand out like beacons against the white cliff face. If the German planes turn up before we reach the bottom of the cliff, we'll be done for." I looked at the beach below and then back at Jock. "If we're going, we'll have to go now."

'Jock put his arms around Archie and Geordie. "'Are we ready, lads?"

'They both nodded. I expect they were too scared to speak.'

'Had any of you had experience of rock climbing?' Bess asked.

'Yes. Jock had climbed before. He led the descent, sandwiching himself between the two younger lads.' Tom gave a laugh. 'Archie and

Geordie were only a year younger than me and Jock, but that was what Jock was like. Always putting the needs of the other lads first.' Tom paused, as if to remember precisely what happened next. 'There were a lot of jagged rocks sticking out of the cliff, which made it easy to get a foothold but damn near impossible to grip with bare hands. Halfway down the cliff there was a narrow ledge. It was the last open place where we'd be vulnerable before the final drop. One by one we leapt onto the ledge and inched our way along the narrow crevice on our bellies, like lizards.' Tom put his head in his hands. 'I'm sorry, Bess.'

'Are you sure you don't want to stop and take a break, Tom?'

'No. It's okay.' Tom took a drink of water and cleared his throat. 'When we heard the drone of planes approaching, Archie and I counted to three and leapt from the cliff. We stayed where we landed. Me on my back and Archie sprawled across me, face down. Jock and Geordie were still on the ledge. Jock had pulled Geordie to his feet and was saying something. I couldn't hear what it was, but Geordie looked down at the beach and shook his head. I'll never forget the look of terror on that boy's face. "Jump, Jock!" I shouted. "Bring the boy with you. Time's running out. Jump or you'll die up there."

'Jock didn't hear me – how could he? But he must have heard the planes, because I saw him look up. Geordie looked up too, but he was still shaking his head. Next thing, Jock punched him on the chin and when the lad lost his balance Jock put his arms around him and leapt. They landed at the bottom of the cliff as the yellow noses of two Messerschmitts came over the top and began firing into the ledge we'd been on minutes earlier. Bullets ricocheted off the cliff and landed all around us, sending clouds of sand swirling into the air. I couldn't see properly. My face was burnt and my mouth was so full of sand I thought I'd choke. I tried breathing through my nose, but it was no good, I still inhaled sand. We lay on that scorching sand for what seemed like hours. Finally, when the shooting had stopped and the planes were gone, we crawled across the beach to Dunkirk's harbour and the pier.'

'Thank goodness you managed to get out of the sun and firing line,' Bess said.

'Oh we were out of the sun, all right. It was dark and dank, and we were up to our waists in oil and sewage. But you're right, for the first time in ages we were safe from German bullets. Anyway, Jock spotted some old boats tied together at the far end of the pier. So we waded through a mass of seaweed and God only knows what else was in the water, which we didn't want to think about.

'Jock pressed down on each boat and we watched water seep into every one of them – except the last. The floor of the small vessel at the end of the row stayed dry, so we untied it and dragged it to the edge of the pier into the light. I tried to start the engine, but it just

257

croaked. None of us had any experience with boats, but you know what I'm like with cars. I didn't think it could be that different, so I began to strip the engine. It was damp, but not from sea water, which is corrosive. Someone must have tried to start it earlier and flooded the engine. It only needed drying out.

'The first couple of attempts to start the boat failed, so we left it for half an hour – we didn't want to flood the engine again. On the third attempt, which had to be our last because the sun had begun to set, the boat spluttered into life. Now all we had to do was keep the motor running and when the sun went down, but before the Germans began their night bombing, make our escape.

'I jumped into the boat and Archie followed. But when Geordie tried to board, his legs gave way and he sank to his knees. Jock pulled him to his feet. "We're going home, lad," he said, but Geordie couldn't stand. He had a gash in his side. He'd landed on a jagged piece of rock when he jumped off the cliff. So Jock lifted him up like a baby and put him into the boat beside Archie. Then he took off his coat. "Put this over him, keep him warm, he's lost a lot of blood," he said.

'Suddenly, two soldiers appeared out of nowhere carrying an unconscious friend. "He caught one in the back," the first one explained. "We've got to get him out, he won't survive another night," the other one said.

'Jock took the injured soldier from his friends and lowered him into the boat next to Geordie. His face was grey. One of the other soldiers tried to climb aboard. "Your friend's the last passenger," Jock shouted. "The boat's full. Stand clear." The soldier hung onto the boat and it tipped to the left. "It'll capsize, son," Jock said gruffly. He prised the crying soldier's hands from the side of the small craft and it levelled. He kept his arm round the boy to comfort him as well as restrain him. "Go on, Tom, get out of here, or it'll be too late," Jock shouted.

'"I'm not leaving without you," I shouted back to him.

'"Oh yes you are, my friend," Jock said, and he pushed the boat from under the pier. "If you don't want Gerry to see you you'd better get a move on."

Tom cuffed tears from his eyes. 'The last thing Jock said to me was, "I'll see you on my way to the Highlands," and I shouted, "I'll be waiting." Then I opened the throttle and the engine roared – and so did I. I roared with anger and frustration and the injustice of war. But most of all I roared to block out the cries for help from the dozens of soldiers who were swimming against the tide. The current was too strong. It was dragging them – some alive and some dead – back to the beach. There was nothing I could do but swerve to miss them. I retched at the sight. But I didn't stop. I kept going, and I kept roaring.

'I steered the boat round the harbour wall and had to swerve again, this time to avoid a fleet of small boats. I couldn't believe my eyes. There were hundreds of fishing boats and sailing boats. Some that didn't look seaworthy enough to cross the Channel, let alone sail full pelt into a battle zone, were heading for Dunkirk's beaches. "Jock and the others will be rescued," I shouted to Archie and Geordie, and we cheered.'

Tom lowered his head and began to cry.

'Tom, do you want to stop?' Bess asked, but he didn't reply. 'I'll make a pot of tea. See how you feel after you've had a hot drink,' she said, and went to the kitchen. What a pathetic thing to say, she thought, as she filled the kettle. Tom looked so tired. She wanted to give him some time on his own, to decide whether he wanted to carry on talking, or go to bed.

While the kettle boiled, Bess went to the bathroom. She was tired too. She splashed cold water on her face and felt refreshed. When she went back to the kitchen to make the tea, it was four o'clock.

Bess returned to the living room with two cups of tea and a plate of Rich Tea biscuits on a tray. 'I've put a couple of sugars in yours. I found Mam's secret stash,' she joked, handing Tom his tea. 'Drink it while it's hot. I found a few biscuits too. I don't know about you but I'm peckish. Want one?'

Tom shook his head but took his tea. For a while he drank in silence. 'One plane!' he said

260

at last. 'A Stuka dive bomber came out of the clouds. I didn't see it and I didn't hear it. I didn't hear anything until the explosion. I looked back and the pier was in flames. The boats under it were going up, one after another, and the sea was on fire. I wanted to turn the boat around and go back for Jock, but I didn't. I knew if I took the boat back, I'd be taking Archie, Geordie, and the other soldier to their deaths. I was full of anger and fear, and riddled with guilt, because I was alive and my best friend wasn't, but I held the throttle open and drove that speedboat as fast as I could until we were over the horizon.

'The next morning I woke up on the deck of HMS Manxman. My clothes were soaked, I was shivering with cold, and the stench of Dunkirk's sewers was still in my nostrils. But I was looking at the White Cliffs of Dover!

'Archie and I carried Geordie from the ship to a Red Cross tent on the quay at Dover. There was a young nurse sitting in the entrance taking the names and rank of the servicemen who needed medical attention. She took one look at Geordie and shouted for help. A couple of tired-looking hospital auxiliaries came dashing out, lifted Geordie onto a stretcher and disappeared inside.'

'Do you know what happened to the injured soldier that Jock gave his place to, in the boat?' Bess asked.

'He didn't make it. He died on the Manxman.' Tom rubbed his eyes and sighed. 'Such a bloody waste. Jock would have been

261

home in the Highlands by now. Anyway,' he said, after a few moments, 'a doctor came out and said Geordie needed to go to hospital. He said there was nothing either of us could do and told us to go to the camp and get some rest.

'Archie said he was going to stick around for a bit, go with Geordie if they'd let him. He said I'd done enough getting them out of Dunkirk, so we shook hands and swore we'd never forget Jock. I didn't want to leave them, but I'd started to shiver badly and thought I'd better get out of my wet uniform. So I left Archie on the quayside, joined the rest of the soldiers that had disembarked from the Manxman and marched through Dover to the Army barracks.'

'Was it far?'

'I don't know. I recall women standing outside their houses, clapping and cheering and offering us food and drink as we marched past, but I couldn't see properly. Everything was blurred. My eyes were smarting and I remember thinking I must have salt in them, but it was sweat. My teeth ached. I was so cold I couldn't stop them chattering. A girl offered me tea from a big metal urn. She said it would warm me up, but I was shivering so much, I couldn't hold the cup. Then, I don't know why, I remembered the two shillings you'd sent me at Christmas, wrapped in your letter. I should have destroyed it, but I'd forgotten it was in my breast pocket. Anyway, I asked her if she'd send a telegram to let

Mam know I was alive, and I gave her the two shillings and your letter. And that was the last thing I remember until I woke up in Ashford hospital a few days later with pneumonia.'

CHAPTER EIGHTEEN

Bess jumped down from the tractor to join Laura, who was sitting astride a five-bar gate that separated Larks Meadow from a field of carrots, as Annabel and James arrived on horseback. 'Hello Annabel. James!' Bess said, startled by the handsome vision towering above her on Sultan.

'Annabel's been showing me around the west wing. You've done a great job, Bess. It's so comfortable the lads won't want to leave.'

Bess, overwhelmed at seeing James, blushed. 'It's a shame the sheep don't feel the same way about their quarters,' she said, nodding towards a field of carrots. 'They'll have chomped their way through the entire crop by teatime.'

'Can we help you to catch them while we're here?' James asked.

'Thank you, but no. Polly's gone to get--' Before Bess had time to say his name, Garth Davies and his collie arrived and, after a short exchange, Garth ordered his dog into the field. Within minutes the dog, barking in short sharp bursts, had driven the sheep back to the adjoining field. The hole in the fence was now even bigger.

'Well, if there's nothing we can do,' James said, 'we'll--'

'You could repair the fence,' Laura said, 'while we try to salvage the carrots. I've put the new section and a ball of twine next to the hole - you can't miss it.

'Leave it to us,' James said, and left at a trot with Annabel close behind.

Bess watched James as he showed Annabel how to secure the new piece of fence to the damaged fence by twisting the edges of new round the old, before securing it by weaving the twine in and out of both old and new. They looked happy together. They were working hard, but they were having fun. It was obvious that Annabel loved James. Bess could see it in her eyes when she looked at him. She could tell that James was fond of Annabel too. No wonder Lady Foxden saw Annabel as a potential daughter-in-law. I would, Bess thought, if I was her.

Walking back to the gate after checking several rows of carrot tops, Laura shouted, 'Not a lot of damage done. A drop of rain, a bit of sun-- Are you all right, Bess?'

'What? Oh, yes, I'm fine. I'm a bit tired, that's all. There's nothing more we can do here. Let's get the tractor back and call it a day,' she said, straightening the grain sacks on the seat before climbing onto it. 'Well done, you two,' she called over to James and Annabel. 'It'll take a bull to get through that fence now.'

'That's praise indeed coming from you, Bess,' James said, laughing.

'I'm serious. Thank you,' she said, starting the tractor.

'If you really want to thank us, you can come for a drink to the Crown tonight. You too, Laura. Because it's Tom's last night of freedom we thought we'd make a night of it. Give him a good send off,' James said.

'What a good idea,' Annabel said. 'Do say you'll both come. James is meeting Tom at seven. I'll be bored by eight, when they start talking about cars and aeroplanes and this wretched war.'

'I'd love to. Thanks,' Laura said. 'You'll come too, won't you, Bess? Bess--?'

'What? Yes, of course. See you both at seven.'

'Are you sure you're all right?' Laura asked, as they drove back to the Hall.

'Yes, I'm fine. I'm just worried that Tom's going back to his regiment too soon after-- I hope he's ready.'

Of the two public houses in the village of Woodcote, The Crown and The Black Horse, the Dudley family favoured the Crown because it was the nearest to walk to and, more importantly, to walk home from. It also had a piano that the landlady, Mrs Hanley, could be persuaded to play on Saturday nights.

By the time Bess and Laura arrived the pub was packed. There was a dance at the village hall and because the hall didn't have a licence to sell alcohol everyone piled into one or other of the pubs at the interval. Bess and Laura spotted James, Annabel and Tom sitting under the window on the far side of the room near the piano. They pushed their way through the crowd to join them.

'Come on, Tom! Give us a song,' someone shouted across the smoky saloon bar.

Everyone cheered and chanted. 'Give us a song, Tom! Give us a song!' Tom had no choice but to ask the pub landlady if she'd play the piano for him.

'Not tonight, Tommy. I'm too busy.'

'Sorry, lads, I haven't got a pianist. Can't sing without a pianist, can I?'

'I'll play for you, Tom,' Annabel said. 'What do you want me to play?'

'Oh, something slow to start with, to get me warmed up. Do you know "I'll Be Seeing You"?'

Annabel laughed. 'I know it, I'm not sure I can play it. Don't worry, if I lose my way I'll busk.'

As Tom began to sing, the customers in the pub stopped talking until there was silence. When the song came to an end, everyone cheered and called for more. James bought a round of drinks, which he managed to carry across the room on a tray without spilling, and Laura joined Tom and Annabel at the piano and sang, "There'll Always Be An England". Suddenly, Bess and James were sitting at the table on their own.

'They make a lovely couple,' Bess said.

'Who, Tom and Annabel?'

'No, Tom and Laura.' Bess was smiling as she watched her brother and her friend sing "Wish Me Luck As You Wave Me Goodbye", and clapped loudly when they'd finished.

James put his arm along the back of Bess's seat and spoke softly into her ear. 'Are you matchmaking, Bess Dudley?'

'No! Well maybe a little,' she said, laughing. 'I like Laura. I think she'd be good for Tom.'

'And who would be good for Bess?' James asked.

Bess felt her pulse fasten and her cheeks flush. She wanted to say, you James, you! Instead, in a flash of comic inspiration, she said, 'Mr Porter!'

James laughed. 'Mr Porter?'

'Why not? He's good with horses, works hard and doesn't get under my feet. In my book that's a perfect man. Ah, Laura's coming back,' she said, applauding Laura when she returned to her seat.

At closing time Tom sang "Roses of Picardy" unaccompanied and dedicated it to his lovely pianist, Annabel.

A hush spread through the saloon bar as Tom sang words as relevant in 1940 as they had been when they were written in 1916, during the First World War. The landlord put the bar towels over the beer pumps instead of calling time, and when they'd finished drinking, the customers left silently.

The following morning, before Bess had time to talk to Tom, Annabel arrived and

268

insisted on taking him to the station, saying it was the least she could do after Tom had done such a marvellous job of servicing her car.

'Take care, Tom,' Bess told him. 'It hasn't been long since-- You are sure you're feeling well enough to go back, aren't you? They'd understand if--'

'Don't worry, Sis. I'm as right as rain now. Thanks to you,' he said, holding her tightly for a long minute before kissing her goodbye.

Bess and Laura were ploughing an outlying field by the time Annabel returned from Rugby station. Already dressed in jodhpurs and rainproof riding jacket, she tied Sultan to the gate, climbed over it, and ran across the field. 'James has returned to the aerodrome, Tom is on his way to Kent. I've checked on the servicemen and no one needs me. So put me to work, Bess!'

'I would if you could plough a straight furrow,' Bess said.

'I could learn. I'll tell you what. You teach me how to plough a furrow, and I'll teach you how to drive a car.'

'Go on,' Laura said. 'Sounds like a good deal.'

Bess laughed. 'What would Tom say if I picked him up from the station the next time he comes home on leave?' Bess had wanted to learn how to drive since the day Tom chased her into the kitchen with greasy hands.

Of the land girls there was only Laura who could drive, and for some reason Mr Porter was reluctant to lend her his truck. The more she thought about it the more she liked the idea. 'All right,' Bess said, jumping down from the seat of the tractor onto the mudguard. 'Sit up here. I'll teach you how to plough.'

Annabel didn't find driving the new Fordson difficult. She had accompanied Laura on several occasions and driven the tractor once or twice when they'd been delivering animal feed to the Estate farms. But she had never attempted to plough a furrow, let alone a straight one. 'It's damn near impossible!' she shouted.

Driving a car also had its tricky moments. During Bess's first lesson, the following day, her foot slipped off the clutch while she was practising a three-point turn. Annabel and Bess laughed until they ached when the car kangarooed into a drainage ditch that was so overgrown with weeds that it was impossible to see where the grass verge ended and the ditch began. Luckily the channel was shallow so there was no damage done – except to Bess's pride when she had to walk all the way back to the Hall and ask Mr Porter to get the tractor and rescue the car.

Annabel learned to plough a straight furrow, but her main work was with the servicemen in the west wing. She wasn't fazed by gory dressings and didn't flinch at the sight of an infected wound or amputated limb, which was something neither Bess nor Laura could have coped with. Bess noticed that Annabel was patient, and she listened. But she didn't pity the injured servicemen, and she didn't patronise them.

Getting to know Annabel had helped Bess to turn the love she felt for James into friendship. After her shameful experience in London, a relationship with James would be short lived, or it would mean a lifetime of lies. She was damaged, and there was nothing she could do to change that. If she told James the truth, she would risk losing him. If she didn't tell him, and he found out, he would think she'd tricked him and he would hate her for it. Either way, James would be out of her life forever, and she couldn't bear that; she loved him too much. This way they would always be friends. She wouldn't have to lie to him and she wouldn't have to betray Annabel.

July had been one of the hottest and driest months since records began and according to the BBC's long-range weather forecast September was going to be one of the wettest.

The harvest had dominated the lives of Woodcote's men, women and children for as long as anyone could remember and this year was no different, except for the added workload involved in harvesting Foxden Acres. Instead of meadows and pastures there were fields of corn, wheat and oats, forage maize and cow cabbage.

Kitty and Fanny started work at High Fields Farm at five o'clock in the morning. After milking the cows they took the churns to Lowarth dairy. By the time they returned the herd was grazing in a nearby field and Ethan Baylis had washed down the stalls. During the harvest, Ethan paid a couple of local lads to help him in the evenings, so Kitty and Fanny could work on Foxden's harvest.

Iris and Mavis spent most of the summer months working at Foxden, because Charity Farm's busiest times were the lambing season in February and the shearing in April. In July, Garth Davies's sons, fourteen year old John and David, who was twelve – naturals at all things agricultural – broke up from school and took over Iris and Mavis's chores.

Mr Porter bought a combine harvester for the Estate. The other farmers preferred the traditional binder. Foxden's arable land was considerably bigger than the farms, so both methods were used. High Fields dairy farm laid claim to the first ten acres of Foxden's harvest, and the remainder was split between a hayrick and winter fodder stored in the Estate's barns.

The land girls worked from dawn until dusk. The sun burned and blistered whatever parts of their bodies were exposed. Their arms, legs and backs ached from wielding pitchforks and hay rakes. They were bitten and stung, and they itched and scratched until they were sore. Haymaking was hot, dirty work, and the nightly ritual of picking hayseeds out of their hair and clothes became very tedious. Then one night the dusty, itchy lives of Foxden's Land Army changed forever.

Returning to the Hall exhausted after a day's haymaking, Bess and the land girls found Mr Porter in the rick-yard hammering nails into large pieces of wood.

'I've made a screen around the water pump. Thought you might like to wash the worst of the day's dust off before you go indoors,' he announced to the small gathering of dirty and bemused young women. 'You can put your feet into these buckets and pump cold water onto them – cool you down a treat,' he beamed.

And it did. As soon as Mr Porter was out of sight the girls stripped to their underwear, filled the buckets with cold water from the well and washed the dust from their arms and legs. Then they sat in a row on the low wall in their undies, put their feet into the buckets and let the evening sun dry their bodies.

'Hey!' Kitty said to Fanny. 'Watch it, you're soaking me.'

'Sorry, I was trying to splash water on my face. I'm so hot!'

'I'll cool you down,' Kitty said. Flicking water at Fanny, she splashed Polly.

Polly retaliated by picking up her bucket and throwing its contents over Kitty, and in the process wet the other girls, who then picked up their buckets and threw water at Polly. Soon the girls were running round laughing and screaming, and emptying their buckets over one another.

Eventually the novelty of splashing each other wore off, but washing off the worst of the day's dirt and relaxing with their feet in buckets of cold water didn't.

By early September, by the time the rain came, the harvest was in and the girls were given a long weekend off.

'I think we should celebrate,' Bess said to Mr Porter at breakfast. 'Let's have a party. Everyone has worked so hard and it wouldn't cost much. We could have a barn dance, like they used to do in the old days. What do you think, Mr Porter?'

'I think it's a wonderful idea,' Mrs Hartley called from the scullery.

'Now there's a surprise,' Mr Porter muttered. 'It'll take a lot of organising. I don't know that I've got the time.'

'Not to worry,' Bess said. 'If you can't do it I'm sure with the help of a couple of the girls Mrs Hartley and I can sort something out.'

Mrs Hartley came back into the kitchen, nodding. 'Yes, between us--'

'All right, you two, steady up. I didn't say I couldn't do it. It'll just take a bit of arranging, that's all.' He looked up at them with a twinkle in his eye. 'If we must have a shindig, it might as well be done properly.'

The party started at three o'clock on Saturday afternoon. The farmers and their wives brought the bulk of the food, with a substantial contribution from Mrs Hartley's larder. Everyone who had worked on the harvest was there – farm workers, land girls, villagers and their children. In the evening Arthur Hanley brought a barrel of beer and several flagons of cider. 'With his Lordship's compliments,' he announced to assorted hoots and cheers.

The women sat and gossiped, the children played and squabbled, and the men drank their fill of ale. But for Bess the party began when Tom arrived.

'What are you doing here? I thought you didn't have any leave left,' Bess said, hugging her brother.

I haven't! I've brought a Major General up to Laughton Manor in Northampton. There's a big powwow going on and dozens of the top brass are there. I've never seen so many medals in one place. Anyway, the MG said he didn't mind if I came home for a couple of hours, so long as I was back to pick him up at seven sharp. So here I am!' Tom looked around. 'I think I'll go and say hello to the lads in the west wing. Won't be long.'

One of the older men took a harmonica from his pocket, another produced a squeezebox and someone took a fiddle from its case. While the Barn Dance Trio blew, squeezed and fiddled old country songs, as well as a few modern tunes, the partygoers sang and danced.

Bess had just slipped out of the barn to check the horses as it started to rain. She stopped halfway across the yard, looked up and closed her eyes. She could feel the fine rain on her face and smell the warm scent of newly mown hay – and she was satisfied that the harvest was a job well done. Bess still had a long way to go, but she was happy with what she'd achieved since she'd been back at Foxden. And she was more content and at ease with herself than she had been for a long time. Any doubts she had on the night James visited her in London, when he'd asked her to come back and turn the Estate into arable land, had gone.

There was still a great deal of work to do before winter, but Bess was determined to go to London for Molly's baby's christening and while she was there, visit her friends Natalie and Anton Goldman. But first she had a barn dance to go to.

CHAPTER NINETEEN

Bess stared at her old lodgings, too numb to move. She felt sure her legs would give way at any second. 'Molly! Elizabeth!' she cried, tears stinging her eyes.

'Edna?' An elderly man grabbed Bess's arm. 'Where have you been?' he asked affectionately, shaking his head as if she was a mischievous child. 'We've been worried.'

'I'm sorry,' Bess said, 'I'm not Edna.'

The look of disappointment in the old man's eyes when he realised Bess was not who he was looking for distressed her so much she began to cry. 'I'm so sorry…'

The old man shook his head again, muttered something Bess couldn't hear and shuffled off in his carpet slippers.

She was still watching the old man when a younger man in pyjamas carrying a little girl in a pink nightdress ran past. The little girl dropped her teddy bear and began to cry, 'Daddy, stop!' But her daddy didn't hear her above the noise of wailing sirens and collapsing houses. The little girl twisted her small body until she was able to look over her father's shoulder at her fallen comforter on the ground. She reached out and, like the halfpenny crane game on the end of the pier, her small hands opened and closed in rapid succession. But unlike the jib that picks up the treasure the little girl wasn't near enough to grasp the prize. Tears spilled from the child's eyes but her father didn't stop.

Bess picked up the teddy bear and started after them. She hadn't gone more than a few yards when a young woman, also in nightclothes, stopped her.

'Have you seen two men and a little girl?' The young woman began to choke from the smoke and brick dust. 'One man was older, the other-- That's my little girl's teddy,' she said.

Bess gave the woman the teddy bear and pointed to the opposite side of the road. 'The older man was looking for someone called Edna.'

'Edna was my mother-in-law. We were on our way to the shelter. We crossed the road, father-in-law and me, my husband and our little girl, but Edna went back to get dad's spectacles. She was only in the house a minute. She came out of the front door with the glasses in her hand. She was smiling when the bomb... Dad won't accept she's gone. He keeps saying she's got herself lost and she's waiting for him to find her.'

The woman thanked Bess for the teddy bear and ran off to look for her family. Bess wanted to help her but she had her own loved ones to find.

Two ARP men were cordoning off the area around what remained of numbers seventy-seven and seventy-nine Arcadia Avenue. They were directing people across the road to the church hall, where the women of the Women's Voluntary Service were giving out blankets and cups of tea.

'Move along, Miss,' a tired looking, smoke-stained ARP man shouted at Bess. 'There's an unexploded bomb,' he said, pointing to a huge hole in Mrs McAllister's next door neighbour's front garden.

'You are sure there's no one trapped inside number seventy-nine, aren't you?' Bess asked.

'Positive! Now will you *please* move along!'

'The old gentleman who lived in that house spent his life tending his garden,' Bess said, as much to herself as to the ARP man. 'No matter the season, it was always a profusion of colour.' The ARP man ignored her. He was too busy.

'And this house has been so badly hit it'll collapse any minute, I shouldn't wonder,' the other ARP man said.

A gaping hole, as wide as the front room, went from the hall at the foot of the stairs to the ceiling of the bathroom. Bess was watching rivulets of plaster-dust, like sand in an egg timer, trickle through the floorboards of the upstairs landing when, along with its neighbour, her old lodgings groaned and lurched to the left. Then the stairs she had walked up so many times collapsed, one on top of the other, until there were no stairs left.

When the dust had settled Mrs McAllister's house was no longer a mirror image of its neighbour. The roof was lopsided. It looked like a large black beret that had been put on at an angle. Bedroom ceilings, bowing under the weight, had started to bear down on the outside walls. Suddenly there was a loud splintering sound followed by a terrific crack – and the front bedroom window, along with a panel of plaster, plunged into the front garden. Tears filled Bess's eyes as she looked into Miss Armstrong's bedroom. Miss Armstrong was a private person. It wasn't right that her personal belongings were exposed for everyone to see. Bess turned and walked away.

She needed to get rid of her suitcase. It was heavy. She joined a queue of people going into the church hall. Inside she asked a WVS lady who was serving tea if she would keep an eye on her case while she looked for her friends. The woman put the suitcase under the table and said she would do her best, but warned there were opportunist thieves about, so she couldn't guarantee the case would be there when Bess returned. Bess said she'd risk it. After searching the hall for her friends – and not finding them – she left.

Outside the noise of exploding bombs and collapsing houses was deafening – and the dust and smoke created by the debris made it difficult to see. Bess cupped her hands over her nose and mouth and zigzagged her way through the queue of people going into the hall. 'Can you tell me where the nearest shelter is?' she asked an ARP man who was running towards her.

'Fifty yards along the avenue on the left,' he shouted without stopping. 'Follow me.'

Bess turned and fell into step behind the man. But before she was able to get into her stride an ear-shattering explosion lifted her off her feet and threw her to the ground. From where she landed she could see fire and smoke coming from a gaping hole where the garden of number seventy-seven used to be. The bomb had exploded. Fire took hold of the semi-detached house, spreading quickly to number seventy-nine. Flames licked at the remaining windows, causing them to shatter and shower the road with glass. Bess put her hand up to shield her eyes as the roof of her old lodgings collapsed into the bedrooms. Within seconds the weight had forced the upstairs floors to give way and the upper half of the house crashed into the inferno that was once Mrs McAllister's sitting room. Finally the whole house disappeared into the cellar, taking with it the hornbeam – a sapling when Bess first came to number seventy-nine – the post box that stood on the pavement, and the street light.

Bess stumbled to her feet and rubbed the dust from her eyes to see more clearly the devastation the German bombs had wrought on this quiet suburb of London. There were no factories or military installations in Kensington. There were only people. Ordinary people living in ordinary houses.

People who took pride in their vinegar-clean windows, scrubbed front door steps and neat gardens.

As she neared the Anderson shelter closest to number seventy-nine people were beginning to leave. She searched the face of every dazed and disorientated person as they left the safety of the shelter for the uncertainty of the street, but her friends were not among them. Bess sat on the kerb, exhausted. After a few minutes she decided to go back to the beginning of the avenue and start the search again. She stood up and stretched – and she heard a baby cry.

'Molly...' Bess shouted frantically, 'Miss Armstrong, Mrs McAllister…'

'Bess, we're here!' Molly came running out of the shelter into Bess's arms. 'Have you seen Mrs Mac? She went home to fetch Elizabeth another bottle, but she didn't come back.'

'No, I'm sorry. I haven't seen her. She's probably in one of the other shelters,' Bess said, hugging Molly. 'Miss Armstrong, thank goodness you're safe,' Bess said, holding her hand out to her friend as she came out of the shelter with Molly's baby in her arms. 'I can't tell you how good it is to see you. And this must be Elizabeth?' Bess smiled at her little goddaughter. 'She's beautiful, Molly. Let's get her out of this smoke.'

'We can't leave, Bess. We have to be here when Mrs Mac gets back. If we're not here she'll worry.' Molly began to cry.

'We can't stay here, Molly. Besides, Mrs Mac's probably in the church hall by now, looking for you. Come on, let's go and see, shall we?'

Molly didn't want to leave, but because Miss Armstrong agreed with Bess she gave in on the condition they called at number seventy-nine first, to make sure Mrs Mac hadn't returned there.

Bess tried to persuade Molly not to go to the house, that Mrs Mac wasn't there, but Molly insisted on seeing for herself. When she saw the destruction the bombs had caused, Molly fell to her knees and howled.

Bess knelt down in front of her friend and put her arms around her. 'There's nothing we can do tonight.' She helped Molly to her feet. 'Let's go to the church hall and get some rest and first thing in the morning we'll look for Mrs Mac. She can't have gone far.'

Reluctantly, Molly let Bess lead her across the road to the church hall, where the ladies of the WVS gave them each a blanket and directed them to a row of thin single mattresses before bringing them cups of hot sweet tea. As worn out as she was, Molly wouldn't rest. While Miss Armstrong gave Elizabeth the last of her bottle, Bess collected her suitcase and Molly searched the room. When she was satisfied that Mrs McAllister was not in the hall, she returned to Bess and Miss Armstrong and, with her little daughter in her arms, fell asleep.

The morning sun did nothing to disperse the pungent smell of acrid smoke, even though the fires had been extinguished for several hours. The Auxiliary Fire Service had left the area, leaving the ARP men to clear paths through the rubble and tape off the areas that remained dangerous. The man who had moved Bess on the night before – and probably saved her life – looked exhausted as he roped off a house further along the avenue. He smiled wearily as Bess approached.

'We're looking for our friend,' Bess said. 'She lived at number seventy-nine. She came back to the house last night during the bombing raid, but didn't return to the shelter. Have you seen her? She's my height, in her late fifties with light brown hair and she has a Scottish accent.'

'She was wearing a navy blue hat and coat,' Miss Armstrong added.

'There was so much going on last night we didn't get that far down the avenue until after the house was hit. Sorry ladies, I didn't see anyone of that description when I arrived, or afterwards,' the ARP man said.

'Is there another shelter she could have gone to, in the other direction perhaps?'

'There's only the church hall, miss.'

'We've just come from there.'

'The only thing I can suggest is that you give the WVS a description of your friend and they'll circulate it to the other voluntary services.'

'We've done that too, but thank you,' Bess said.

The three women walked along Arcadia Avenue and turned left into Kensington High Street without looking back. Elizabeth was hungry and cried continuously and Bess's arms felt as if they were going to drop off with the weight of her suitcase.

Bess suggested they stopped for something to eat. 'I've got plenty of coupons, so if we can find somewhere to have breakfast--'

'Keep your coupons, Bess, and cross the road,' Miss Armstrong said. 'We'll go to the restaurant in Denton and Christie. The manager owes me a favour.'

Half a dozen shop assistants with smart haircuts, dressed in black skirts and crisp white blouses, stood open-mouthed when Miss Armstrong, in her most authoritative voice, requested that the senior sales person escort her to the office of Mr Markham, the department store's manager.

Bess had never seen Miss Armstrong act in such an assertive way and realised that she too had her mouth open. By the time the shop assistants had finished discussing the forceful lady with the smoke-stained face and dirty clothes, Miss Armstrong had returned, looking rather pleased with herself.

'This is Miss Simpson. The person Mr Markham replaced me with when I was… made redundant,' Miss Armstrong said. 'And it is Miss Simpson who is going to show us where we can have a wash and smarten ourselves up.'

In the staff cloakroom there was scented soap, soft towels and fine talcum powder. Bess couldn't remember the last time she'd used talc but it was before rationing, and she sprinkled it on liberally. Molly and Miss Armstrong were taken to the ladies' fashion department and invited to take whatever they needed. Bess declined the offer, because she had a suitcase full of clothes that only needed ironing.

'Oh, Bess,' Molly called, running from the Mother and Child department, followed by several young shop assistants loaded down with Carnation milk, bottles and bibs, nappies, vests, bonnets, booties, and dresses. 'Look what they've given me for Elizabeth. I told them I couldn't pay for it, that we'd lost our ration books and clothes coupons when the house was bombed, but--'

Miss Simpson was suddenly at Molly's side. 'Miss Armstrong has paid for everything in that basket and a lot more besides with hours of dedicated work when she was an employee of Denton and Christie,' she said.

'Thank you,' Molly whispered.

'You're welcome. Now, if you will excuse me.' Miss Simpson turned and clapped her hands, twice. 'Back to your posts, girls, there's work to be done.'

After a breakfast of scrambled egg on toast, and a couple of pots of tea, Bess telephoned her friend Natalie Goldman. After explaining what had happened the night before, Natalie insisted that they all stay with her and Anton in north London.

The small party of homeless women carrying an assortment of bags and boxes arrived at Natalie Goldman's front door in the early afternoon. Natalie welcomed them and, after taking their coats, led them through to the sitting room where a fire roared in the hearth and where Nanny Friel was laying the table for lunch. When she had finished, Nanny strode across the room and mimed to Molly that she, Molly, should take her bags upstairs while Nanny - she pointed to herself - would take Elizabeth to the kitchen and give her a feed. Molly knew from Bess that she could trust the Goldman's Nanny and handed over her hungry little pink bundle. Nanny's broad Germanic face, usually set in a frown around strangers, broke into a smile that would have won a gurning competition and she left the room singing "Schönes Baby, reizendes kleines Mädchen".

While Nanny gave Elizabeth her bottle, Natalie took Miss Armstrong and Molly upstairs to show them where they would be sleeping. Bess said she'd make do with a blanket on the settee. She was so tired she would sleep anywhere. By the time they returned, Bess and Nanny Friel were watching over Elizabeth, who was sleeping contentedly on the settee, secured by cushions that Nanny Friel had placed along the edge of the seat.

'Thank you,' Molly said to her. 'Mrs McAllister said babies can turn over in their sleep and fall off a settee. Elizabeth's probably too little to move that far, but you can never be too careful, Mrs Mac said.' Nanny Friel, straining to understand what Molly was saying, nodded and smiled along with everyone else.

In the days that followed, Molly and Elizabeth stayed at home with Nanny Friel and Nurse Ambler, and Bess, Natalie and Miss Armstrong went out and looked for Mrs McAllister. They took a dozen or more copies of Mrs Mac's description with them each day, which described her fully: her age, height, size, hair colour and Scottish accent – and on the bottom of each copy was Natalie's telephone number in London and Bess's at Foxden.

Between them, the three women visited every displaced person's centre, homeless shelter and hostel – as well as the hospitals, from Queen Charlotte and St. Stephen's in Fulham to the Brompton Hospital off Old Brompton Road, and from St. Mary's Paddington and St. George's at Hyde Park to St. Thomas's on Westminster Bridge, which had been bombed on September 8th, the day after Arcadia Avenue.

Bess's sister Margaret and her husband Bill, who lodged with the Goldman's and worked in the West End, distributed Mrs McAllister's description to central London's police and ambulance stations, as well as the hospitals in the area. No one had seen or heard of anyone fitting Mrs McAllister's description. It was as if she had never existed.

Bess put down the telephone and returned to the kitchen and her friends, who were already seated, eating breakfast. 'I'm going back,' she said. 'That was Lady Foxden on the telephone. She reminded me that I have been away longer than agreed. She said she understood that I had responsibilities in London, but I also have responsibilities at Foxden.'

'When will you leave?' Natalie asked.

'Tomorrow.'

'Tomorrow? What about Mrs Mac?' Molly said.

'There's isn't anything else I can do - any of us can do – until she's found, Molly. So I asked Lady Foxden if Miss Armstrong and you and Elizabeth could come back to Foxden with me. And she agreed. I've already spoken to Miss Armstrong, asked her if she'd take on the job of Estate bookkeeper, but she says she'll only come if you and Elizabeth come too. So what do you say, Molly? It'll be safer and healthier for Elizabeth – no bombs and lots of fresh air.'

Molly thought for a minute and then said, 'I'd like to go with you, and I know it would be better for Elizabeth, but what if Mrs Mac comes looking for us? How will she know where we are?'

'Well, she knew I was coming to London, so she'll put two and two together and realise you've come home with me.'

'What if she can't remember where you live?' Molly asked.

'Sweetheart, Mrs Mac has known my address at Foxden since before I came to lodge with her. And it's been on every letter since I moved back. But if she has forgotten, all she has to do is go into the nearest police station. My name and telephone number is on every poster in every police station, hospital, hostel and voluntary organisation in west and central London. If Mrs Mac is found--'

'What do you mean, *if* Mrs Mac is found?'

'I didn't mean if, I meant, when--'

'Why did you say it then? Why did you say "if"?' Molly looked at Bess, her eyes wild and accusing. 'You think she's dead, don't you?' she shouted.

'No, Molly, of course I don't think she's dead.' Bess put her arms around her young friend and held her until she was calm. 'When Mrs Mac is found the authorities will probably notify Natalie first, because she lives in London. Natalie will telephone me, and I'll come down to London straight away and bring her back to Foxden – I promise.'

'And I promise to keep looking for your friend,' Natalie said. 'And when I find her, I will bring her here and look after her until Bess arrives. But today I think you should take Elizabeth to the country, where she will be safe.'

Natalie's calm reasoning did the trick and Molly agreed to go to Foxden on condition she, like Miss Armstrong, worked to earn her and Elizabeth's keep.

Bess laughed. 'You might regret the offer, Moll. There's tons of work to do on the Estate.'

'Thank you, Natalie,' Bess said. 'Once again I don't know what I'd have done without you. If there is ever anything ....'

Natalie took hold of Bess's hands. Her eyes were brimming with tears. 'There is something, Bess. Would you take Rebekah and the boys with you? Please? Would you take them to the country, so they too will be safe?'

Bess would have said yes, immediately, but it wasn't up to her. Taking adults who could work was one thing, but three children... 'I'm sure Her Ladyship won't mind, but I'd better telephone first.'

'Thank you Bess. Please tell your Lady that the children will not be any trouble. Nanny Friel and Nurse Ambler will come also, to look after them. And tell her that Anton will arrange money to be sent every week.'

Bess wasn't sure whether adding two adults to the party would make things better or worse. She telephoned Lady Foxden, explained that since September 7th the bombing of London had been relentless, and asked if she could bring her friend's three children back with her.

Lady Foxden had serious doubts about children living at the Hall. 'We don't have the staff to look after three children, Bess.'

'You're right, Lady Foxden,' Bess said. 'Perhaps it would be better if their nanny and nurse came with them. The children will be at school during the day, so Nanny could help Molly with Elizabeth. And to have a fully qualified nurse living at the Hall would be a real asset to the west wing.' Bess paused to let the idea of a trained nurse looking after the servicemen in the west wing – her Ladyship's favourite project – sink in. 'And they won't be a strain on the Estate's finances. Every week my friend's husband will deposit an agreed amount of money in the bank to pay for their board and lodging.'

Saving money, or acquiring it, was always a decisive factor where Lady Foxden was concerned. 'Very well, but they are your responsibility, Bess. As long as your friends and their children don't get in the way of your work on the Estate, I'm sure something can be arranged. I'll leave the details to you and Porter. Goodbye,' she said, and hung up.

Bess dialled the number again and while she waited for Mr Porter to come to the telephone, she gave Natalie the thumbs up. 'I bamboozled Lady Foxden into accepting Nanny Friel and Nurse Ambler. I didn't give her a chance to draw breath, never mind voice her objections, which I'm sure she had by the cart load,' she said. Mr Porter came on the line and although he showed little enthusiasm, he agreed to ask a couple of the girls to prepare five bedrooms – one with a cot – and arrange transport to collect nine people from Rugby station.

'Thank you, Natalie. I don't know what we'd have done without your help and your hospitality,' Bess said, biting back the tears as she prepared to leave.

'Nor me without you, Bess. I don't know what our family would have done without you,' Natalie said again, kissing Bess on both cheeks. 'Goodbye, darling Nanny, and dear Nurse Ambler, look after my children for me?'

Great pear-shaped tears fell from Nanny Friel's eyes onto her plump cheeks, which she mopped up with a large white handkerchief. Unable to speak, she threw her arms around Natalie and held her in a bear hug before kissing her goodbye.

Nurse Ambler, saddened to see how distraught Nanny was, said, 'Don't worry, Mrs Goldman, Nanny and I will look after the children, won't we, Nanny?'

'Ja, ja. Kommen jetzt, Krankenschwester Ambler, der Zug wird nicht warten auf Sie.'

Natalie was about to translate when Nurse Ambler, seeing how upset Nanny was, shook her head. 'There's no need, Mrs Goldman. I'll catch her up, make sure she's all right. Goodbye!' Nurse Ambler put out her hand and Natalie Goldman shook it warmly. 'We'll wait for the children in the car,' she said, and hurried off after Nanny.

Having opened the front passenger door for Nanny Friel and the back door for Nurse Ambler, Anton loaded the suitcases into the boot of his car, and then returned to his seat to wait for the children. The taxi driver, after helping Miss Armstrong, Molly and baby Elizabeth into the back of his cab, stood by the passenger door and waited for Bess.

Natalie bent down and kissed each of her children. 'Be brave, my darlings. And be good for Bess,' she said, chucking Samuel under the chin. 'I promise that the minute this horrible war is over Daddy and I will come for you and bring you home. Until then, my precious ones, remember we love you.'

'I'm sorry, Natalie.' Bess looked at her wristwatch. 'If we're going to catch the train…'

A sob caught in Natalie's throat. 'Yes, of course. It's time for you to go, children,' she said. 'Rebekah, will you take the boys to the car?'

Rebekah took her arms from around her mother's waist and stepped back, but her brothers clung on like young branches clinging to a tree. 'My heart is breaking,' she mouthed to Bess. 'You will look after my children for me, won't you?' she said.

Nodding and trying not to cry herself, Bess said, 'Of course.'

Rebekah put her arm around her oldest brother's shoulder. 'Come on, Benjamin,' she said. Benjamin looked up at his mother and smiled, and then let go of her. But Samuel, his eyes wide and pleading, clung to his mother, kicking and screaming when his brother and sister tried to pull him from her.

'Samuel, if we don't leave now we're going to miss the train,' Bess said in a firm but sympathetic voice.

'Mama, Mama,' Natalie's youngest son cried as Bess lifted him up and carried him to his father's car.

'Shalom, my friend,' Natalie Goldman whispered through her tears. 'Shalom.'

CHAPTER TWENTY

The northbound platforms at Euston Station heaved with people waiting to board trains to the Midlands and the North. Fights broke out as people pushed their way to the front of the queue, arguing that they had been first in line and waiting the longest.

Bess, Miss Armstrong, Nanny Friel and Nurse Ambler stood in a rigid semi-circle behind Molly and the children. No matter who pushed, or how hard they pushed, the four women stood firm and held their ground. Except for moving forward after each train had picked up its passengers and left the station, the four women didn't budge. It was the only way to protect Molly and the children from being crushed, as well as keep their place in the queue, and it worked. At one o'clock that afternoon Bess and her party boarded the train to Rugby.

The train was as crowded and noisy – and almost as hazardous – as the platform had been. Men pushed, shoved and struggled to hold onto their bags and suitcases, while mothers tried to pacify their frightened and often crying children. Unable to take any more of Elizabeth's howls, a man sitting in the compartment next to the corridor where Bess and the Goldman party were standing got up and gave Molly his seat. About time too, Bess thought, and she smiled as he pushed past.

The journey north was stressful – and took much longer than expected. But the Goldman children turned the journey into an adventure. Even Samuel stopped crying and joined in the fun. He couldn't remember the words to the songs, nor spell when they played I-spy, which made everyone laugh, including their young nurse, Ruth Ambler. For Nanny Friel, who hadn't spent any time away from Natalie and Anton Goldman since coming to England, it was a terrifying experience.

'Am I pleased to see you!' Bess called to Laura and Polly when she saw them on the platform at Rugby station. 'We have a little more luggage and a few more people than originally planned,' she said, handing bags and boxes to the two land girls who stood open-mouthed as they watched more and more people get off the train.

'This is Miss Armstrong, Molly, and baby Elizabeth,' Bess said to the two land girls, 'my friends from my student days. And this is Polly and Laura, two of Foxden's hard-working Land Army girls – and my friends.'

'Pleased to meet you. We've heard a lot about you,' Laura said.

'We've been looking forward to meeting you,' Polly added.

'And this is Nanny Friel, Nurse Amber and... Oh, you can introduce yourselves,' Bess said to the giggling children standing before her.

'Welcome to the country, everyone,' Laura shouted above the hullabaloo.

'Good job your dad got the manager of the foundry to lend us their bus,' Polly said, laughing. 'Come on kids, your charabanc awaits. And, on the left!' she shouted, marching off with the children falling in step behind her. 'Come on, keep up!' she called, leading them down the tunnel to the street and the bus.

Mrs Hartley, standing in the doorway of her kitchen when Foxden's newest residents arrived, shouted, 'This way if you're hungry.' The land girls cheered, saying, 'We're starving,' and 'Save some for us.' But the Goldman children, looking around wide-eyed and standing together as if they were glued to each other, said nothing.

'In you come then, my lovelies,' Mrs Hartley said. 'Are you hungry?' Not waiting for an answer, she continued. 'We've got jelly for afters. And,' she said to Samuel, 'when you've had your tea, I bet one of these lovely ladies will take you to see the ponies. Do you like ponies?' she asked Benjamin, who nodded. 'I bet you do too, darling,' she said to Rebekah. 'Now then, sit where you like. We're all friends here.'

After tea, Iris took the children to see the horses and then entertained them in James's old playroom while the adults unpacked.

'Are you sure you'll be all right with this motley crew?' Bess joked.

'Oh yes. We're already friends, thanks to her Ladyship's ponies, which I've promised to take them to see again tomorrow. And,' she said to Samuel, 'I bet if you're good, her Ladyship will let you ride one of them. Would you like that?'

'Yes,' Samuel said, making cow eyes at Iris.

'I think you've got an admirer,' Bess whispered.

Iris looked down at the little boy. 'The feeling's mutual.'

Lingering for longer than was good for her heart, Bess thought of James as a little boy and imagined him playing with the colourful wooden train that Samuel was playing with now. 'I'll leave you to it then. If you need any help, you've only got to shout. Nanny Friel's room is just along the corridor,' Bess said before closing the door on the excited brood.

'Shush!' Bess put her hand up. 'Sorry, but what's that noise?' The land girls, in the middle of their supper, put down their knives and forks and listened in silence.

'Sounds like aircraft,' Laura whispered.

'Yes, low flying aircraft,' Bess added. Getting up from the table, she ran to the door. Before opening it, she put out the light.

'Not again,' Mrs Hartley said. Followed by the land girls, Bess ran into the rick-yard where Mr Porter was looking up at the sky. Bess followed his gaze. Advancing toward Foxden were hundreds of German bomber planes. Formation after formation approached the Estate from the east before turning in a broad sweep, like a swarm of locusts, and heading west.

At first, Foxden's residents hadn't braved the cold November night. They had put out their lights and watched from behind their blackout curtains. Now everyone was in the yard.

'They're heading for Birmingham,' Mr Porter shouted.

Bess shook her head. 'Coventry!' she said, as the city's air raid sirens began to wail. 'We wouldn't be able to hear Birmingham's sirens. It's Coventry,' she said again.

Too shocked to speak, they stood and listened to the high-pitched wail of Coventry's air raid sirens, followed by the rumble of explosives and the rat-a-tat-tat of anti-aircraft guns. Within minutes the first crump of bombs was followed by the second, then the third – and so it went on. Shivering in the bitterly cold mid-November night air, Bess watched the sky above Coventry turn red as wave after wave of German incendiary bombs tore through the city.

The air strike had happened almost without warning. The sirens were supposed to wail fifteen minutes before the bombing began, to give people time to get to their shelters. That hadn't been the case tonight.

Bess feared people wouldn't have had time to get to a shelter – and if they had, they'd have to face the heartbreak of seeing their homes reduced to rubble, or losing family and friends, as Miss Armstrong and

Molly had done. Molly still cried for Mrs McAllister at night. Molly…

'Molly? Has anyone seen Molly?'

'Bess, we've got to take shelter in the cellar,' Mr Porter shouted. 'There might be stragglers about. If any planes have strayed from the flight path they'll need to offload their bombs before they return.'

'I've got to find Molly.'

'She's already down there. Now come on!' he ordered.

The ferocious and unrelenting bombardment of Coventry carried on through the night. There were so many bombs exploding at the same time that it was impossible to distinguish one explosion from another.

Bess put her arms round Molly and rocked her. 'Shush, now,' she said, as Molly howled. 'Shush,' but Molly was inconsolable. It was as if she was back in Arcadia Avenue on the night Mrs McAllister's house was bombed.

Molly cried all night and most of the following day, refusing to undress when she went to bed in case the German bombers came back. Miss Armstrong spent the next two days looking after her, as well as Elizabeth. Only when she had put Elizabeth down for the night did she go downstairs to the kitchen and eat something. The rest of the night she spent in the armchair in Molly's bedroom, in case either of them needed her.

Work on the Acres was put on hold for a week. Laura drove Bess's father to Coventry to see if Bill's parents needed any help, which they didn't. Their house was so far out of the city centre that, except for a few broken windows, it was still in one piece.

After telephoning Natalie and Anton Goldman and assuring them that their children, nanny and nurse were safe, Bess helped Mr Porter and Polly to clear the wine cellar. There were two floors – the lower had deep recesses, ideal to store the wine and the upper was large enough to sleep everyone. It had been built in the fourteenth century as a chantry for Benedictine monks to pray for the soul of the first Lord Foxden. Today, with its five-foot thick walls, the cellar's purpose was to protect the residents of Foxden if the German bombers returned – which could happen, because the Estate was sandwiched between two RAF aerodromes – Bitteswell and Bruntingthorpe.

CHAPTER TWENTY-ONE

The week before Christmas a large hamper arrived from the Goldmans, containing three tins of ham, plum puddings, a fruitcake, bags of mixed fruit, chocolate bars, letters for the children – and a card wishing Bess and the residents of Foxden a happy holiday. The card also said that, although they did not celebrate Christmas or exchange gifts, they wanted to show their gratitude in a practical way. Natalie Goldman added: "PS. Dearest Bess, please do not give the children ham. With fondest love, Natalie and Anton Goldman."

After placing Natalie and Anton's card on the mantle shelf, Bess read a card from her sister Margaret. "Dear Bess, It's all go here. Being an usherette I get to watch the show every night. I've learned all the dances and songs. I'm also helping to make the costumes. And guess what? After the first night party at the Prince Albert Club, the girls from the show persuaded me to sing a song with the band. I went down a storm. I wish you'd been there. Must sign off now. Happy Christmas from Bill and me. Love Margaret." Bess laughed at Margaret's modern turn of phrase, but shuddered remembering the first night party she had been to at the Albert Club. In her reply, Bess said she too wished she'd have been there – which couldn't have been further from the truth. She'd have loved to see her sister singing with the band, but she wasn't ready to return to the Prince Albert Club.

'Timber!' Polly called as she felled a fir tree.

'You know this is theft, don't you?' Laura said, helping Polly to haul the tree onto the back of the horse-drawn cart.

'And you're aiding and abetting,' Polly replied, laughing.

'What are we going to do with it now we've got it? We don't have any decorations.'

'Oh ye of little faith.' Polly stepped up onto the wooden seat of the cart. 'The Foxdens must have tons of decorations. The place would have been wall to wall with them at Christmas and New Year in the Thirties. Think of all the parties they must have thrown before the war.'

'But what if we can't find them?'

'Then we'll make some!' Polly said, flicking on the reins. 'Walk on.'

As Polly and Laura turned into the Estate, Annabel was getting out of her car.

'Pip your horn, Annabel!' Polly shouted. 'We need helpers to unload the tree.'

Annabel leant into her car and sounded the horn several times. By the time Polly and Laura had brought the horse and cart to the front of the Hall, Bess and the children were running down the steps.

'Annabel! I didn't think you were coming up this year,' Bess shouted above the children's squeals of excitement.

'I can only stay for a couple of days, but I wouldn't have missed Christmas at Foxden for the world. Help me, would you, Bess?' Annabel ran to the back of the car and opened the boot. It was full of food and packages wrapped in coloured paper.

'Annabel, you're an angel,' Bess exclaimed. Then, turning to Polly and Laura and seeing the huge fir tree, she asked, 'What on earth have you two been up to?'

Trying not to giggle, they looked up at Bess, pretending they didn't know what she was talking about.

'Children,' Bess called. 'Would you help Annabel to unload her car – and please be careful,' she added, as each child clambered to help.

'Well done, you two,' Bess said. 'It wouldn't be Christmas without a tree.'

'I can't make all the decorations on my own,' Annabel said. 'Hands up who wants to help.'

'Me, me, me,' everyone shouted, putting their hands in the air.

'We'll need something to stand the tree in,' Bess said.

'I'll go and see Mr Porter. He's bound to have something suitable.' Laura disappeared through the main door.

'Can we put it in the window?' asked Samuel. 'Then we can see it when we're outside playing.'

'We can't have it on show darling, because of the blackout. Besides, it's too big to go in the window. We'll stand it here and tie the top to the banister upstairs. And,' Bess said, kneeling down so her face was level with the little boy's, 'you can put the star on top, how about that?'

'Hooray! I'm going to put the star on top of the tree,' Samuel said to Polly. 'I'm going to tell Benjamin.'

'Not tonight, though,' Polly called after him, but the little boy was so excited he didn't hear her.

Until the war there had always been a Christmas tree in the marble hall at Foxden. Bess smiled, remembering New Year's Eve 1938, when she had been leaving the library and bumped into James. So much had happened - changed - since that night.

A clanging sound brought Bess back to the present. Laura was carrying an old red fireman's bucket. 'Mr Porter said we need to pack soil round the trunk of the tree after we put it in the bucket. And put some heavy stones on top so it doesn't fall over.' Polly went upstairs and held the top of the tree while Laura and Bess lifted it into the bucket. 'Hold on to it, Bess, while I fill the bucket with soil,' Laura said. 'And Polly,' she shouted, 'tie the top of the tree to the banister, will you?'

Laura went off to find stones to use as ballast for the bucket, and Bess and Polly joined Annabel and the children. When the decorations were made they would be ready for Christmas. Mr Porter had laid fires in all the fireplaces. A giant fir tree stood in the hall. And Annabel had turned up with enough food to feed a small army.

When the children were in bed Mrs Hartley arrived with a plate of mince pies, followed by Mr Porter carrying a large jug of mulled wine.

'There is something we must do before we settle down to enjoy ourselves,' Annabel said. 'Follow me.'

After several light-hearted protests, the women trailed outside. At her car, Annabel opened the back door to reveal several large brown paper bags, each containing a number of smaller parcels.

'Let's get these inside and under the tree before anyone sees us.'

Speechless, the women stood and stared at Annabel.

'What?' she said, smiling. 'Well, I wasn't sure Father Christmas would make it this far up the country, what with all the transport disruptions, so I persuaded my parents and some of their friends to help him on his way.'

Without putting the lights on, the women crept into the hall giggling like naughty children and placed the presents under the Christmas tree.

'I'd like to propose a toast,' Bess said, when they were back in the sitting room. 'To Annabel.'

'To Annabel!'

Christmas morning, after church, Bess's mother and father and her sisters Ena and Claire walked up to the Hall. The Dudley women went to the kitchen to help Mrs Hartley prepare Christmas dinner. Bess's father joined Bess and Mr Porter in the music room where Annabel and the Goldman children's nurse, Ruth were rehearsing the children for the afternoon concert.

'I'm worried what Natalie and Anton would think about their children singing Christmas carols, Ruth,' Bess said to Nurse Ambler. 'And I don't want to offend you or Nanny.'

Nurse Ambler shook her head. 'Children singing Christmas songs won't offend us. We're evacuees living in a Christian house. We expect it. Besides, it wouldn't be fair on the other children.'

'Because you're here you won't be celebrating Hanukkah this year, will you?'

'Not in the way we would if we were in London, no, but--'

'That's it!' Bess said. 'Rebekah, Benjamin and Samuel can celebrate Hanukkah, by singing songs that are relevant to their faith – and they can teach the village children some of the words. What do you think, Ruth?'

'I think that's a wonderful idea for the children to sing each other's songs, especially in these terrible times. We have some lovely children's songs. I'll find out which songs the children know best, and write down the words of the chorus so the other children can join in.'

'Thank you, Ruth.'

'My pleasure. Leave it with me.'

Returning with her father a little later, Bess saw Rebekah Goldman in one corner of the room teaching a little girl from the village the words to a Jewish song called, "Oh Chanukah, Oh Chanukah", while in the opposite corner David Davies was teaching Benjamin and Samuel Goldman "Good King Wenceslas". When it came to practising the songs with the piano, the girls sang "Oh Chanukah, Oh Chanukah, Come light the Menorah, Let's have a party, We'll all dance the Horah" beautifully. When the Goldman boys rehearsed "Good King Wenceslas", instead of singing, "When the snow lay round about, deep and crisp and even" they sang, "He turned his breeches inside out, 'cause he thought he'd weed them".

Hearing the revised lyrics, Bess's father shouted, 'Stop this nonsense at once!' Summoning David Davies, he said, 'At your age you should be setting an example to the younger children, not teaching them rubbish. Now tell them the right words, or I'll fetch your father.'

His older brother Jonathan sniggered, but David daren't move. 'Sorry, Mr Dudley,' he said, and began immediately to tell the Goldman boys the correct words.

'I liked the words better before,' Samuel said. 'They were funny.'

'They weren't funny. They were rude,' his older brother said.

'I don't care, I liked them,' he said, and carried on singing the first version.

When the fuss had died down Bess's father sought out Mr Porter. 'Time to come outside for a smoke?'

'I should think so,' Mr Porter said. 'You don't mind, do you, Bess?'

'Not at all. I'll come with you. Get a breath of fresh air.'

After lighting his own cigarette, Mr Porter offered his cupped hands to Bess's father. 'It's a rum game, this war, Thomas.'

'It certainly is,' Thomas agreed, leaning over and lighting his cigarette.

'But the papers say our boys are putting up a good fight on every front. France, Italy...'

'Then why are the Germans defeating us?' Bess asked, walking across the yard behind the men.

'The papers only tell us what the government wants us to know,' her father said.

'Aye, that's true,' Mr Porter agreed.

'Haven't heard from Tom for a couple of weeks. In his last letter he said his regiment was going overseas again in January.'

'I hope he's well enough to go back to the front,' Bess said, as much to herself as to her father and Ernest Porter.

Both men stopped walking. 'Will he get home before he goes abroad?'

Bess's father shook his head. 'He's got forty-eight hours' leave over the New Year, but what with the petrol shortage and public transport being so bad, I shouldn't think he'll be able to come home. Lily's worried to death, of course, we both are. He was lucky to get out of Dunkirk alive, you know.'

Bess was worried too, but decided not to voice her opinion. 'Come on, it's time we were getting back. You two are integral to the success of the concert, so will you both please put on your happy faces? If not for me, for the children.'

Bess's father, smiling, said, 'Of course. But I can't help worrying about Tom and all the other boys. We seem to be losing ground and Hitler's gaining it.'

'It's not like you to be negative, Dad. Anyway, now Mr Churchill's in charge things will get better, you see if they don't,' Bess added, with more conviction than she felt. 'In the meantime,' she said, changing the subject. 'we have a Christmas concert to put on.' Bess linked her arm through her father's arm and looked up into his face. 'You know what Margaret would say? The show must go on!'

Nodding, he said, 'I wish she was here to say it.'

Both men nipped the end of their cigarettes and followed Bess.

'Right,' she said, entering the music room. 'Annabel will tell you when to open the curtains, which I think is before and after each child's party piece. Then when you're satisfied that you know what you're doing – and more importantly, Annabel is satisfied – I'd like you to put the trestle tables up, ready for lunch.'

'Dinner is about to be served, children. Would you please find your name on the table and sit in the chair nearest to it,' Bess announced. She had made small place settings from leftover scraps of wrapping paper, placing each child strategically next to an adult. There would be less chance of the children playing around and more chance of them eating that way.

To cheers and applause, Mrs Hartley and Bess's mother carried in two large chickens, a gift from Low Farm, with homemade sage and onion stuffing from Mrs Hartley's vegetable and herb garden. 'We'll put a bird at either end, Lily,' Mrs Hartley said. 'Thomas and Mr Porter are carving.' Ena and Claire brought dishes of vegetables followed by Laura and Polly carrying large jugs of gravy.

Lunch was as chaotic as it was fun. And the tongue-in-cheek threat of not opening any presents until they had eaten every scrap of food on their plates worked so well that by the time they'd finished their main course, the children were full. So Bess suggested they leave the Christmas pudding and the fruitcake until teatime and open their Christmas presents.

Baby Elizabeth, at only six months old, was more interested in the brightly coloured wrapping paper than the teddy bear inside, which she tried to eat - as she did everything within her reach.

'Look at all these toys,' Bess exclaimed. 'You must have been very good children for Father Christmas to bring you such lovely toys.'

The girls had dolls, floppy-eared puppy dogs and coloured ribbons. The boys had bats and balls, hoops and penny whistles. 'You can go and play outside if you want to, boys,' Bess said to the Davies brothers, who were now very protective of their new friends from London. 'But put your outdoor coats on, and your scarves and gloves. And don't wander off. Stay close to each other, and to the Hall - it'll be dark soon.'

'Who is Father Christmas?' Samuel Goldman asked, as Bess wrapped his scarf round his neck.

'He's the one who brought you the toys,' David Davies piped up. 'He lives across the sea where it snows all the time. He flies through the air on a sleigh pulled by reindeer and if you've been good he comes down your chimney while you're asleep and leaves presents at the bottom of your bed, in one of your mam's old stockings – or he puts them under the Christmas tree, if you're rich enough to have a tree,' he added.

'He doesn't come to our house in London,' Samuel said.

313

'You must be bad then,' David replied with authority.

Samuel's bottom lip began to quiver.

'Of course you're not bad, Samuel, David's only teasing,' Bess said, pulling the little boy's woolly hat over his dark curls. 'Jonathan,' she said to David's older brother, 'will you take the boys outside to play? The fresh air will do you all good. And you!' she said to David Davies. 'Behave yourself.'

Rebekah was still reading the letter she had received from her parents. Some of the girls were playing with their dolls and a couple were at the piano with Annabel when Jonathan and David Davies, followed by Benjamin and Samuel, came crashing back through the front door. 'Bess! Come quick!' Jonathan shouted. 'There's an Army lorry in the ditch at the bottom of Shaft Hill.'

'All right, calm down, boys. Laura, you come with me, and Annabel, Polly, you keep the party going.' Bess shouted as she grabbed her coat from the stand in the foyer.

'Yes, of course,' Polly replied.

'Be careful!' Annabel called.

'We'll show you where it is,' Jonathan said, following Bess.

'No. I want you boys to stay here. You shouldn't have been down Shaft Hill in the first place. David, take the boys inside and Jonathan, go and find my father and Mr Porter. Tell them what's happened and ask them to come as quickly as they can. And then go to the kitchen and ask Mrs Hartley to make lots of strong tea.'

Shaft Hill was steep and halfway down there was a sharp bend. If drivers didn't know the road, and didn't slow down as they approached the bend, they often ended up in the ditch opposite. Because it was getting dark, the driver of the lorry probably didn't see the bend until it was too late.

As they ran down the hill, they saw the lorry. 'Anyone hurt?' Bess called.

'Yes, me, nurse,' said one young soldier. 'I think I've died and gone to heaven,' said another, and 'There is a Father Christmas after all.'

'All right, lads, let's have some respect, shall we? Only a few bumps and bruises Miss, nothing to worry about,' the young sergeant in charge said.

'What can we do to help?' Laura asked, to which the replies were saucy and many.

'Thank you!' the sergeant said loudly - for the benefit of the men in his charge, not Bess and Laura. 'We'll be fine. Once we get the lorry out of the ditch we'll be on our way.'

'Hello there,' Mr Porter hollered, as he and Bess's father came round the bend on the tractor. They pulled up in front of the lorry and jumped down. 'Tie this to the back bumper,' he said, throwing a thick rope to the sergeant. 'The rest of you lads go to the front of the lorry and prepare to push. We'll have you out of that ditch in no time.'

The soldiers did as instructed. Each stood with their right shoulder against the lorry while the sergeant – the driver – jumped into the cab, switched on the ignition and put the lorry in reverse gear.

'On the count of three, Ernest,' Bess's dad shouted. 'One – two – three!'

The tractor moved slowly across the road until it picked up the slack in the rope.

'And, two, three!' Bess's father called again.

The sergeant let the clutch out slowly and at the same time put his foot down gently on the accelerator – and the soldiers pushed with all their strength until the lorry began to move. At first it was slow going, but finally the lorry's back wheels cleared the ditch and the lorry began to make its ascent.

'Keep going boys, you're nearly there.' Bess's father spoke too soon. The engine made a whining noise, the wheels began to spin in the mud and the lorry slid back into the ditch.

'Stop!' Bess shouted. Running over to the tractor, she took half a dozen empty grain sacks from behind the seat and passed half to Laura. 'Pack these round the wheels on the other side of the lorry. I'll do the same on this side. It'll stop them from sliding.'

'Let's try again, but quickly, I can smell petrol!' Bess shouted, as soon as Laura was clear of the lorry. 'One, two, three, heave.'

The lorry began to move, and this time the wheels gripped the sacks and rolled slowly over the sodden earth.

'Come on! One last push!' she called again. And suddenly the back wheels, and then the front, flew over the top of the ditch.

While the soldiers stood around thanking their civilian friends, the sergeant checked and tightened the straps around the jerry cans on the side of the lorry. 'Could you do with some petrol?' he asked Bess, over the bonnet. 'I need to offload this five gallon can.'

'Yes, we're desperate for petrol,' Bess said.

'I'll leave it here then,' he said, unbuckling the can and pushing it down into the mud in the ditch. 'Daren't travel it, it's too dangerous,' he said, pointing to the bottom of the spout. 'Hairline crack! It would get bigger on the move, but it'll be safe enough here overnight – as long as it's standing upright.'

'I don't know how to thank you,' Bess said. 'I'll come down and transfer it into another can tomorrow, first thing. We'll put it to good use, I promise. Thank you,' she said again.

The soldiers piled into the back of the lorry, cheering and shouting their goodbyes. After untying the rope from the lorry's bumper, the young sergeant thanked Bess and Laura, Mr Porter and Bess's father, and climbed into the lorry's cab.

'Wait a minute, Sergeant,' Bess shouted, jumping onto the step at the driver's door.

'There is a way we can thank you for the petrol. How would you all like to come up to the Hall for some refreshment? It's only at the top of the hill. You'd be very welcome.'

'Well… it has been a long day and the lads are tired.' Looking at his watch, he said, 'I don't see that another hour will make any difference. After all, if it hadn't been for you, we might have been in that ditch all night.'

The sergeant drove slowly behind the tractor while Bess and Laura, having declined a lift in the back of the lorry, followed on foot.

From the outside, the Hall appeared to be in darkness, but once they were inside it was a different story.

'Bloody hell,' one private murmured, before his mate nudged him and told him to watch his language.

The soldiers trooped through the foyer, past the huge Christmas tree and into the warm brightly decorated music room. Mrs Hartley and Bess's mother were laying the trestle tables with chicken and ham sandwiches, fruitcake and Christmas puddings. Ena and Claire brought in two pots of tea and a tray of cups and saucers – and giggled when the soldiers flirted and teased.

'Sit down, boys, and tuck in,' Mrs Hartley said. 'We've had ours. It's a shame you weren't here a few hours ago, while the chicken was still hot,' she said, pouring each of them a cup of tea.

While the soldiers ate their meal Annabel gathered the children round the piano and they sang a selection of Christmas carols. When the soldiers had finished eating, the concert proper began.

The curtains opened on the Nativity. Rebekah, dressed in a simple white gown, played the part of Mary, standing protectively by the side of a Moses basket and the baby Jesus, played perfectly by a sleeping baby Elizabeth. Benjamin, wearing one of Mr Porter's old leather aprons and sporting a beard made of cotton wool, played Joseph; David and Jonathan Davies carried crooks as the shepherds and Samuel, just visible behind a huge cardboard star, was the star of the east. Then, after much clearing of throats and straightening of song sheets, the children sang, "Oh Little Town of Bethlehem" followed by "Oh Chanukah, Oh Chanukah".

The children sang songs, recited poems and nursery rhymes, and danced jigs – and Bess's dad and Mr Porter got every curtain call on cue. The concert ended with everyone on their feet singing "Give A Little Whistle", followed by "Hands, Knees and Boomps-a-Daisy". The soldiers, clapping their hands when they should have slapping their knees, made everyone laugh. Coincidentally they conquered the moves at exactly the same time and everyone cheered. Finally, after taking theatrical bows, all but one of the soldiers returned to their seats.

The sergeant stood at the top of the table and looked around the room until there was hush. 'On behalf of myself and the lads, I would like to thank you all. It's been a long time since any of us have sat down with friends and eaten a meal. And, because we're going overseas in the New Year, it may be a long time until we do it again. I think I speak for every soldier here when I say we will never forget what you did for us today. And the next time we sit down with friends, wherever it is and whenever it is, we'll remember today and every one of you.' He looked at his fellow soldiers. 'Look sharp, lads, it's time we were on our way.'

The soldiers pushed back their chairs and stood to attention. As they made their way to the door they thanked Mrs Hartley, Bess's father and Mr Porter, shook the hands of the children who were nearest to them and saluted those who were further away. At the door they turned as one and saluted Bess, Laura, Polly and Annabel, who were standing by the piano.

An anticlimactic feeling hung in the air when the soldiers had gone. The party had fallen flat - until Samuel Goldman said, 'Can I have my Christmas pudding now?'

'No, silly,' his brother replied, 'the soldiers have eaten it.'

'But I ate all my dinner, and Bess said--'

'Anybody that's hungry can come with me to my kitchen. I'm sure I can rustle up something if your tummy's rumbling,' Mrs Hartley said to Samuel and Benjamin. 'And tomorrow, I'll make a chocolate cake for tea, how's that?' she said, leaving the room followed closely by two happy little boys who had enjoyed their first Christmas.

CHAPTER TWENTY-TWO

The winter was harsh. Snow fell almost every day. For much of the time the temperature was below zero. Black ice caused havoc on the roads, the farm machinery seized up, and food and water had to be transported to animals in outlying fields by horse and cart. But the children loved it, especially the children from London who weren't used to seeing the kind of heavy snowfalls and drifts that children in the country took for granted.

It was snowing heavily when Bess, walking across the rick-yard from the barn to the kitchen, heard a vehicle coming up the drive. She doubled back to see who it was that had been so brave - or so stupid - to drive in such a heavy snowstorm. Sheltering beneath the thatched roof of the unused foaling stable, she saw an RAF Jeep pull up. It was James! She stepped back into the doorway and watched him walk over to Benjamin and Samuel Goldman, who were building a snowman.

Bess didn't know James was coming home for New Year. Annabel couldn't have known either, or she wouldn't have gone back to Kent. Perhaps it was a last minute thing and he didn't have time to tell her. An involuntary smile crept across her face and she felt the butterflies of excitement in the pit of her stomach, as she had done on the eve of 1939.

Secretly pleased that James was going to be at Foxden when Annabel wasn't, Bess watched him turn and trudge through the snow to the Hall. The boys waited for a few minutes, but soon returned to the business of decorating the snowman's face with assorted root vegetables. Bess was more patient and waited, out of sight.

She put her hand to her mouth to stop herself from laughing out loud as James, in an old bowler hat and swinging a walking stick like Charlie Chaplin, came down the steps from the Hall. Then, with an exaggerated sad expression like Chaplin often had in his films, he leant his stick against the body of the snowman and put the bowler hat on his head. The boys clapped as James waddled back to the Hall. Before he entered he turned and saluted the boys who, together, saluted him back.

Walking back to the barn, it struck Bess that she'd never seen James interact with children before – at least, not since they themselves were children. She felt her cheeks glowing in the cold air and smiled at the memory. Strange, she thought, that she'd imagined him in every scenario possible, but never with children. By the way he behaved with Samuel and Benjamin it was obvious that he liked them – and after seeing the smiles on their faces, they liked him too. James would make a lovely father, Bess thought, wiping away a tear.

Village children came to the Hall to play with their friends from London almost every day during the Christmas holiday. They played hide and seek in the woods, built snowmen and had snowball fights, calling themselves The Mighty Midlanders and The Super Southerners. But it was the lake that was the most popular source of entertainment for both the children and the land girls, especially for Kitty and Molly who had never seen a frozen lake until they came to Foxden, and were eager to learn how to skate. No matter how many times they fell over, they got up and tried again, and again.

Polly, Laura and Sylvia, who were good at all sports, particularly the outdoor kind, were accomplished skaters. Like lifeguards – whose job it was to help swimmers in distress – the girls skated round the edge of the lake, so they were on hand if anyone needed help.

The lake reminded Bess of her childhood, when she and Margaret taught Claire and Ena how to skate. The Dudley girls took to skating like ducks to water, but Tom didn't take it seriously. He spent most of his time with James, messing around and putting the girls off their stride. Tom wasn't a bad skater, but James spent more time on his bottom than he did on his feet. Bess, on the other hand, took to ice-skating with the same enthusiasm as she did to horse riding, and rarely fell over.

James joined the party, as Bess hoped he would, but was immediately dragged onto the lake by Polly and Laura. 'Be gentle with me, girls, it's been a long time since I've skated,' James shouted, as the two land girls led him round the lake. At first they were gentle, and skated slowly, but by the time they'd lapped the lake and returned to the Peacock lawn, to where Bess and the others were sitting, they'd picked up speed. As they approached the onlookers, the girls let go of James's hands, turned their feet slightly to the side to slow down, and came to a halt at the edge of the lake. James, imitating a tap-dancing windmill, ended up on his bottom.

Mr Porter arrived with two jugs of hot chocolate and Mrs Hartley, hard on her old friend's heels, carried a tray of cups and a tin of roasted chestnuts, which Iris counted out into three-cornered paper bags. Mr Porter banged the empty roasting tin like a gong and shouted, 'Come and get it.' And when everyone was safely sitting on the tarpaulin, Mrs Hartley gave them each a bag of chestnuts and a cup of hot chocolate.

Bess had never had so much fun on New Year's Eve before. The land girls who had stayed for Christmas, or who had returned in time for the New Year, made sure of that. Everyone missed Annabel, of course, who had returned to Kent on Boxing Day. She didn't tell Bess, or anyone else, why she had to go back. Not that it mattered. The servicemen had either gone home for Christmas, or back to their regiments, so she wasn't needed in the west wing. Even so, Bess thought it strange that she'd left Foxden without seeing James.

As the afternoon wore on the temperature dropped. Snow clouds filled the sky and as darkness fell, so did the snow – and the party came to an end. It had been a long day, which everyone had enjoyed. The parents of the village children arrived and after a few minutes – it was too cold to stand about chatting – they took their tired offspring home. Mr Porter and James, deep in conversation, strolled round the grounds, and Nanny Friel and Nurse Ambler rounded up the children, who looked worn out and for once didn't argue about going to bed. Polly, Iris and Mavis made a final check of the lawn for rubbish before going to their billet, and Mrs Hartley, Laura, Sylvia and Bess took the plates and mugs to the kitchen and washed them up.

'Why don't you go up, Mrs Hartley? Bess said. 'We'll finish off down here. You look tired and you have to be up early in the morning.'

'Well, if you're sure,' Mrs Hartley said, taking off her pinafore and yawning. 'Thank you for your help, girls. See you in the morning.'

'Goodnight,' the girls said in unison.

As soon as the washing up was finished Sylvia said, 'I think I'll turn in too.' She bowled the tea towel that she'd used at the row of hooks where it usually hung and by some miracle it caught on the first hook and held fast.

Laura and Bess had seen the incredible fluke and began to laugh. Sylvia polished the nails of her right hand on an imaginary lapel and waited to be congratulated. Instead Laura pushed her out of the door, laughing.

After she had put the last of the dishes away, Bess walked across the room to the kitchen door. She reached out and was just about to lock it when she heard footsteps outside. She caught her breath. 'Laura? Sylvia? Is that you?'

'No, it's me – James. Sorry to call so late, but it's such a lovely night, I didn't feel like turning in.'

Relieved that the caller wasn't an intruder, Bess opened the door.

'I know you check on the horses last thing, and wondered if I might accompany you?' James said.

'Of course, I was just on my way to the stables,' she lied. Mr Porter would have checked on the horses while she was clearing away the dishes.

'Sable's getting older,' Bess said, as they walked across the yard. 'I put a blanket on her on cold nights.' She unbolted the top of Sultan and Sable's door and both horses came to her. Sable was wearing her blanket.

'Good old Mr Porter,' Bess said, stroking Sable's nose. 'He looks after you doesn't he, girl?'

'Good old Mr Porter? You've changed your tune,' James teased.

'Yes, I have,' Bess admitted. 'I didn't really know him before we worked together. But now I know him, I understand him, and I like him very much. I'll let you into a secret. I couldn't do the job I'm doing here without him.' Bess gave both Sable and Sultan a carrot before closing their doors.

'You are the most remarkable woman, Bess Dudley,' James said. 'Do you think of everything?'

'No, I don't think I do, but I try to remember things that I think are important,' Bess replied.

'Like horses and children. Your sisters, Tom, Molly, the land girls, Mr--'

'Stop! You're embarrassing me,' Bess said, putting her hand up to James's mouth. His lips were cold but his breath was warm on her fingers. She looked into his eyes, unable to move. Her heart was drumming. She had an uncontrollable desire to put her arms around him, to replace her hand with her mouth, to feel his lips against her lips – and she began to tremble.

'You're shivering – and it's no wonder, it's freezing out here. Let's go inside. Shall we go up to the library for a nightcap?'

'What? I'm so sorry, I was miles away,' she said. 'What did you say?'

'Would you like a nightcap?'

'Yes. Thank you. I'd love a nightcap.'

The fire in the library was almost out, but James found an old newspaper and he and Bess sat on the rug and rolled up each page tightly, before adding a handful of dry sticks and a couple of logs from a brass scuttle. While James went to his father's study to fetch the brandy, Bess pumped air into the newly-laid fire with a pair of bellows until it caught. By the time James returned with a decanter and two glasses, Bess was sitting on the rug warming her hands.

James poured two measures of brandy, gave one to Bess and put the other on the hearth, before taking off his coat and sitting on the rug next to her. 'Come closer,' he said. And as Bess moved towards him, James put his coat round her shoulders.

Deep in thought, Bess stared at the flames flickering in the fireplace. She sipped her brandy, holding the smooth amber liquid in her mouth to savour its rich taste before swallowing.

James picked up his glass and took a drink. 'You look like you're miles away. Are you all right?'

'Yes,' Bess said, 'I'm fine. But I received a letter from the mother of an old friend today. She said her son, Frank, was missing in action, presumed dead. He was a lovely chap. A Lowarth boy. He went to school with Tom, but I don't think you would have known him – he didn't come over this way much.' Bess had walked out with Frank, been fond of him, but decided against sharing that piece of information with James. 'Poor Mrs Donnelly. Frank was her only son, her only child.'

'Poor Bess,' James said, tightening his arm round her protectively. Bess relaxed into the curve of James's body and laid her head on his shoulder. 'Bess worries for everyone, but who worries for Bess?' James asked.

Bess looked up at James, but before she had time to reply, he kissed her.

Bess accepted James's lips - warm now, not cold - and she closed her eyes. If this was a dream, she never wanted to wake from it. James kissed her again. His lips were open and moist. She felt love and need stirring in her stomach, panicked and pulled away. There was a time when she would have given anything in the world to be kissed by James. She used to imagine falling into his arms, giving herself to him and being with him forever – but now, after what had happened in London...

'I'm sorry, Bess, that was presumptuous of me. Forgive me, I thought--'

'There's nothing to forgive. It's me who should be sorry. There was a time when I would have... I'm sorry, James, but I can't,' Bess cried.

'Can't what?' James put his hand under Bess's chin and lifted her face. 'Talk to me, Bess. What is it?'

Embarrassed, Bess turned away so James couldn't see her face. She looked into the fire and focussed on the fingers of flame that crept up the chimney. She took a sip of her brandy – it gave her courage – and in the safety of the warm library, she told James everything that had happened to her on the night she had too much champagne in London. The night she had allowed herself to be taken into a filthy alley and abused by a man she thought was a friend. She told him that she was ashamed of herself for having too much to drink, and for not being able to stop him. 'I hate him for taking advantage of me,' she said, 'but I hate myself more because I couldn't stop him. I was terrified that he'd kill me, so I gave in to him. And now,' she sobbed, 'everything is spoiled, I'm spoiled, and I don't deserve to be loved.'

James held Bess in his arms and rocked her gently until she stopped crying. He told her that what her abuser had done to her, what he had forced her to do, was terrible, horrific, but it wasn't her fault. She was not to blame. And he told her that it didn't change who she was, or how he felt about her.

'Thank you,' she whispered.

'Thank *you*, Bess,' he said, kissing her on the forehead. 'Thank you for trusting me enough to tell me.'

Bess closed her eyes and for the first time since that night she wanted to be held, to be kissed, to be loved.

At first their kisses were tentative, guarded. Then they became passionate until neither of them was able to control what was happening. James pulled the ribbon from Bess's hair and when it fell in loose curls onto her shoulders, he gently pushed it away and kissed the lobe of her ear. Bess caught her breath and closed her eyes. Tingles ran down her spine as James kissed her neck. He unbuttoned her blouse and slowly pulled it down until her shoulders were bare. He kissed her shoulders and then her breasts – and Bess knew that if she didn't want James to make love to her, she would have to stop him now. But she did want him to make love to her. She wanted him as much as he wanted her. She looked into his eyes and smiled her consent, and James kissed her again. With little kisses, no more than pecks, he asked, 'Are you sure?'

Bess was sure, she had never been so sure of anything in her life. She had dreamed of this night for as long as she could remember. She stood in front of the fire and, as if it was the most natural thing in the world, she unbuttoned her skirt and let it fall to the floor. James went to her and held her in his arms, all the while searching her face for signs of uncertainty, but there were none. He eased the straps of her underskirt from her shoulders and the underskirt slipped over her hips to join her skirt.

Giving herself to James felt right. She had loved him for as long as she could remember. She loved him before she knew what love was. She felt abandoned when he went away to boarding school, and would stand at her bedroom window for hours just to catch a glimpse of him riding past the cottage on his horse in the summer holidays. She had loved him so much that she daren't say his name in front of Tom or her sisters, for fear they would see the love in her face. There was a time when even friendship between a servant's daughter and the master's son would have been frowned upon. But the war had changed that. Class differences were becoming less important. Even so, Bess still wasn't able to show her feelings for James, because of Annabel. Annabel? Dear Lord, what was she doing in the arms of Annabel's fiancé?

Bess looked into James's eyes. So many rules, prejudices, and people had come between them over the years, but not anymore. Nothing and no one was ever going to come between them again. She had given James her heart a long time ago; now she was ready to give him all of herself.

James took off his clothes and pulled Bess to him again. She could feel his heart beating, his arousal, and she closed her eyes. With his arm firmly round her waist, James lowered her to the floor. She felt his warm breath on her cheek, her breasts, and she welcomed his love. They made love slowly and gently at first, and then James lifted her to him. Bess arched her back and felt him deep inside her. They shared the same rhythm until neither could bear the intensity of it any longer. Exhausted and happy, they slept in each other's arms on the rug in front of the library fire.

Bess woke first the following morning but didn't stir. She lay on her side and watched the soft pale light of early morning creep across James's handsome profile. Still half asleep, James pulled her to him and smiled contentedly. 'Good morning. Are you cold?' he asked, pulling his overcoat up and round Bess's shoulders.

Bess shook her head. 'I don't think I'll ever be cold again.'

James kissed her on the tip of her nose and then on her lips.

'I must go,' Bess said, still flushed with love.

'Stay a little longer,' James whispered.

'I can't,' she said, as she slipped from beneath his coat. 'I have to go to work. I wish I could stay, but it wouldn't be fair on the others.' Which was true – but what was really worrying her was someone might come into the library and catch them. What had happened between them was beautiful, but not everyone would see it that way. Some people would think making love on the library floor was sordid, and she was common. Bess didn't want anyone to know she'd spent the night with James. Apart from hating gossip, Bess didn't want Annabel to hear about it. If anyone was going to tell Annabel, it had to be James. Bess knelt down beside him. She couldn't say the words, so she kissed him goodbye.

CHAPTER TWENTY-THREE

Bess took Garth Davies to Larks Meadow to feed his sheep in Foxden's hay wain. Garth's cart had lost a wheel a couple of days earlier in frozen ruts and was at the wheelwrights in Lowarth.

As Garth forked hay from the back of the wain and Bess broke the ice on the water trough, a fleet of Wellington bombers roared overhead.

Bess waved and the plane leading the formation tipped its wing.

'That'll be young Foxden,' Garth shouted.

'Yes,' Bess called back. 'I didn't think they'd be flying tonight.'

'A night operation tests the mettle of the lads and the Wellingtons, especially in this weather. See what man and machine are made of,' he said.

Fear, like a flame, spread through Bess's body. Why hadn't James told her he was flying today? And why hadn't she told him how she felt about him last night when she had the chance?

'You all right, Bess?'

'What? Yes, I'm fine,' she said, sitting upright, trying to pull herself together. 'I've broken the ice on the trough. I'll turn the hay wain round.'

'You looked as if you'd seen a ghost,' Garth said, climbing up and sitting beside her. 'You're coming down with something. Here, give me those reins. I think we'd best get you back to the Hall. Besides, it'll be dark soon and by the looks of those clouds there's another snowstorm brewing.'

Bess went straight up to her room, threw herself onto the bed and buried her head in the pillow. She cried herself to sleep. She dreamed that she was falling, spiralling through the air. It was dark, but she could see the earth. It was getting nearer. Branches of trees were reaching out to her. Just before she hit the ground, she heard a loud knock followed by two sharper knocks. Her body jerked and she woke. She opened her eyes, but for a moment didn't know where she was. She sat up and looked around. She was in her bedroom and she was safe. 'It was only a dream,' she said with relief, 'a bad dream.'

'Bess, it's Laura. Are you all right?'

'I don't think I am,' Bess replied. She had no idea how long she'd been asleep, but it had grown dark. 'Hang on a minute.' She crossed the room and closed the blackout curtains before switching on the light. 'Come in Laura, the door's open.'

'What's the matter?' Laura asked when she saw Bess had been crying. 'Is it James?'

'What makes you think it's James?'

'I've seen the way you two look at each other. Last night he couldn't take his eyes off you. Has he done something to upset you?'

'No,' Bess said. 'Last night was the most wonderful night of my life.'

'Is it Annabel?'

'No. Yes. I mean-- I don't want to hurt Annabel, I respect her and I like her very much. But that's not why I'm upset. I'm frightened, Laura. Frightened for James. I watched his squadron fly off this afternoon and I had a terrible feeling that I'll never see him again,' she said, and burst into tears.

Laura put her arms round her friend.

'I love him so much, Laura, I always have. When I was a girl, I used to dream of being his sweetheart and walking out with him. Of course, it could never have happened. Until last night, I could only imagine what it would be like to be loved by James, but now... Oh Laura, I love James and he feels the same way about me. I don't want to lose him. Not to Annabel and not to this bloody war.'

'And you won't. It's obvious that the chap's crazy about you.'

'I think he is,' Bess said, laughing and crying at the same time.

'C'mon, dry your eyes. Let's go downstairs and raid Mrs Hartley's pantry. If there's anyone down there, we'll bring the spoils up here.'

In the early hours of the morning, Bess heard James's squadron return. She ran to the window and in the clear night sky she watched the planes come home. One after another, like big grumbling birds, the Wellingtons came into view and made their descent to Bitteswell. Nine planes flew out of the aerodrome and nine returned. Bess lay on her bed and she cried again – with happiness.

During January James visited Foxden several times and each time he and Bess found a way to be alone. They'd walk across the yard to the stables or the barn, discussing the horses, or farm business, but once inside they would fall into each other's arms and hold each other as if their lives depended on the few minutes they had together.

At the beginning of February, the young sergeant who had driven James to collect Bess from the gate on the night of the aerodrome's Christmas dance arrived with a letter. Bess opened her mouth to speak, but fear took the words. 'I'll wait for your reply by the car, Miss,' the sergeant said, handing Bess the letter before turning and walking away. Bess sighed with relief and after taking the single sheet of Air Force note paper from its envelope read, "My dearest Bess, I've had the most incredible bit of luck. I've been given forty-eight hours' leave starting on Friday 14th - St. Valentine's Day. No, it isn't a joke. Will you come away with me for the weekend? We can go wherever you like. My only request is that I have you all to myself. If you can get away, meet me in the barn at 7.30 on the 14th. Please say you'll come. With love, James."

Bess's reply was short and took only seconds to write. "I'm counting the days."

In the afternoon on the Friday Bess and James were going away for the weekend, Bess and Laura were repairing a dry-stone wall on the Lowarth to Woodcote Road when Annabel drove by.

'I didn't know Annabel was coming up this weekend,' Laura said.

Bess watched Annabel's car turn into Foxden's drive. 'Nor did I.'

'Do you think she's come up to surprise James, with it being St. Valentine's?'

It would be just my luck, Bess thought, and serve me right too, for having an affair with my friend's fiancé. 'She's probably come up because there are new patients in the west wing.'

'I thought Nurse Ambler was looking after them.'

'She is, but Annabel's in charge of things. Besides, she has every right to be here.'

'I know. But what about your weekend away with James? You will still be able to go, won't you?' Laura asked.

'I don't know.' Guilt had overtaken Bess's disappointment at seeing Annabel. 'Let's just get this wall finished.'

Bess and Laura returned to the Hall and a message from Annabel saying she hoped they were free that evening to go with her for a drink to the Crown – and that she'd be in Mrs Hartley's kitchen around seven.

Bess would normally have gone up and welcomed Annabel, but today, knowing that she had come all the way from Kent to see the man she loved, who Bess also loved, Bess couldn't face her. What a mess. If Annabel ever found out that she and James loved each other and were going away for the weekend together, it would break her heart. It would break Bess's heart, if she were in Annabel's place. Bess hated herself for deceiving her friend but her love for James was too strong to ignore. She loved him so much that nothing else in the world mattered. So, fighting to put Annabel out of her mind, she packed a weekend bag with her best clothes and slipped out of the hall to meet James in the barn.

Bess was half an hour early. It was only seven o'clock, but she couldn't risk being in the kitchen when Annabel and the girls met to go to the Crown. She hid her bag behind the door and, keeping in the shadows, edged her way along the side of the barn to wait for James. It was then that she saw them: James and Annabel. They were standing on top of the circular steps leading down to the drive, embracing. Unable to move, Bess watched as Annabel stood on tiptoe, put her arms around James's neck and kissed him. Then James, his face half hidden in Annabel's hair, lifted her off her feet and swung her round.

Bess stared in disbelief, unable to take in what she was seeing. How could James pretend he cared for her when he clearly still loved Annabel? Bess wanted to scream from the pain, shout with anger. Instead she turned and took a shuddering, but calming, breath. As if she was sleepwalking she made her way to the stables, opened Sable's door, and led her quietly across the courtyard. When was sure she couldn't be seen or heard, she mounted and rode Sable bareback across Foxden Acres. Tears stung and blinded her and the icy wind chafed her face, but she didn't stop until she was at the river.

'Poor Sable,' Bess said. Crying and shivering, she dismounted. 'I should never have brought you out on such a cold night.' Sable lowered her head and nudged Bess, which made her cry more. 'Come on, girl,' she said, giving Sable a loving pat, 'let's go home.'

James went to the barn at seven-thirty, as arranged, and waited. When Bess hadn't arrived by eight he began to worry. He knew she hadn't gone to the Crown with Annabel, Laura and Polly, because he'd seen them leave in Annabel's car at quarter past seven.

He searched the Hall. He visited the soldiers in the west wing and when he didn't find her there he went to the library. He went up to his old nursery under the pretence of finding out if the children needed anything. He called on Molly and Miss Armstrong, and asked Mrs Hartley outright if she'd seen Bess. By the time Laura, Polly and Annabel came back from the pub, James was out of his mind with worry.

'Have you seen Bess?' he asked Laura, who was first out of Annabel's car.

'No. I thought she was with you.'

'She didn't turn up and she's nowhere to be found.'

'Well, something important must have come up. Bess wouldn't let you down without a good reason.'

James left the three women and went up to his bedroom in his mother's apartment. He threw himself onto the bed. If something had happened, if Bess had to go to her parents, she would have got a message to him somehow. She wouldn't have just stood him up. He daren't think she'd changed her mind. Why would she? Bess loved him as much as he loved her.

While James lay staring at the ceiling in one part of the Hall, Bess had returned and lay unable to sleep in another. What a mess I've made of everything, she thought. I've knowingly betrayed my friend by making love with the man she plans to marry, so what right have I to feel betrayed when he leaves me for her? I've lost the man I love, and because of him, I'll lose Annabel's friendship and Laura and Polly's respect. Bess stared at the ceiling and sobbed.

Relieved to see Sable hadn't suffered from her late night excursion, Bess led her out of the stables.

'I'll catch you up, Bess,' Mr Porter said, saddling Sultan.

'Bess! Bess!' James shouted. 'Wait!'

Bess heard James calling her, but she didn't look back. She mounted Sable and galloped off.

'Thank you, Mr Porter,' James said, pulling the reins out of the old man's hands before jumping on Sultan and chasing after Bess.

Bess rode as if the devil himself was after her. She didn't want to see James or speak to him. She was afraid she might weaken and... 'James... How could you do this to me?' she screamed.

'Whoa, girl.' Sable faltered, and when Bess brought her to a halt she hobbled. 'What's the matter, girl?' she said, dismounting.

'Bess, what's wrong?' James asked when he caught up with her at the river.

'Sable's got a stone in her hoof.'

'I don't mean with Sable,' James said, dismounting to examine Sable's hoof. 'I mean with you. Why didn't you come to the barn last night? We were supposed to go away for the weekend.'

'I changed my mind,' Bess lied. She wasn't going to give James Foxden the satisfaction of knowing he had made a fool of her.

'You changed your mind? I don't believe you, Bess. You were looking forward to going away - to us spending time together, alone - as much as I was!'

Bess fought for the right words, as well as to stop her tears. 'I was, but...'

'But what? What could possibly have happened to make you change your mind?'

'I don't want to talk about it! I've changed my mind! That's all there is to it!'

James took a knife from his jacket pocket and carefully hooked a stone out of Sable's hoof. 'There you are, girl,' he said, holding onto the horse's reins to steady her, and looking at Bess.

'Thank you,' Bess said, and mounted.

'I love you, Bess. I thought you loved me.'

'I thought so too,' Bess replied sharply. 'I was wrong.'

'What do you mean, you were wrong? You loved me on New Year's Eve. What's changed?'

'New Year's Eve was a mistake!' Bess snapped.

'How can you say that? For Christ's sake, Bess, tell me what it is I've done!' James shouted, still holding Sable's reins.

'It's over, James. I've made up my mind.'

'But I love you, Bess. I want to marry you.'

Tears streamed down Bess's face. She wanted to fall into his arms, say I love you too, that I want nothing more than to marry you, to be your wife. But she knew she would never be able to get the image of James kissing Annabel out of her mind. 'It's too late!' she shouted. 'Now let go of Sable's reins!'

Startled by the depth of anger in Bess's voice, James let go of Sable's reins – and she galloped away.

CHAPTER TWENTY-FOUR

'Can I help you?' Bess called, wiping tears from her eyes as she approached two strangers standing next to a black saloon motorcar in front of the Hall.

'Perhaps you can,' the taller of the men said. 'We're looking for a young woman named Molly McKenna.'

Bess looked from one to the other of the men. 'May I ask what business you have with Miss McKenna?'

'We're employed by the solicitors of Mr Shaunessy McKenna to find his niece.'

Bess was suddenly on her guard. 'What makes you think Miss McKenna is here?'

'In our search for Miss McKenna we found the lady she lodged with before--'

'You found Mrs McAllister?' Bess screamed.

'Yes. It was Mrs McAllister who thought Miss McKenna might be staying here with a young woman named Bess Dudley.'

'Molly is here. She's well and she's safe. But what of Mrs McAllister?' Bess asked frantically. 'When did you see her? How was she? Do you know where she is now?'

'I'm here, Bess,' a familiar voice called from inside the car.

'Mrs McAllister!' Bess cried. 'Is it really you?' Bess helped her old friend out of the car and threw her arms around her. 'We searched for days. We looked everywhere for you.'

'I know, dear. I took a blow to the head in the bombing and lost my memory. I wandered from place to place. Then one day these gentlemen found me. I'm fully recovered now and it's thanks to Molly's uncle.'

'Molly's uncle?'

'Yes, dear! I'll tell you all about it later, but first I must keep the promise I made to him.'

Bess took the small party from London up to the sitting room and invited the two gentlemen to take a seat while she and Mrs McAllister went to the nursery. Molly and Elizabeth were in the playroom with Nurse Ambler. Molly was sitting on the floor with Elizabeth, building a tower out of colourful bricks. Every time she carefully balanced the last brick on top of the stack, Elizabeth knocked the tower down and squealed with joy.

With her forefinger at her lips, Bess beckoned Nurse Ambler. 'Would you ask Miss Armstrong to come up, please? You'll find her on the ground floor, in the small office next to his Lordship's study.'

Nurse Ambler nodded. 'It's time I brought the children in for lunch. I'll tell her on my way.'

'Thank you,' Bess said, and when the nurse had left, she went into the nursery. 'Molly, there's someone here to see you.'

'Who is it?' Molly asked, jumping up.

'It's me, Molly dear,' Mrs McAllister said, entering the room behind Bess.

Molly stood for a long moment, wide-eyed and open-mouthed, before flying into Mrs McAllister's arms.

'I'll go and rustle up some tea,' Bess said to Miss Armstrong, who had dashed upstairs after hearing the description of the visitor and was standing beside Bess watching the reunion of Molly and Mrs Mac. 'I'll take it to the sitting room. Come along when you're ready,' Bess said, and left her old friends from London to get re-acquainted.

Molly and Miss Armstrong sat either side of Mrs McAllister while Mrs Mac cuddled Elizabeth. Elizabeth gave her new friend a broad smile, showing off her two front teeth, before snuggling down with her thumb in her mouth against Mrs Mac's now not so ample chest. Content in Mrs Mac's arms, the little girl closed her eyes and went to sleep.

After tea one of the men from the solicitors asked Molly if he could speak to her alone.

Molly quite firmly said that anything he had to say to her could be said in front of her friends. 'We have no secrets from one another,' she added.

'As you wish,' the man said, and cleared his throat. 'While your uncle, Mr Shaunessy McKenna, who had been ill for some time, was convalescing in a sanatorium on the west coast of Ireland, he heard on the wireless that the Luftwaffe had bombed parts of Kensington. He telephoned your lodgings, but there was no reply, so he returned to London

347

immediately. He went to Arcadia Avenue, to the house where you had lived but, as you know, it was no longer there. He knocked on every door of every house that was still standing in the avenue, and asked everyone he met if they knew where you or any of the other residents from number seventy-nine were. No one knew of your whereabouts.

'Your uncle was frantic with worry for you and the baby but his health was failing so he employed us, his solicitors, to find you. And it was while we were looking for you that we found Mrs McAllister.'

'I'd been ill too,' Mrs McAllister explained. 'Not in the same way as your uncle, but after the house was bombed I suffered a sort of shell shock. I lost my memory and was very confused. I tramped the streets for months, walking from one hostel to another, looking for someone. I knew I had lost someone that was dear to me, and I was determined to find them, but I didn't know who it was. I didn't know who I was at the time. But I ended up back in west London, living in a hostel for homeless women, and that's where these gentlemen found me.'

'Mr McKenna insisted that Mrs McAllister was brought to his house in Surrey, where he provided round-the-clock nursing until she was well again. And, as Mrs McAllister's health improved, she began to remember what had happened on the night of the bombing.'

'Yes,' Mrs McAllister cut in. 'It all came back to me - the bombs, Molly and Elizabeth, Miss Armstrong, and Bess. I remembered Bess came from a village near Lowarth. I also remembered that she was coming to London for Elizabeth's christening, which should have taken place the day after the bombing.' Mrs McAllister turned and smiled at Bess. 'I knew she'd have taken you and the baby and Miss Armstrong back to the country with her, where you'd be safe. So here we are.'

'And my uncle?' Molly asked. 'When can I see him?'

'I'm afraid your uncle passed away, miss.'

Molly's eyes filled with tears. 'No, please don't say that. He was the only family I had, until I lodged with Mrs McAllister,' she said, as if somehow that piece of information would change what the solicitor had told her.

Mrs Mac put her arms round her young friend. 'And he loved you very much.'

'Poor uncle. Now I'll never be able to ask him to forgive me.'

'My dear child,' Mrs McAllister said, looking into Molly's big blue eyes. 'Your uncle told me that he deeply regretted turning you away when you told him you were having a baby. He said he wanted so much to be part of your life, and Elizabeth's. And he made me promise to tell you how much he loved you, and how very sorry he was that he'd let you down when you needed him most. He hoped you would forgive him.'

'There's nothing to forgive,' Molly said.

349

'Miss McKenna, we would like you to come to our offices in London as soon as it's convenient,' the shorter of the two men said, handing Molly a business card. 'As sole beneficiary of your late uncle's estate there are papers you must sign. The house in Surrey--'

'My uncle's house?'

'It's your house now, miss,' the man said.

'My house? Did you hear that, Mrs McAllister? We have a home again. I can't believe it,' Molly said, taking hold of Mrs Mac's hand and holding out her other hand to Miss Armstrong, who joined them as they hugged each other.

'Why had you been crying this morning?' Miss Armstrong asked Bess after she had looked in on Molly and Elizabeth, who were both sound asleep.

'It was emotional seeing Mrs Mac again.'

'I mean earlier. You'd been crying before you saw Mrs McAllister,' Miss Armstrong said, with concern in her voice.

Bess wasn't sure if Miss Armstrong knew about her relationship with James. If she did, she probably wouldn't approve. Laura knew; she had noticed the way Bess and James looked at each other, even before Bess had told her that she and James were in love. Thinking about it, the land girls probably suspected something was going on. They had stopped talking once or twice when Bess entered the dorm, or changed the subject abruptly and loudly, which was always a giveaway. 'I'd seen James,' Bess said at last.

'And what did he do or say that upset you so terribly?'

'He told me he loved me and asked me to marry him.'

'What's so terrible about that?' Miss Armstrong asked.

'He isn't free. James is betrothed, or whatever it is the upper classes call it, to Annabel. Their parents want them to marry.'

'Does James want to marry Annabel?'

Bess shrugged her shoulders.

'Does he love her?'

'I don't know, but I saw them embracing last night, on St. Valentine's.'

'There could be a dozen reasons for that.'

'And he kissed her.'

'Have you spoken to James? Asked him why he kissed Annabel?'

'No.'

'Have you spoken to Annabel?'

'No, I couldn't. She looked so happy to be back from Kent. I couldn't take that away from her.' Bess lowered her eyes. 'I felt bad enough about loving James before I knew Annabel. Now we're friends, good friends, I'm ashamed that I've been disloyal to her. If she knew that James and I...' Bess shook her head. 'It would break her heart.'

'Let me get this straight. You love James and James loves you. He has asked you to marry him, but you've turned him down because you think Annabel loves him. Don't you know?'

'No. We've never talked about James in that way. We've talked light-heartedly about what James and my brother Tom used to get up to when they were young. We've talked about horses, the war, the west wing, and of course, Foxden Acres. Even when the girls talk about their sweethearts, Annabel never says anything about James.'

'Bess, you're not being fair to yourself, or to James – or to Annabel, for that matter. If you end your relationship with James and he marries Annabel, you won't only be responsible for breaking his heart – and your own – you'll be responsible for breaking Annabel's heart too, if James doesn't love her.

'Go and talk to him, Bess. Don't throw the love you have for each other away. To give James up because you think it's the right thing to do, or because it's what his family want, is absolute tosh. I know from bitter experience that doing the right thing doesn't make things better, it makes them worse. Do you love James, Bess?'

'Yes I do, very much.'

'Then tell him. If you don't you'll regret it for the rest of your life. Believe me, I know what I'm talking about.'

'What do you mean?'

'I've been in love,' Miss Armstrong confided, 'secretly, for several years. The man I love, Cyril, my boss at Mademoiselle Modes, was married. I'd known for as long as

I'd worked with him that he and his wife led separate lives but, like you, I felt guilty. So rather than be responsible for breaking up his marriage, I told him I didn't love him.'

'Poor man,' Bess said. 'What happened to him?'

'He was heartbroken. He moved to work for Denton and Christie. I missed him terribly, so I selfishly followed him. He gave me a job as Senior Sales Supervisor, but he couldn't cope with seeing me every day. So when I was on leave, he brought Miss Simpson in from another department and gave her my job. The week before I was due to return to work, I received a letter saying there had been a drop in sales, because of rationing, and I had been made redundant.

'The humiliation I felt coloured my feelings towards Cyril. I began to hate him. But when I saw him again on the day we went to Denton and Christie, after number seventy-nine had been bombed, I knew I still loved him.'

'And his wife?'

'She ran away with a door-to-door salesman.'

Both women laughed. 'So where do you go from here?' Bess asked.

'We've been writing to each other. Cyril has decided to ignore his male pride and divorce his wife for adultery. So when he's free, we're going to be married.' Miss Armstrong took Bess's hands in hers. 'Everyone deserves to be happy, Bess, to love

353

and to be loved. Life is short enough, but because of this damn war, no one knows what's round the corner. Don't throw away what you and James have. Go to him, tell him how you feel and give him the chance to explain.'

'Thank you, Miss Armstrong, I will,' Bess said. 'I'll go to see him first thing tomorrow.'

Bess said goodbye to her friends Molly and baby Elizabeth, Miss Armstrong and Mrs McAllister on Sunday morning – and had every intention of taking Miss Armstrong's advice and telling James how much she loved him. First she needed to do what she believed was right. She needed to tell Annabel.

As she walked towards the Hall, Bess could see Annabel sitting in the bay window of the ballroom reading the Sunday newspaper to Frank Donnelly, Bess's old boyfriend who, until six weeks ago, was missing in action, presumed dead. Frank had come to Foxden from the Walsgrave hospital in Coventry to recover after having an operation to remove his left eye. He wasn't able to see, but his spirits were high and he was looking forward to having his bandages removed.

Annabel welcomed Bess with a warm smile.

'Hello, Frank,' Bess said, including Annabel in the greeting. 'Do you mind if I steal Annabel for a few minutes? I won't keep her long.'

'And I thought you'd come to see me,' Frank joked.

'What is it, Bess?' Annabel asked when she and Bess were out of earshot of the other soldiers in the ballroom.

'I have something important to tell you, Annabel.'

'Go on,' Annabel said, fearing Bess was the bearer of bad news.

'I am in love with James.'

'Oh my God,' Annabel said. 'I--'

'And James loves me!'

'I know! I know James loves you,' Annabel said, laughing. 'I probably knew before he did. I certainly knew before you did.'

'And you don't mind?' Bess asked, puzzled.

'Mind? Why should I mind?'

'Because I thought .... You and James ...?' Bess stuttered. 'I saw you kissing on Friday night, St. Valentine's--'

'Yes, I did kiss James, outside the Hall, but not for the reasons you think. I had some news I wanted to share with him - with you both. That's why I invited you to the Crown. But because you and James were going away and wouldn't be there, I told James before I went to the pub with Laura and Polly.'

'I don't understand,' Bess said.

'The reason James kissed me was to congratulate me on my marriage.'

'Marriage?' Bess stood, open-mouthed. 'Who have you married?'

'Tom. We were married in the New Year, before he went overseas. That's why I went back to Kent,' Annabel said, holding out her hand to show Bess her wedding ring.'

'Tom? My brother Tom?'

'Yes, didn't Laura tell you?'

'I haven't seen her.'

'Surely James--?'

'No. I haven't seen him either.'

'We became close when we met again in Ashford hospital, when Tom came back from Dunkirk. But I fell in love with him on the night he sang "Roses of Picardy" to me in the Crown,' Annabel said, smiling at the memory.

'I thought your family wanted you to marry James?'

Annabel laughed. 'They did, until I told them how much I loved Tom. They weren't happy at first - and they were furious when they found out that we had married in secret. Tom only had forty-eight hours' leave, so it was all a bit of a rush. Anyway, they've come to terms with it now and they've accepted him. James knew I loved Tom, but I couldn't tell him we were married until I'd told my parents.'

'I'm sorry, Annabel. I thought you loved James.'

'I do love James, I always have. It might have been more than brotherly love once, but that was a long time ago when we were in our teens. Now I love James in the same way that you love Tom - like a brother.'

'James looked so happy when you kissed him,' Bess said.

'He was happy. He was telling me how much he loved you. He said he was taking you away for a romantic weekend, and he was going to ask you to marry him.'

'Oh my God, Annabel, what have I done?' Bess cried. 'I turned him down.'

'You did what?' Annabel fumed. 'James loves you so much!'

'And I love him, with all my heart,' Bess cried.

'Then you must tell him. Tell him before he goes up tonight. From what he said on Friday - or rather, from what he didn't say - his squadron is about to see action again. He said he wouldn't be able to get home to Foxden for some time. That's why he was given leave. If you go now, you might just catch him. Take my car.'

Bess pulled up outside the main security gate at Bitteswell Aerodrome. 'I need to see Flying Officer Foxden. It's urgent.'

'Can I see your pass, miss?' the military policeman asked.

'I don't have a pass, but it's very important. If you phone through I'm sure--'

'Sorry miss, you're too late. They're preparing for take-off,' the MP said.

Bess jumped into the car and drove round to the side gate. She could see the planes clearly, see the engineers working on them, hear the whirr of the propellers. Two airmen were lighting cigarettes outside the canteen.

Bess watched them walk away and then stop to speak to a group of men. James was not one of them. She looked back at the canteen and her heart almost stopped. James and another officer were standing in the doorway. Bess waved frantically, willing James to look her way, but it wasn't until he walked onto the runway with the sun behind him that he saw her.

'James,' Bess shouted. 'I love you! I will marry you!'

James waved briefly, turned and spoke to the officer he had left the canteen with, and then jumped into a Jeep and drove at speed to her.

'James, I'm sorry. I saw you kissing Annabel and I thought .... Can you ever forgive me? I want to be your wife more than anything in the world.'

'It doesn't matter, darling. The only thing that matters is that you'll marry me. Oh, Bess, I do love you!' James said, holding her hands through the gate.

'I love you too.'

'I have to go, darling. Will you wait for me?'

'For as long as it takes,' Bess said, not wanting to let go of James's hand. 'Please be careful.'

James laughed. 'Gerry can't hurt me now, I'm invincible. I'm in love with the most beautiful girl in the world and she's going to marry me!' he shouted to the guard, as he climbed over the gate.

The young military policeman looked the other way as James and Bess kissed each other passionately.

'I love you,' James said.

'And I love you, more than anything,' Bess replied.

'Then will you wear my ring until this damn war is over, or until I can put a wedding ring on your finger?' James took off the signet ring his grandfather had given to him on his twenty-first birthday and slipped it onto Bess's wedding finger.

'But James, this is your family ring. It has the Foxden crest on it. It shouldn't be worn by anyone except the heir to the Foxden Estate,' Bess said.

'Then you'd better take good care of it for me, hadn't you, like you do the Estate.'

'I will, I promise,' Bess said, and they kissed again.

The young MP cleared his throat.

'Goodbye my love,' James said, as he tore himself away from Bess.

The planes were lining up on the runway as James sped back to his aeroplane. As he climbed into the cockpit he turned and waved, and Bess blew him a kiss.

'I love you!' she shouted. She knew James couldn't hear her; she could hardly hear herself above the noise of the aeroplanes.

Leading the formation, James's Wellington thundered down the runway ahead of the other planes and was first to lift off. The second and third planes followed closely behind him, then the fourth, fifth and sixth planes left the runway in quick succession with the last four planes bringing up the rear. James flashed his tail-light, and Bess waved until he was out of sight.

Bess was so excited she couldn't sleep. She lay in bed looking at James's ring on her finger. She relived every kiss they had shared, and recalled again and again how James had asked her to wait for him – and how happy he was when she said she would marry him. In the morning, Bess wondered whether she should hide the ring, wear it round her neck perhaps, but she decided against taking it off. The man she loved had put his ring on her finger and she had promised to wear it until he returned – and she would.

Bess went down to breakfast, but was too excited to eat.

'Bess Dudley, what have you got on your wedding finger?' Mrs Hartley asked. Her old friend had spotted James's ring and as tears of happiness welled up in her eyes, she hugged Bess to her. 'I am so pleased for you, Bess. I knew Master James loved you. I could see it in his eyes every time he looked at you. Even afore this damn war, I could see that he loved you.'

'And I loved him, Mrs Hartley,' Bess confided, 'but I never dared to hope that one day ....'

'What will be will be, my dear girl! Don't they say it's fate, what happens to us in this life? Now eat your breakfast, you need to keep your strength up. You've got a lot of work to do, lass – and a lot of plans to make,' she said, with a wink. The land girls tumbled through the kitchen door, having intercepted the postman, and sat down to breakfast with their letters.

Kitty opened a letter from her mother who, she said, was living at the Black Swan, the pub in London's East End where she was a barmaid. 'She's got a new gentleman friend and she's old enough to be his mother by what she says in this letter,' Kitty said, laughing. 'It was always good fun at the Black Swan. When I used to go there, I was never short of gentlemen friends. Problem was, if I took a fella home me mam would introduce herself as me sister and try to pinch him off me. She's a real gal, my mam is,' Kitty said proudly.

'My mother's praying for my virginity at chapel,' Fanny said.

'Blimey!' Kitty looked serious. 'It'd do no good if the whole bloomin' congregation prayed for mine,' she said, and everyone laughed.

'Kitty, you are terrible!' Polly said.

'It's true,' she replied, tucking into a thick slice of toast with jam.

'Changing the subject,' Sylvia said pointedly, 'my sister has moved to Portsmouth. She's got a teaching job down there so she can be there when her husband comes home on leave – he's in the Navy.'

361

Everyone discussed the letters they'd received and there was a great deal of laughter as a result.

Bess took her breakfast dishes to the sink, washed them, and left the room before any of the girls noticed James's ring. There would be plenty of time to tell them her news later.

It was a sunny spring morning, when the young sergeant delivered James's letter.

'I'm sorry, Miss.'

'Sorry, sergeant?' Bess said. 'Sorry for what?'

The young sergeant lowered his head. 'If there's anything?' he said.

Anything-'

Bess heard a small voice that sounded like her own say, 'Thank you.' She watched the young sergeant walk across the courtyard, get into his car and slowly drive off. I should be cutting spring cabbage, she thought as she opened the letter and read,

My dear Bess,

This letter is the hardest that I have ever had to write and one that I had hoped you would never have to read. However, my darling, if fate has dictated that you must read it, it is because I cannot be with you to tell you how much I love you.

Don't cry, my darling. We were lucky to have found each other, and to have known real

love. Some people spend a lifetime looking for the kind of love that we had and never find it.

Take care of yourself, Bess, and don't be sad. Remember me with love and with happiness, not with tears.

Think of me sometimes when you're riding across the Foxden Acres.

Forever yours,

James.

EPILOGUE

The loudspeaker on the platform, which hadn't been in use since the war began, crackled and sprang into life. Several people cheered while others called for quiet. An elderly woman opened the door to hear the message more clearly, by which time the cafeteria was in silence. "THE NEXT TRAIN TO ARRIVE ON PLATFORM TWO IS THE ONE-O-FIVE FROM LONDON EUSTON."

Bess and Annabel jumped up and looked at each another. Simultaneously they began to speak, then stopped. Neither could hear what the other was saying. There was so much noise as people leapt out of their seats and rushed to the door. Bess caught sight of herself in the glass of a signed photograph of Vera Lynn but decided to ignore her unruly curls, while Annabel rummaged through her handbag and found her lipstick and powder. She applied a little lipstick but put the powder back into her bag – there was no time. The two women laughed. They laughed with excitement and with relief. The waiting was almost over. Bess knelt down and wiped a speck of chocolate from Charlotte's mouth before gathering her up in her arms and following Annabel, who was already making her way through the crowds to the southern end of the platform.

Bess watched Annabel's red trilby disappear amid a rainbow of hats, berets and brightly coloured scarves. Someone shouted, 'The train's coming!' and the crowd surged forward. With Charlotte still in her arms, Bess took advantage of the space available and moved to the northern end of the platform.

At their new location, Charlotte was no longer in danger of being squashed and Bess had a better view of Annabel – or would have when Annabel arrived at the opposite end of the platform. Bess lifted Charlotte onto a large wooden crate and held her firmly while she scanned the ever-growing crowd for her friend. Her gaze locked onto a familiar face. 'Laura?' she called. Bess craned her neck to see more clearly. The young woman was tall and slender, and had the same blonde sun-streaked hair and bronzed complexion from working in the fields but, as she turned her face fully towards her, Bess could see she was not Laura.

Bess hugged Charlotte to her and wondered where the women of Foxden's Land Army were. Sylvia had moved to Portsmouth to be near her sister after her sister's husband was killed in the Battle of the Atlantic, and had returned to teaching. Fanny had gone home to Wales to be with her mother, who was mourning the loss of Fanny's grandmother. And Kitty - where was she now? Bess worried for Kitty. Had she gone back to her old lifestyle of living off her wits and the generosity of gentlemen? Bess hoped not.

A young woman standing close to Bess burst into tears. She was nervously twisting a thin gold wedding band round her finger. Bess took a clean handkerchief from her pocket and gave it to her. She accepted it without lifting her head. When at last she stopped crying she took a deep, shuddering breath and said, 'Thank you.'

Most of the women were happy, excited. Many, like Bess and Annabel, had waited years to see their loved ones return. Even so, the lives of every woman here would have changed in some respect, while their men had been away. Women who had once looked forward to a future as a wife and mother now knew how to assemble an aeroplane engine and de-grease a magneto, drive a tractor, plough a field, and run a business. Women who had been dependent on their husbands financially had been earning their own money, making their own decisions – and for some there would be no going back.

Bess was deep in thought when she noticed someone frantically waving a red trilby at the south end of the platform. That was the signal. The train was approaching. Bess waved back, wondering whether her friend was able to distinguish her hand from the dozens of others being waved. She probably couldn't, but it didn't matter.

Bess at one end of the platform and Annabel at the other searched the faces of the soldiers and sailors who were looking out of the windows or hanging out of the doors. Many of them were injured. Some had bandages round their heads, others their eyes. One soldier in a carriage near to where Bess was standing had lost an arm. The empty sleeve of his jacket had been pinned to the padding on his shoulder. The boy next to him shook uncontrollably; unaware of what was going on around him. Another stared out of the window, but seemed to see nothing. Bess's heart broke at the sight before her, but she kept looking. Somewhere among the hundreds of exhausted and wounded young servicemen was Charlotte's father.

Bess lifted her hand and looked at the ring on her engagement finger, bearing the Foxden crest. It had been four years since James put his ring on her finger and asked her to marry him.

Some weeks after James's plane had gone down, Lord and Lady Foxden sent a message with Mr Porter asking Bess if she would go up to the Hall when convenient.

Welcoming her warmly, Lady Foxden offered her tea. 'Or something stronger,' Lord Foxden said.

Bess thanked them, refusing both, and slipped James's ring from her finger, holding it in the palm of her hand for what she thought was the last time.

Emotion choking his words, Lord Foxden said, 'We are going to have a memorial service for James, and...'

'And,' Lady Foxden continued, 'as James's fiancé we'd like you to sit with us, Bess. When the Air Force finds James and brings him home, we'll bury him properly. But we want to mark his pass-- passing now.'

Numb with grief, Bess nodded. She tried to say thank you, but her throat was so tight with emotion she was unable to speak. She opened her hand and offered its contents to Lord Foxden, who shook his head. 'My son gave you his ring, Bess. We'd like you to keep it.'

James didn't come home. His body was never found. Bess bit back the tears. It had been almost six years since the night James visited her in her small London apartment and asked her to go back to Foxden and turn the Estate into arable land. During that time there had been five good harvests, as well as a constant supply of seasonal produce – none of which would have been possible without the hardworking women of Foxden's Land Army. Old friends like Molly, Miss Armstrong, Mrs McAllister and the Goldman children had made Foxden their home for varying lengths of time. And there had been hundreds of servicemen come to Foxden to recover from injuries that were physical or mental – and sometimes both.

One young soldier who had spent time convalescing at Foxden was Bess's old friend, Frank Donnelly. Frank had lost an eye when his unit came under fire in the Italian Alps. Everyone in the company ran for cover except a young corporal who was paralysed with fear. Frank scrambled out of his makeshift dugout, ran to the boy and dragged him to safety. He saved the boy's life, but almost lost his own when he was shot in the temple.

Several months later, on the day his bandages came off, Frank told Bess that he had always loved her and asked her to marry him.

Bess liked Frank and in the years that followed she grew to love him. She didn't have the same passion for Frank as she'd had for James. James was her first love and Frank understood that. Frank was sensitive and caring and told Bess that he would wait for her and when she was ready, he would do his best to make her happy.

Bess took James's ring from her engagement finger and put it on the corresponding finger on her right hand. I'll always love you, James, but now the war's over, it's time I let go of the pain and –

'Is that my daddy?' Charlotte was tapping Bess's shoulder. 'Is that my daddy?'

'Yes, darling, that's your daddy,' Bess said, lifting Charlotte from the crate. Moments later Tom caught sight of Bess and his little daughter. He dropped to his knees and opened his arms.

'Take my hand, sweetheart,' Bess said to her niece, sensing that the child was anxious. 'We'll welcome your daddy home together, shall we?'

Charlotte took several tentative steps towards her father, and stopped. 'You're not my daddy. I want my daddy in the picture,' she cried.

Tom no longer looked like his photograph. Five years of war had changed him drastically. He had lost a lot of weight. He had dark shadows under his eyes and his face was brown, unshaven, and gaunt.

Still on his knees and smiling through his tears, he said, 'I'll soon look like my picture again now I'm home with you and Mummy, I promise.'

'Go on, sweetheart,' Bess said, kneeling down beside her niece. She let go of Charlotte's small hand.

Looking very small, Charlotte stood in the middle of the platform for what seemed like an age. The brakes on the empty train squealed as it stopped in the sidings and the little girl jumped. She turned to Bess for reassurance, and Bess nodded.

'Daddy, Daddy,' Charlotte called, and ran into her father's arms.

Tom lifted his little daughter up as if she was a feather, hugged her and cried with joy. Annabel put her arms round them both, and then beckoned Bess.

'Welcome home, Tom,' Bess said. 'I've missed you so much.'

'I've missed you too,' he said, kissing his sister. 'And you,' he said, kissing Charlotte. 'And you,' he whispered lovingly to Annabel, holding her with his eyes.

'Come on, Charlotte, let's go and get the car and we'll take Mummy and Daddy home,' Bess said, lifting the little girl from her father's arms.

As she entered the tunnel that led from the platform to the street, Bess looked back. The northbound platform was deserted but for Tom and Annabel, and the elderly ticket collector who doffed his cap as he passed.

'After we've taken Mummy and Daddy home, would you like to come with me to tell Nanny and Grandpa Dudley that Daddy's back?'

'Will Uncle Frank be there?' Charlotte asked.

'Yes, I think so,' Bess replied.

'I like Uncle Frank.'

'Yes,' Bess said. 'So do I.'

THE END

Outlines of the other Books in the Dudley Sisters Saga

The second book, working title, **Applause**, is Margaret Dudley's story. At the beginning of World War II, Margaret marries her childhood sweetheart and leaves rural Leicestershire to live with him in London. Fiercely ambitious "Margot" works her way from being an usherette in a West End theatre, to leading lady of the show. However, she soon finds herself caught up in a web of deceit, black-market racketeers, Nazis, drugs and alcohol.

The third book, **China Blue**, is about love and courage – and is Claire Dudley's story. While in the WAAF Claire is seconded to the Royal Air Force's Advanced Air Strike Force. She falls in love with Mitchell 'Mitch' McKenzie, an American Airman who is shot down while parachuting into France. At the end of the war, while working in a liberated POW camp in Hamburg she is told that Mitch is still alive. Do miracles happen?

The fourth book, working title, **The Bletchley Secret**, is about strength and determination – and is the story of Ena, the youngest of the Dudley sisters. Ena works in a local factory. She is one of several young women who build components for machines bound for Bletchley Park during World War II. The Bletchley Secret costs her the love of her life. Some years after the war has ended, Ena, now happily married, is running a hotel with her husband when she encounters someone from her past.

ABOUT THE AUTHOR

Madalyn Morgan has been an actress for more than thirty years, working in repertory theatre, the West End and television. She is a radio presenter and journalist, and has written articles for newspapers and magazines.

Madalyn was brought up in, The Fox Inn, a busy working class pub in the market town of Lutterworth in Leicestershire. As a pub-kid, life was not always pop and crisps, but it was a great place for an aspiring actress and writer to live. There were so many wonderful characters to study and accents learn. At twenty-four Madalyn gave up a successful hairdressing salon and wig-hire business for a place at E15 Drama College, and a career as an actress.

In 2000, with fewer parts available for older actresses, Madalyn reinvented herself. She learned how to touch type, completed two-years with The Writer's Bureau, and began writing. After living and working in London for thirty-six years, Madalyn has now returned to her home town of Lutterworth, swapping two window boxes and a mortgage, for a garden and the freedom to write.

Visit Madalyn Morgan online:

The Foxden Acres Website:
https://sites.google.com/site/foxdenacresbymada
lynmorgan/home

Non-Fiction Blog:
http://madalynmorgan.blogspot.co.uk/

Fiction Blog:
http://madalynmorgansfiction.blogspot.co.uk/

Actress website:
http://www.madalynmorgan.com/

16390973R00214

Printed in Poland
by Amazon Fulfillment
Poland Sp. z o.o., Wrocław